FORBIDDEN WATERS

CW01508370

BY THE SAME AUTHOR

CAM KILLICK MYSTERY SERIES

The Troubled Deep

AVAILABLE ON EBOOK

Far From the Tree
The Only Truly Dead
And Your Enemies Closer

FORBIDDEN WATERS

Rob Parker

RAVEN BOOKS

LONDON · OXFORD · NEW YORK · NEW DELHI · SYDNEY

RAVEN BOOKS
Bloomsbury Publishing Plc
50 Bedford Square, London, WC1B 3DP, UK
Bloomsbury Publishing Ireland Limited,
29 Earlsfort Terrace, Dublin 2, D02 AY28, Ireland

BLOOMSBURY, RAVEN BOOKS and the Raven Books logo
are trademarks of Bloomsbury Publishing Plc

First published in Great Britain 2026

Copyright © Rob Parker, 2026

Rob Parker is identified as the author of this work in accordance with the Copyright,
Designs and Patents Act 1988

This is a work of fiction. Names, characters and organisations are the product of the
author's imagination. Any resemblance to actual persons, living or
dead, is entirely coincidental

All rights reserved. No part of this publication may be: i) reproduced or transmitted
in any form, electronic or mechanical, including photocopying, recording or by
means of any information storage or retrieval system without prior permission in
writing from the publishers; or ii) used or reproduced in any way for the training,
development or operation of artificial intelligence (AI) technologies, including
generative AI technologies. The rights holders expressly reserve this
publication from the text and data mining exception as per Article 4(3)
of the Digital Single Market Directive (EU) 2019/790

A catalogue record for this book is available from the British Library

ISBN: HB: 978-1-5266-8369-4; EBOOK: 978-1-5266-8364-9

2 4 6 8 10 9 7 5 3 1

Typeset by Six Red Marbles India
Printed and bound in Great Britain by Clays Ltd, Elcograf S.p.A

To find out more about our authors and books visit www.bloomsbury.com
and sign up for our newsletters
For product-safety-related questions contact productsafety@bloomsbury.com

To everyone reading these words:
thank you.

And to Becky, always.

Some Time Ago

The float, which resembled a thick pencil with one end dipped in fluorescent orange paint, suddenly stood on end – a beacon in the morning light. The angler stood in his boat, his knees quivering, and his heart suddenly made a charge for his throat and mouth. Breath wouldn't come.

The float had been lying flat thirty metres away, drifting gently this way and that in the early shimmer, when suddenly it all changed. Hours had slipped by with no suggestion that anything was beneath the surface at all, yet now, this abrupt movement felt like an explosion.

So much hope through stillness – but it can all change in an instant. That was fishing, the angler thought with excited knowing.

He reached for the rod, nestled in the rod rest attached to the panel of the boat he'd borrowed for this very occasion. He held it, and watched the float with keen focus. His eyes watered with expectation, and he forced himself to take a deep breath.

It didn't move.

Maybe something had dislodged the bait, which was a dead herring. Maybe another fish had blundered into the line, or hidden currents had forced debris to intervene.

He strained, and covered his eyes from the overhead sun.

The tip began to twirl, clockwise.

The angler had to check, to see if it was really happening. He wiped his eyes, removed all the moisture that had materialised through the excitement, and strained.

Yes. It was twirling.

Then it popped down, then back up again.

It was definite, clear, and somehow deafening.

His bait had been picked up.

He made two turns of the reel to pick up the slack, in case he had to strike quickly.

But the float still stood on end, its previous dart downwards forgotten.

If it was a bite, which it surely had to be, it was a very tentative one. But that could be a good sign. The big ones had a reputation for being more finicky the bigger they got. They made minimal movements, preserving energy.

Please be one of the big ones, he thought.

Then the float started to drift to the left.

Then, ever so slowly, down. It slipped beneath the surface, out of sight.

What was it the man in the bait shop had told him, all those years ago, when he was a kid picking out his first predator fishing rod?

'How will I know when I've got a bite?' he'd asked.

'Well, what are you using as bait?' the man in the tackle shop had said.

'A dead fish.'

'So, why would it move?'

'If it's been picked up by another fish?'

'That's right – because dead bait don't move.'

That's what he told all the kids who went in.

Dead bait don't move.

But his bait was.

The angler bent forward, then swung up and back with all his might, sweeping the rod up and to the right, in the opposite direction to the float's run – just like he'd been taught.

He felt firm opposition immediately, a thick immovable weight, like trying to pull down a brick wall with dental floss. The water, a few metres to the left of where the float had plummeted away, frothed as something heavy moved through it, not far beneath the surface.

The angler couldn't help a shocked half-smile from playing across his face, and his fingertips tingled with hot swathes of pure adrenaline.

The fish surged, and stripped line at an astonishing rate. The angler had set the reel's drag resistance fairly stoutly, but this creature had no problem in ripping clean line from it, sending the line spool screaming as it darted.

This was a serious fish.

The angler looked at his feet, to make sure everything was ready.

Net was within reaching distance by the bow. Unhooking mat was laid out ready.

Now, where were the needle nose pliers, the long ones… there they were. The fish slowed as it made a break for the far bank, and began to turn back.

The angler hissed: 'Come on, come on, come on,' as he frantically reeled to make up the metres of suddenly slack line. He was using barbless hooks, as were the rules of being here, and if you didn't keep the line tight, the hooks might slide right out.

He pumped the reel, and the line caught up.

'Please be there, please be there…' he whispered through teeth gritted so tightly he had jaw ache.

And it was. The fish was still attached.

The run had tired it.

It had shown its raw power, but in doing so had spent a lot of energy, and the angler began to pull the beast towards him. He couldn't get it to rise. It hugged the bottom for its life, which, he assumed, the fish thought was at stake.

The angler had no intention of killing the fish, however. He merely wanted to marvel at it, spend time in its glorious presence, know that he'd taken on nature in a battle of wits and craft. That was all – plus some photos. And then, he'd slide it back into the depths, none the worse for its jaunt above the surface. That was all the plan.

It was still low, but nearly at the boat now. It wasn't all that deep here, maybe five feet – surely he would see it any second now?

He lowered to his knees, net in his left hand, rod in his right, ready to scoop the fish in as soon as he saw it. In position, he stared at the water, hoping. Desperate just for a glance of a fin or tail.

The line was getting closer and closer.

He could see something beneath the surface, a flash of colour.

The float! Yes, it was there. It was coming up. Closer to the surface… Closer still. The fish would appear any second.

He honestly didn't know if his heart could stand the excitement.

With a sudden splash the surface was broken – but he didn't see anything. The float was still under the surface, darting this way and that under the invisible fish's struggles.

Something else had come up.

It lunged at the side of the boat, in a spiral of wet hair.

And hit him. Smack in the chest.

His hands loosened, and the fish gained ground again. It was ploughing away through the water.

No! He hadn't even seen it.

As he watched the line tear away, he slowly became aware that there was a huge mass clinging to the side of the boat, and that whatever had hit him, it wasn't the fish.

He looked down – and saw a knife in his chest. Dead centre. Bull's-eye.

The rod slipped from his hand, and sprang down into the water. Like the float before it, it arrowed beneath the surface like a javelin, and raced off to the depths, after the magnificent fish that he would never see.

Because he had a knife in his chest.

His attacker watched him with detachment from the side of the boat, as blood started to pump out in quaint little spurts.

It watched the angler reach for the handle, which was embedded as far as it would go. He pulled it out, but that only made the pressure in his body release, and he fell, blood coming faster now, the knife tinkling over the side, into the eager drink.

He tried to put his hands out to ease his fall, but they wouldn't move. His eyes couldn't keep focus.

The angler watched the attacker climb into the boat, as he fell back. The figure was huge, exuding raw, demonic power. The sky overhead was a beautiful grey-blue haze.

A lovely day was coming.

But a beast stood over him, blocking it out for good.

The mists parted at the entrance to Upton Broad to show a corridor of vegetation, wide as a three-lane motorway. There was no traffic, however, just rolling wisps of a fickle haze that would lift quickly now that the sun had risen.

Cam Killick looked up. He still couldn't see the great star itself, but the breeze on the bare skin of his forearms told him that the temperature had lifted in the last few moments, if only by a couple of degrees. Any warmth was useful in the middle of a crisp March.

He stood at the stern of a dinghy that was ancient, crooked, and wrapped in cracked, navy paint. Nala, as ever, stood by his side. Today, her tongue lapped at the air, catching whatever moisture she could from the swirling vapours.

Cam held the throttle at a low turnover, all too aware of the poor visibility, and how the broad sometimes played host to anchored cruisers that stayed fast like oversized buoys, having come off the River Bure to hunker down for the night, or even for an early lunch. At his feet, in the middle of the boat, lay his diving gear, arranged for easy access in order of how he'd put it on when the time came. For now, he wore his wetsuit undone to the waist, underneath a long, black dryrobe, with a pair of pink Crocs on his bare feet – a gift from a mischievous friend.

The deep trees on either side of the channel gave gradual way, leaving a large, misted expanse ahead of him, which gave the impression of puttering through the centre of a huge cloud pocket. He didn't need to be able to see to know where he was going, but he remained keenly vigilant for obstacles as he went.

Cam looked down at his canine companion, watching her tongue flick in and out with fervour.

'You're going to need a wee if you keep drinking like that,' he said, causing Nala to look up at him. 'Then you'll be stuck, won't you? Because you're not doing it on here.'

Nala looked up at him with deep, Bourneville eyes, and huffed. She was compact yet regal, a Shih Tzu-Yorkshire Terrier cross the colour of a Victorian chimney sweep after a particularly busy day. She was Cam's companion, lifeline and right-hand dog. She shook her head, and started biting at the air again, this time with even more determination. She couldn't understand a word he'd just said, of course, but the obviousness of her sudden defiance suggested she must have got *something*.

The tick-over of the engine rolled out across the water's surface, and Cam looked across the expanse of that muddied mirror. *Any time now*, he thought – and no sooner had the notion crossed his mind, that it happened, and the morning fog started to dissipate before his eyes. Columns of bright blue began to appear beyond the lifting mists, revealing the onset of a perfect spring morning. Within moments, all the mist had faded, like an eighties TV set tuning away its static, and suddenly everything was visible, literally clear as day.

Not far ahead of him, along his easterly course, was a rusted gate, embedded in the trees at the side of the broad's bank. A newer padlock held it shut, a gleaming shard of steel in the sudden sun. Subconsciously, he tapped the pocket of his dryrobe, and felt the thick bunch of keys sitting there. He had picked them up late last night, in a pub car park a few miles away – loaned to him by a representative from the Broads Trust; the overarching administrative body that governed the waterways of the area.

Doke End was a short body of water just off Upton Broad, not a million miles from the village of Upton itself, and it had long been under lock and key. It used to be a heronry, where the large, grey predatory birds could nest in peace, away from the boating commotions of the main river. Cam didn't know the score now, only aware that it was still privately owned and operated by the Broads Trust. He approached the gate cautiously, killing the engine with ten metres to go, to allow the dinghy to drift slowly towards his target. Floating forward, he caught the gate with both hands, and unlocked it with a hefty jangle of metal. He pulled it open, planted his feet and used his body as a lever to drag the vessel through. Without letting go, he eased the dinghy into the smaller body of water before padlocking the gate closed behind him, dumping the keys safely back into his robe pocket.

Now through, he turned back to look at Doke End in all its natural glory.

He'd never been in here, and immediately felt grateful that he'd finally been granted the opportunity. It was a spot of untouched beauty, a hundred metres long and seventy metres wide at the middle. Each spot of bank was domi-nated by overhanging trees and unfettered vegetation, over a glassy surface so still it could have been one huge sheet of ice. Cam took a moment to enjoy the sight, and the quiet: cut off, silent, flushed through with natural beauty. He was in awe.

'As call-outs go, this is a bit of a beauty, isn't it?' he said. Even Nala had stilled and, no longer biting air, looked at him. 'Well, best get to it. That thing isn't going to find itself.'

He shifted only fractionally to swap tillers to the electric motor, taking the smaller rubber handle that was protruding just a little further along the stern, and flipped the switch on its tip. It elicited a small clunk as the motor engaged, which sounded monstrous in the pressing silence. The overhanging trees on all sides had created a bowl, which muffled any outside noise, and he found the compressed quiet profoundly relaxing, and comforting.

He felt a smile cross his cheeks.

Cam was a man wedged in the long-term grip of post-traumatic stress disorder, an unwanted hangover and parting gift from his time with the Special Boat Service, fighting for the then Queen and her country. It had left him with myriad symptoms and quirks that he was getting used to, day by day. It was an ongoing balancing act of pharmaceutical intervention, patience, and simply giving things a go and finding what worked. He'd not long ago added therapy into the mix. But hands down the greatest remedy he'd found yet, which soothed his teetering mindset, was the underwater world. In that muffled cool, with his jangling nerves encased in silent compression, he found the closest thing to normal and real relief that he ever experienced. And now, oddly, this wood-shaded bowl in Doke End gave him, for what he was sure was the first time since his diagnosis, the same feeling of decompression and solace.

And it was the first time he'd ever experienced it dry.

Back to work. He checked the tiller handle. Along its rubber column was a series of five small blue lights, revealing the electric motor to be at full charge. The unit didn't betray any sound, despite being ready to roll.

To his left, Cam then clicked on a small screen that had been bolted to the port flank, which flicked into life in a haze of blue. He rotated the handle of the electric motor, and the dinghy silently forged forward – which in turn created dancing cyan shadows on the screen. Beneath man and dog, below the surface, was a lightweight, compact sonar unit and Cam watched the screen intently, alternating with glances up at the bank to his left, as he angled the boat around the edge of Doke End.

Nala settled herself down in the front of the boat on a tired dog bed that Cam had dragged out of his dive van. As a salvage diver, much of the job was searching (for him) and waiting (for her), and Nala knew this all too well. Her eyes were shut before her head hit the faded plaid.

Today, his quarry was a curious one. As far as he understood, someone at the Broads Trust had lent the keys to a friend, and that friend had come in here fishing for the pike that sought quiet out of the main river. Cam could see one now on the sonar screen, presenting itself as a light blue banana shape about three metres from the trees to his left. The angler in question had had no success, because he lost his favourite fishing lure in the process. It was a hand-painted, bespoke piece, imported from America, and the angler had spent a fortune on it, only to lose it. Cam had been hired to find and retrieve it from whatever underwater snag it had become lodged in.

When he was first offered the job, he initially wondered why on earth this guy didn't just buy another one? Was it really worth Cam's call-out fee? A job was ultimately a job, so he hadn't questioned it – but it must've been one expensive lure to justify such lengths in retrieval. Still, if you were going to advertise yourself as a diver for hire with the caveat that no job was too small, you had to take the rough with the smooth.

On the day he'd lost it, the angler had employed an expensive fish finder, similar to Cam's own but with far more detail than the unit he was using now. He claimed to have seen that the lure had gone missing around an underwater log on the left-hand side of Doke End. Cam had wondered why he couldn't be more specific, but it turned out the man had inadvertently complicated the matter by treating himself to a bottle of red wine while on his solo fishing trip, and consequently couldn't remember exactly where this downed log was.

Hence, calling the friendly, neighbourhood diver.

Cam, without looking away from the screen now, angled the boat carefully at low speed past the trees. At the top of the monitor, the staccato blue shadows came down like blocks in Tetris. The exact shape of the log in question would be hard to pinpoint, but it would bear noticeable characteristics, like reaching spindles if it was a downed branch, which is precisely what Cam thought he was dealing with. Wood floated when dry, sure, but leave that wood to get waterlogged and you've got a heavy and huge obstacle. Plus, here, they were found almost everywhere – the number of felled tree limbs Cam had navigated in waters right across the region, that were adorned with coils of fishing line like the barest remains of cut-price tinsel, were beyond sensible statistic. But he couldn't see anything yet, just the undulating hard blue barrier of the sonar bouncing back off the left-hand bank. He became gleefully lost to the task, engrossed by the simplicity of the work and the setting, and time ticked by without him really knowing.

He'd been combing the bank for half an hour when he eventually saw it. A large shape, twenty metres to his left, with so many interconnected branches reaching from a central lump that, even from this distance, on this screen, gave the whole thing a sizeable presence.

He glanced across and looked at the spot itself, having to guesstimate its position, given that there was nothing on the surface that gave away the snag's presence. No reaching wooden fingers through the surface, no obvious hump of trunk breaking into the fresh air like Nessie's breaching flank.

Cam turned the boat to where he thought the tree was, giving a wide enough berth for the sonar to pick it up. The shape on the screen soon reappeared as he got close to the bank, but in far more detail. A rich lightning bolt network of jagged branches was obvious, and even on the screen he saw something amiss.

It was a search principle that he'd adopted from the very beginning of his dive career: when you're looking for something man-made, a straight line is a huge giveaway. And stuck on one of those branches below the waterline was an oblong shape. It stayed put, even as he puttered past, slowed, and reversed.

Cam would put money on it. He'd found the missing lure. He glanced at Nala.

'Time to suit up,' he said – before killing the electric outboard and, with a tug of frayed rope and an echoing splash, dropping the mud weight. Icy water flicked up onto his bare hands.

'It's going to be a cold one,' he said, gritting his teeth.

Nala huffed, partly in agreement, partly as if to say, *better you than me.*

2

The dryrobe was on the deck, the wetsuit up over his shoulders and zipped up tight. The regulator was in place, and the tanks on his back. Cam checked his dive watch, which had all the bells and whistles you could possibly want, and then some you'd never come close to using. Most importantly, it hooked up to his tank via sensors and told Cam how much air he had left. That, and the fact it was a GPS unit, rendered it the single most important thing on his ventures underwater. On his left wrist was his torch, mounted on the back of his hand like one of Batman's gadgets. He didn't know what visibility he'd find down there, but given the surface impression of vending machine coffee circa 1992, he didn't think it would be much.

Mask on, he wasted no time before dropping over the side.

The water swallowed him in a cold voltage of pure invigoration, and sucked him away from the outside world in an instant. He bent his knees on entry, knowing from the sonar screen that it was only five feet deep here: he didn't want to accidentally collide with the bottom and whatever other snags may be lurking. Fancy breathing monitors couldn't do much if you were stuck underwater, apart from provide a ticking clock to your shortening mortality – while the coveted GPS function would only serve as a beacon to help rescuers find your drowned body.

As predicted, the water seemed thick and impenetrable, and offered visibility of maybe a foot. It was like diving blindfolded. He had to pull his watch right up to his nose to read the digits. The tank was full of pressurised air to 200 bar – which would give him an hour. He didn't think he'd need a fraction of that, but it did give him leeway. As did the second tank back up on the dinghy.

Cam was careful, even more so now, after various close calls a few months ago. He stayed slow, purposeful and methodical. He'd even told Jess Tabernacle where he was going, a new addition to his safety protocols that proved he wasn't quite as alone in the world as he once thought – alongside, of course, the pink Crocs that now sat up in the boat with the rest of his dry kit.

Right now, however, he was as alone as he could be – and he loved it. Just himself, the water, the quiet and none of that packing invasiveness that permeated almost every interaction he had on land. It was blissful respite, because even though he had found a degree of cool and happiness, the ghosts of PTSD remained eager as the keenest bailiffs, always knocking on the door to collect on the debt of the memories he was trying so hard to forget.

Cam lowered to his knees, and used his arms to spin in place, turning a full 180 degrees so that his body was positioned ten feet from the downed branch. He had deliberately decided to come from a slight distance, and approach the obstacle gradually and carefully. Dropping straight onto a pile of interwoven branches would be a surefire way of getting snagged up. He started to gradually paddle forward. While it responded and felt like water, the visibility gave him the notion he was swimming through a fine sludge. It wasn't the first time on the Norfolk Broads that Cam wondered how anything on Earth could survive there. All the pike that were rumoured to hunt in here used a sensory panel on their flanks called the lateral line, which was a coiled spring of nerve endings and receptors. All they had to do was feel a splash, any vibration in the water, and they could follow it to prey. The actual use of sight, for elite predators such as these, could be an afterthought.

Cam felt the branches on his arms and hands before he even saw them, his fingers brushing knots of wood which he eagerly grasped to pull himself closer. He used his hands as eyes – considering he himself had no lateral line to work with – and quickly found that the log was heavy and stuck fast. It had to be at least half-buried in the viscous silt that lay on the bottom of the broad bed. Staying slow and methodical, he stuck to his task, and reached in and out of the branches for the lost fishing lure.

Once again, his searching fingers found it before his eyes did, when their tips brushed onto something smooth which gave a rattle to his touch. When he pulled himself closer and finally got a look at the missing lure, now a matter of inches from his nose, he was amazed at the size of it. It was over a foot long, and even in this harsh visibility, it was obviously painstakingly painted to resemble a young pike – the very species the lure was aiming to flummox and coax. He had heard about the pike's proclivities for cannibalism, but this decoy had Cam questioning whether a full-grown pike really could eat something of this size. He realised, despite not being an angler himself, that he'd quite like to see it. It was wrapped tightly in fishing line, which itself was wrapped tightly around one of the thickest branches. The snapped end of the line dangled and floated like a lost kite string in the soft flow.

He started untangling the fishing line which coiled in a clump around one of the smaller branches, but Cam realised quickly that this wasn't the reason the lure had got stuck. The piece itself carried two large treble hooks, which were essentially three hooks joined at the middle by a central shaft, with one in the middle and one at the lure's tail. The furthest hook was deeply embedded in the knotted arm of the downed tree. Cam, however, was prepared and reached for his trusty dive pouch on his waist. He flipped out a pair of pliers which he used to grip the treble's shank and shake the lure free.

Holding it now in his hand he was able to fully appreciate the craftsmanship. Thirteen inches of green iridescence with yellow painted spots, each marking a unique brushstroke. Its two little eyes were ringed with yellow fire, and it had perfect red fins. That was when Cam realised he was able to see it clearer. And as his eyes switched focus to the tree beyond, he could see more of its scale and shape. He could now see that more than half of it was buried in the mulch, and had given the lure a great rotting anchor. It had only taken a minute or so for the visibility to change. The consistency of the water around him had altered almost instantly, and the underwater topography of Doke End was being revealed more with every second. Visibility was three feet, then five feet, ten feet, then more.

This was a tidal phenomenon, but he'd never seen it quite so pronounced before. Cam knew that some eight miles upstream, the inland rivers met the sea at Great Yarmouth, and in front of that was the town, docks and boatyards.

Fairly recently, a new moveable bridge had been opened to allow great seafaring vessels into port, and every time it closed and opened, it had an effect on the underwater ecology and day-to-day workings of the river right up the waterway, miles inland. Fresh and salt water collided with each other in new ways, and fought for dominance in areas where they never had before. Cam thought that this was what was happening right that moment. Maybe the bridge had opened, and miles away, Doke End went clear. It was like the Norfolk Broads' own take on chaos theory, and it rendered the waters of the broad unpredictable and fickle.

In practical terms, the underwater landscape became ever more visible, in what felt like an amazing natural reveal. Cam could see the floor gradually tilting downwards but only by a foot or so, revealing Doke End's primary characteristic was that of a shallow bowl with a dirt base – which made sense since the word 'doke' was a Suffolk term for shallow. The sunlight in the world above pushed through the water in glowing columns. It was nothing less than magical.

Then, without preamble, Cam saw something reflected in the light. Only polished surfaces refracted light. It caught him by surprise, because there had been no other hint of anything artificial or man-made down there. He rose and his head breached the surface. Spinning in place, he saw the boat immediately, and Nala's head popped up on alert having heard the splash. Cam paddled back quickly to the boat, and reached over into the vessel, placing the fishing lure in a box under the rear seat. The last thing he wanted was Nala finding the lure with all its hooks. Without even removing his regulator, he forged back beneath the surface once more.

He was intrigued. Following the compass bearing from moments earlier, he started swimming towards the sparkling item in question.

The overhead shafts from the sun had shifted as the clouds rolled by, but Cam followed his compass course with easy certainty. The shiny thing, whatever it was, had been lying there on the silt, so Cam leaned forward so that his belly was close to the floor, and pulled himself towards it with his hands, his eyes roving ahead so as not to miss it.

It didn't take him long to find it, and it fired a shard of true surprise directly through his body.

Lying there, as if laid out for Cam's own personal presentation and discovery, was a knife.

It was lying on the settled silt, uncovered by dirt, as if it had been placed there with utmost care. The blade was six inches in length, and its gleaming steel seemed otherworldly in the prehistoric underwater of Doke End.

It was a hunting knife. The kind of knife he had used himself when he was in uniform. The black rubberised handle had a wrist strap reaching from it, which helped contribute to an air of purpose, along with its ready shine – or at least it would have if it weren't for the rust near the hilt.

Cam swam around it in a tight circle.

There were many very sensible explanations for why it was here.

But Cam couldn't immediately think of any.

He was going to pick it up, but had learned from experience that it was better to take a record of things in situ first. From his dive pouch, he took out his phone in its underwater case, and took a couple of photographs from different angles.

As he worked to frame the knife effectively, he realised that something wasn't right. It took a few moments, trying to work out what had tripped his alarm, before he found it.

The error had been in his earlier assessment.

That wasn't rust. He had seen enough rust to know its colour underwater in a great range of conditions. But this didn't look like any rust he'd seen.

It reminded Cam of something else he'd seen far too much of, over the years.

Blood.

The more he stared at it, the more he was certain.

What on earth was a bloodstained knife doing here at the bottom of this private body of water? And if that was really blood, how had it not smeared and dissolved away?

Cam tried to think logically. The fact he could even see it suggested that the blood flow that had caused it had to have been significant.

He switched the phone camera from photo to video, and eased up close to it, drifting the lens tight to the smudge.

The smear looked more damning every inch closer he went.

It looked like it had only been put here yesterday, given the fact that the silt hadn't even had time to naturally shift and cover it in any way.

He'd had to come here via a locked gate, the keys to which he'd had to get off that guy from the Broads Trust. You couldn't just hop the fence because there'd be nowhere to stand on the other side. The banks were packed with dense trees, and beyond that were acres of treacherous marshes in all directions.

So, who had access to the keys before him? His mind started racing to the people he knew were connected to them, but there were only two. The angler who hired him, Charlie Lassiter, and the Broads Trust guy – what was his name? Forsyth, that was it.

Did one of them drop this?

This was one of those fifty-fifty calls. Where it could be something, or it could be nothing – but Cam's sense of right and wrong, plus that innate nose he possessed for mischief, told him he wouldn't rest until he'd at least had things checked out.

So... how to get it out of here?

If he was looking at evidence of a serious crime, then preserving it as close to the way it was at discovery was vital.

Cam put the phone back in the dive pouch, and breached the surface once more, taking extra care not to let his flippers disturb the silt around the knife. The last thing he needed was to bury it before he had a chance to get it out.

Seeing that morning sunlight was a world of change after all that concentration in the world of underwater greens and browns, but his eyes quickly adjusted as he swam for the boat. Nala had her paws up on the gunwale ready to welcome him aboard, but despite her obvious eagerness, he remained in the water yet again.

'Just a quick visit,' he said, as he reached up, over into the boat, and grabbed the cool bag from the under the rear seat. From inside, he took out a small cellophane bag, and dumped out the contents. Three sandwiches on granary bread spilled out onto the floor of the boat. Nala took them as a gift from heaven, and snapped them up before

Cam could retrieve them. He could only look at the dog nonplussed.

'We'll talk about this later,' he said, before grabbing a small chunk of Red Leicester that had bounced onto the dinghy floor. Regulator back in mouth, he submerged and swam back to the knife – but things were different down there already. Visibility was turning again, clouding once more, as he supposed the tide was being sucked back, imagining the bridge in Great Yarmouth once again.

Cam thought he was still ten metres away from the knife and couldn't yet see it. He suddenly started to panic about losing it. Panic for him was more rushed and sudden than perhaps for other people. It came fierce, and left just as abruptly, but its potency had great effect on him when it was present. He slowed for a second, and breathed carefully, and deeply.

In for three.

Hold for five.

Out for eight.

Then he told himself, quite clearly, that the knife was inanimate. It couldn't move. It would be there whether he could see it or not, it might just take longer to find.

Better.

Now righted, he tilted forward and swam purposefully, as visibility dropped foot by foot in real time. He checked his compass reading, convinced he was right on line, and – thank God – the knife was suddenly beneath him. He breathed a sigh of relief, then reached down with the chunk of cheese. He eased it onto the pointed tip of the knife. Bringing the sandwich bag up, he fanned it open and used it as a scoop, collecting the knife from the handle, taking water and a little seasoning of silt with it, until he captured the whole lot in the bag. He zipped up the seal, and looked at it one last time, before the changing tide took the spot from sight.

He came back up to the surface, and checked his prize in the midday light.

Yes, he was as sure as he could be.

That was blood, and the knife was caked in it, right up to the hilt.

And he knew just who to take it to — whether she liked it or not.

3

Detective Sergeant Claire Rogers walked into her office at Norwich Constabulary just after lunchtime and placed her coffee on her desk. She had to perch a frosted jam doughnut around its rim because she couldn't frankly be bothered with washing a plate – not when Brophy was sitting in the kitchen eating rabbit food out of one of those bloody Tupperwares. Brophy was also in her fifties, but was a fitness nut – and by god did she like people to know it. If you got stuck in there with her, even just for the amount of time it took for a kettle to boil, you had to hear all about macros, meal prep, electrolytes and protein. If Rogers had to be told one more time about all the dead calories in her jam doughnut, she might end up forcibly inserting said confectionary somewhere very invasive indeed.

She popped out her AirPods and dropped them onto the desk next to her, sending them skittering like rolled dice as she slumped into the chair. She was tired, bone-tired. Out all morning collecting statements pertaining to a warehouse robbery in Rackheath. After checking the crime scene, created overnight at one of the region's biggest fishing equipment warehouses, she'd amassed and collated witness reports and instructed the direction of enquiries. Since her career had been defibrillated in January, the biggest cases now found their way to her with much more ease – although the fact that in Norfolk a 'big case' still more often than not meant nothing more than a fishing equipment heist, kept her feet on the ground.

The tiredness, however, felt begrudgingly good, any awareness of her own bones and how busy they were now raising a smile. She was back on track.

Rogers picked up the phone and dialled the front desk.

'Hi Diana, it's Claire Rogers here. Only got in now from Rackheath, just wanted to check for any messages.'

The voice that came back was tired, and devoid of any jollity. 'Well, DS Rogers, if you'd come in through the front like everyone else, you'd notice you had a visitor.'

Visitor. That was abnormal. 'Now, you can see why I always come in through the garage.' She sighed. 'Who is it?'

'It's that diver bloke.'

Rogers' eyebrows arched. For an area that contained so much water, it could be seen as strange that there was only one diver bloke. And yet.

That description could only fit Cameron Killick. The enigmatic, trouble-magnetised, SBS-traumatised scuba man-for-hire who confounded, infuriated and occasion-ally delighted Detective Sergeant Claire Rogers in equal measure.

'Is he clean?' she asked.

'I'm sorry?'

'Clean. As in the opposite of dirty and wet?'

The line went dead a moment, before the voice returned. 'He's just come straight here from a dive, he says.'

Rogers sighed again. There was no way she was sitting in one of those stuffy interview rooms, with no room and no air, with a guy caked in pondweed and algae. 'Tell him I'll meet him in the car park.'

She put the phone down to end the discussion.

A couple of minutes later, Rogers emerged from the same back door she'd entered through, which was the entrance used by the garage staff and uniformed officers going to and from patrol. Cam Killick was already there, in his standard issue uniform of unseasonal board shorts, dryrobe and near-bovine look on his face – but there was a surprise new addition on his feet.

'What in the frosted hell are those?' she asked, pointing at the pink Crocs.

Killick looked down at himself and appraised his own footwear as if it was the first time any of this had come to his attention.

Rogers shook her head slowly. It never ceased to amaze her that this man, who had seen it all and done god-knows-what all over the globe, in the most high-stakes situations imaginable, could still come across as having the mental aptitude of both the most awkward of teenagers and a newborn giraffe.

'They were a present,' he mumbled and she could see the red ink his cheeks like a beetroot stain. She decided, knowing what she knew about his personal battles, to cut him some slack.

'Well, I'm sure the five-year-old princess you stole them from will be glad to have got rid of them. You wanted to see me?'

Killick reached into his dryrobe, and began to pull something out. 'I found something this morning on a dive,' he said, and he pulled out a plastic bag full of water, like he'd just won a goldfish at a prehistoric local fair.

'What have you bloody got into now?' Rogers began to ask, before her own thoughts stopped when she registered what she was seeing.

Instead of a half-dead goldfish, a thick and mean-looking knife sat in the grotty water, with an orange blob over the pointed end, presumably to stop it puncturing the bag it was housed in.

'That's a knife,' she said.

'Yep,' replied Killick. 'Pretty sure there's blood on it.'

'I can see that.'

'But that bit on the end, that's a bit of cheese. That's mine.'

Not for the first time in Killick's presence, Rogers felt compelled to sigh in exasperation. 'Thank you for the clarification.'

Rogers' naturally inquisitive mind flooded with questions – not least why there would be any cheese in this conversation at all – but procedure was immediately the most pertinent issue at hand.

'Well, don't just stand there, come with me.' And she turned and bustled back into the building.

Moments later, they sat in an interview room in the bowels of the police station. The bag filled with knife, blood, water and cheese sat in a plastic tray in the middle of a small table.

Rogers knew this might be something and nothing, but if the knife was connected to a crime, it was better to properly document everything at the start, rather than try to bodge things together later on.

'Killick, do you have any objection to me recording this conversation?'

'Is that normal?' he asked.

'No – but then again neither are you. You haven't exactly brought this to police attention via the most conventional of ways, and well, it seems a good idea to avoid any balls ups.'

'Umm, no then,' he said.

Tape rolling, introductions made, Rogers opened the conversation with that same eye on the future.

'Tell me Mr Killick, where did you get this? For the benefit of the tape, on the table is a sandwich bag full of water which also contains a knife with a piece of what appears to be Red Leicester over its point.'

Rogers guided Cam through some preliminary questions, during which time he showed her some fancy fishing lure bedecked with nasty-looking hooks, and a set of keys so fat they barely fit in any pocket. He told her how he'd been hired to find the former, gaining access with the latter. The location he'd found it in was unfamiliar to her, but when he said that it was locked off from the public, she sat up straight. She didn't doubt a word Killick said; he told it like it was. He'd long stopped, in her presence, trying to doll up his diving stories to make it sound like he was responsible, or even took the most basic of precautions. You could lead the man to water, quite literally, but you couldn't make him drink nor behave appropriately when he got into it.

'And you bagged the knife in an old sandwich bag?' she asked with an arched eyebrow.

'It was a new sandwich bag,' Killick replied. 'Fresh this morning. Ham and cheese.'

'I'm sure the forensic techs will appreciate that information.' Rogers leaned forward to take a closer look at the unlikely bag of water and deadly item. 'And you put a piece of cheese on the end of the knife?'

'It would have cut the bag instantly if I hadn't.'

Rogers didn't know whether this was an act of admirable improvisation, or the behaviour of an Olympic-level moron. At the very least, she recognised there was a fine line here between the two.

'And you're sure that's blood?' she asked.

'I've seen enough of it to know.'

Rogers knew that was the truth and moved on. 'You're not thinking it could be animal?'

'Could be. A poacher, maybe. But it was out in the middle of a locked body of water. I can't see it.'

'I was unaware it could stay so intact once submerged,' said Rogers.

'In my experience, it depends on a bunch of things,' replied Killick. 'The consistency of the water. How much blood there was originally.'

'What do you mean?'

Killick spoke impassively. 'Well. Blood is really sticky and thick if there's enough of it. Hard to get off things.'

Rogers grimaced. 'Thank you for the charming imagery.'

'We couldn't get any DNA from it, I'm guessing?' Killick asked.

'Hold onto your horses. That used to be the case – or so we thought. We'd always been told that once blood hit water, it lost its ability to hold DNA – so you couldn't extract it and run tests from it, things like that.'

'But that's changed now?'

'Well, not exactly – the properties of blood haven't changed – but advancements in science have. I believe there's now a test that can determine if DNA is present, but you have to catch it within five days.'

'What does that mean?' asked Killick.

'It means,' Rogers said carefully. 'In water, DNA disappears after around five days of submersion. If there's going to be DNA on there, it will have been put on the blade within the last five days.'

'Right, so if we find DNA on that knife, it will have been used to hurt someone within the last five days tops?' asked Killick.

'He's caught up, well done,' said Rogers.

'And you could find out who the blood belongs to?'

'If we get a DNA profile which matches someone on file, yes.'

'Can you order that test?'

Rogers looked hard at the knife in its balloon-like packaging. Then looked at Killick. His eyes were set.

She grabbed her phone. 'Let's do it.'

4

Cam left Norwich Police Station on foot and headed
back to the side street where he had parked his trusty
Volkswagen T5 Transporter. He hopped in the driver's
side, and immediately turned to look back between the
headrests. All the usual goodies you'd find in this particular model had been pulled out, replaced with shelves and
racks – for all his scuba equipment, and a dog bed to
accommodate Nala, who looked up at him now. It used
to be a beauty, but it had been relegated a banger overnight, with no amount of repairs hiding the battering it
had taken when some ne'er-do-wells had decided to take
their frustration out on it. Once in, he locked the car door
with a chirpy peep-poop which didn't fit the tiredness of
its appearance. Nala squeezed up front from the back, and
looked at Cam expectantly.

'I think we did the right thing, my chum,' he said,
patting her on the head.

He checked his watch, and was relieved to find he was
still right on schedule for the main appointment of the
day, a forty-minute drive away in Diss. He took the A140
away from Norwich, and forged arrow-straight south past
a host of the most wonderfully Norfolk-sounding places

imaginable. Newton Flotman, Saxlingham Nethergate, Wacton, Forncett St Peter, Tivetshall St Mary, Dickleburgh.

Some of those had to have been made up, he mused. It was like wandering through *Bedknobs and Broomsticks*.

Nevertheless, he soon made it to Diss, parked up, got Nala settled, and made his way to Diss Mere, a six-acre body of water whose exact depth, rumour told, nobody knew. It was Cam's first visit here, and he immediately liked it – although diving it would be a real challenge, considering the water looked murkier than liquid pottery clay.

Pam was there, waiting for him by the small rental hut.

'I picked a blue one,' she said, walking towards the water with a ticket stub.

'Is that because of its calming qualities?' Cam asked.

'Oh, ha ha ha,' she replied sarcastically.

The standard assumption of therapy was two people, sitting opposite each other on comfortable chairs, in a small clinic room somewhere urban. There'd be a low coffee table between them, on which usually sat either a reed diffuser or a box of Kleenex. Sometimes it was both. One of the people present would have a tissue clutched in one hand, while the other sat with one leg up and crossed over the other.

That wasn't the case with Pam.

And goddamn it, despite his best efforts, the confounding of expectation had actually got Cam Killick talking. For the first time ever.

'How have you been?' Pam asked, as if they'd been mates for years, and the answer to the question wasn't the reason Cam was paying her to meet with him once a week.

'All right thanks,' he replied.

They gently pumped their feet in a pedalo which had just left the mere's left bank, and carved their way past a handful of ducks who diligently waited for them to throw bread that was never coming. Cam had been so reluctant to sit in an office and let the four walls try to choke him, that Pam had had the genius idea that they do something while they talk. Other activities they'd done included the driving range, a long Ferris wheel ride over Great Yarmouth pier, and pony-riding on Cromer Beach.

The latter of those three really tested the limits of how awkward Cam could feel, stuck almost static on a steed that was as stubborn as he was, but he realised he really didn't care. Something significant had changed in him, where therapy was concerned. He embraced it now, owned it, and found that the honesty it brought caused him to respect it greatly.

He still needed encouraging at times, but he found himself trusting of Pam, and found her insight frighteningly surgical. It shocked him, just how much she could see to the root of a problem, and even in the short period of two months, she had located and lanced a number of psychological boils with a precision the special forces would be proud of.

'How's the sleep?' Pam asked, as they wound a counterclockwise course, now heading under the overhanging café of Diss Publishing, the local bookshop.

'It's better I think, in that it's less disturbed,' he said. He found that eye contact was tough when he spoke with Pam, so this side-by-side seating in the plastic pedalo was a real help. 'I still wake up, and don't know why. I hear things that aren't there. But, I don't know, I think I'm quicker to dismiss those moments and move on from them. Like… I don't lie there gasping and sweating. I just think *Oh this again* and move on quickly. Something like that I think.'

The steering of the pedalo was achieved via one of the occupants pedalling quicker than the other, so, if you didn't talk, it had to be done by a symbiotic understanding of where they wanted to go. Cam found it the mildest battle of wills, and assumed that it was all part of Pam's assessment of him, but still opted for the path of least resistance.

'Have you managed not to end up in the bath yet?' she asked. There was a playful tone to her voice, as if they were both in on the joke that his sleeping habits were weird at best.

'I feel like there'll be one day I wake up, and I'll be in my own bed, but I won't know what to do,' he replied quietly. 'It's been so long since... normal, you know?'

'That will surely give you a huge sense of achievement,' Pam said. 'Even the fact you're thinking about that possibility, of sleeping in your own bed, shows how far you're coming.'

'If you say so,' he said, dubiously, but he recognised her point. He was making progress, slowly but ever more surely. He didn't know what his future looked like, but it held a promise that maybe he wouldn't end up waking in tepid water in his bathtub every night.

'How's work treating you?'

'Good.'

She folded her arms next to him, and he knew she wouldn't long stand for such a monosyllabic answer. It didn't take long. 'Would you like to expand on that in any way?'

He could hear her unasked questions lining up. He decided he'd beat her to it. 'You always find something that makes you think. Whether it's something man-made, or a rock that shouldn't be there. I remember once finding a chunk of quartz down near St Benet's Abbey – had no business being there. But these things have me asking questions. Made me go looking, and thinking, and I found that the chunk of quartz had come from the gift shop at the Sea Life Centre. I'm assuming the owner of the rock had been to the aquarium, then come back to one of the river cruisers as part of the holiday and it fell out of their pocket. Simple enough. But my point is, when you're down there, and you're by yourself, you can't help letting your mind wander when something out of the ordinary pops up.'

Pam leapt to the inference like a seasoned long jumper. 'So, what else did you find that made you ask questions?'

Cam cursed himself for being so transparent, and he spent a moment considering how to answer.

What was it Jess said? Honesty. Honesty was what was going to make therapy work. He'd taken it to heart, and yeah, he'd felt the positives.

Bugger it, he thought.

'A knife,' he said. 'Blood on it.'

Pam was usually so impassive, but he saw her pause pedalling, just for a second. The loss of rhythm meant they turned a touch to the left before normal directional service resumed.

'Were you OK with the blood?' Pam asked.

It was Cam's turn to stop pedalling for a moment. He hadn't expected that. Surely, for him and Rogers, the presence of the blood was a catalyst towards investigation – something it seemed they both needed, although admitting they were any kind of kindred spirits would irk the detective sergeant no end.

But blood, itself?

Cam had seen enough of it. He was numb, for the most part, to its colour and meaning. The sight of it should induce panic and horror. It shouldn't be outside the veins and arteries, and the fact that it's before your eyes meant that somewhere, at some point, something had gone very wrong. But for Cam, it no longer did, and all that was left was the question: *why*. Why was it there?

He remembered reading about an experiment, involving a live brain scan on diagnosed psychopaths. They were shown a series of images, some of which were occasionally ghastly.

It turns out the part of a psychopath's brain that lights up at the sight of those images isn't the part associated with fear or disgust – it's the part that fires when normal people are interested and challenged. Psychopaths look at blood and gore how normal people would look at a crossword.

Cam often wondered where he would sit on such a scale, and guessed unhappily that he'd be somewhere in between. Disquieted by the sight, but acknowledging that its presence caused a bit of a conundrum.

'No problem with blood,' he replied, unable to put any of these thoughts into words.

'Would you say you are more comfortable with it than you would like?' Pam asked.

'Probably,' he replied.

They chatted on a little bit more, as the ducks followed them in determined hope. They talked about Cam's breathing techniques, and how they helped calm him, but she also gave him some ideas of what to think at the same time. Calming images he could twin with the rhythm to bring him back quicker. He promised he'd give it a try.

Their hour went by in a blur, and before they knew it, they were back at the bank, ready to hop out.

'So,' said Pam. 'Where shall we meet next week?'

Cam shrugged. 'I'm easy-going.'

'OK, I'd noticed that. So...' Pam rooted in her handbag, and pulled out a magazine cutting with frayed edges, evidently torn out in a moment of inspiration. 'I've got a list.'

She held out the scrap. It had a checklist, with a bold title which read *Fifty things to do in Norfolk!* 'So, how about Merrivale Model Village, this time next week?'

Cam smiled despite himself. 'Okay, deal.'

5

Back in the van and reunited with Nala, they travelled in a north-easterly direction back up to Norwich then through Wroxham and past Horning to a place called Rollesby. There was no early-afternoon traffic to speak of, the roads barely dusted by cars.

Rollesby was a small settlement between Ludham and Great Yarmouth, with a couple of wide broads on either side of the road preceding it. There was a village hall, a water treatment plant and a garden centre, and to the outsider, that seemed about it. Cam followed his satnav off down one of the gravel side roads, and it ushered him to its very bottom, where the trees reached over the top of the van and potholes sent him and Nala bouncing towards the roof of the car.

If the road presented itself with discretion, the house at the end most certainly didn't. Lassiter's Barn was a converted boathouse that hovered over Rollesby Great Broad in one of the most sought-after spots one could imagine. It was a triumph of modern engineering, poured into the mould of the antiquated, old meeting new with traditional features coexisting peacefully with cutting-edge technology. Vast solar panels hung near centuries-old beams, with sleek CCTV lenses and control panels on traditional stone.

With such features on display, Cam couldn't work out for the life of him why the road was such a mess, when some good old-fashioned tarmac would do everyone's suspension the world of good.

He parked alongside the steps in a carport beneath the high balcony that ran around the front of the property — or was it the back? After all, the other side was where the impressive view was. Acres of water, with no other buildings in sight. It was like a glimpse at a Mesozoic marsh, only missing pterodactyls wheeling overhead.

Cam killed the engine and hopped out, and before he knew it, he felt eyes on him. He glanced up, his old senses guiding him, that feeling of being watched something he'd honed on much further shores than these. In the eaves of the carport, he spotted the watchful eye of a security camera. Suddenly feeling exposed, he gave it a little wave that even he might describe as awkward.

As if by magic, a hidden speaker answered. 'Oh, it's you,' the voice said. 'Come on up.'

Cam didn't know if there was a microphone around to catch his response, but he guessed there had to be given the lack of expense spared everywhere else. Already embarrassed by his wave, and feeling the social heat kick up a couple of notches because of it, he kept his mouth shut and offered a little nod to the lens. He spotted steps at the back of the carport, and quickly took them, winding up and around onto the balcony.

The view up there was even more impressive. Looking down as he took the stairs, the water clarity was glacier fresh, and shoals of roach swirled in the shadow of the floating platform.

As soon as he stepped onto the raised decking, he heard an aggressive hiss, like a rattlesnake, and stopped sharp.

He couldn't see anything, but a second hiss made him look upwards.

There on the roof of the house was a handful of Egyptian geese. They stared down at Cam with hostile intent and tiny focused beads for eyes, their necks craned and poised to follow his every move.

Mercifully, directly below the geese, a door opened. It wasn't a conventional front door but a set of bifold windows, one of which opened wide with a costly swish. Out stepped a man who Cam hadn't met before, but assumed he'd spoken with.

'Well, Mr Diver, what have you got for me?' He was in his late seventies, to Cam's estimation. A ring of spongey white hair frosted the tops of his ears. He wore a fashion-ably tired lumberjack shirt, emblazoned with the name of a fancy country lifestyle brand. Cam guessed that name was also somewhere on the designer jeans, and the furred moccasins that sat on his feet that looked like they'd been in a shoebox under his bed since the colonial wars.

Cam couldn't speak, instead looking up at the geese. They were still watching him intently. The man caught Cam's distraction, and looked up over his own head.

'Oh, ignore them,' he said. 'They've claimed the roof as their own, for reasons I don't understand – mainly, I think, because they're thick as pig shit. They're always sitting up there hissing at everyone. They won't come down.'

'Right,' Cam said. The unconventionality of it all was throwing him, jarring his calm.

He didn't know whether to step forward to shake his customer's hand, and risk getting his eye pecked out from above. Instead, he stayed where he was. Eventually, he felt so much like a lemon he had to speak.

'Mr Lassiter?' he asked, unzipping his dryrobe and pulling out a Roys carrier bag.

'Yes, yes,' replied the man, who carried that harried countenance of someone for whom twenty-four was an insufficient number of hours in the day to achieve all the mad stuff he had planned. The kind of person where you were left in no doubt as to how they'd got so successful, but were 100 per cent sure they'd be a nightmare to work for. 'Did you find it?'

'I think I did,' Cam replied, dipping his fingers slowly into the open mouth of the carrier bag, again being careful not to get stabbed by all the hooks he knew were in there. He pulled out the lure with a rattle, and held it up for Lassiter to see.

In the blazing sunlight, the craftsmanship of the lure was even more obvious and impressive. It was even beautiful, in its own way.

Lassiter's face opened up with childlike joy, his hands reaching out for the item while his eyebrows danced with glee. 'You did find it!'

Cam simply nodded as he handed the lure over, relieved to have returned it, and in that sense completed his mission. That was the way he looked at these things. Every little job was another mission. Another box to tick, another objective met. It helped the old soldier in him, but it also helped to establish a goal-oriented routine on which the vagaries of his mental state could cling to. But, of course, here he had another goal in mind – one that he was keen to move on to.

'I can see why you wanted it back,' he said to Lassiter, who was now holding the lure up to the light as if it was the first time he'd ever laid eyes on it. He'd fallen into another silence which gave Cam the sweats. 'Mr Lassiter?' he asked after a couple of excruciatingly quiet moments.

The man seemed lost. Before darting back to the present.

Yes, thought Cam, *definitely a nightmare to work for.*

'Yes, of course,' said Lassiter. 'I bought it from a chap who runs fishing charters on Lake Michigan. He really uses them for zander... ummm, bloody hell, yes, walleye over there... and makes them himself. He hand-paints every scale, and rather than insist you put it on display or whatnot, he's adamant not only that his customers should use them, but that they are the most efficient catching tool available.'

'Yes, it seems a shame not to put it on the wall,' Cam said in reply.

'You see, that would go against the whole spirit of the thing.'

'Well...' said Cam, feeling he was reaching the end of the small talk part of the conversation – and also the limit of awkwardness he could handle. It immediately sent heat up his neck to the sides and back of his head. Any awkwardness, any hint of cringe, sent embarrassment flares to his brain, and those in turn put him at risk of a panic attack.

For Cam those kind of mental booby traps were too easy to stumble into. He didn't want to do that now, especially knowing that if he asked a couple of questions, the right questions, he might get a little bit of info that could go a long way to establishing inroads into the other issue – the one that was, in truth, the real reason he was here. He could have waited until he was next passing to drop off the recovered cargo; could have arranged a meeting at both their convenience.

But he wanted to start gathering information in case that really was human blood on that blade.

'Did you happen to lose anything else out at Doke End?' he asked, trying to seem as inconspicuous as he could. Alas James Bond he was not – no matter how much he tried to be, when he really needed it, coolness seemed in short supply.

Lassiter looked away, and furrowed his brow. He returned his gaze to Cam, and said: 'I don't know, did I?'

The look he gave Cam was full of a broad openness, offering only genuine question and confusion. The answer and its directness threw Cam off and extinguished a great deal of the hope that answers might be easy to come by. He pressed on regardless.

'I found something else down there, not too far away from where I found the lure. Very different mind you. Seemed brand new, or close to it. And looked like it hadn't been down there for very long.'

Cam watched Lassiter closely, looking for any signs of a twitch or tell that would give away his knowledge of the bloody knife. However, there was nothing. His eyes were blank coin slots through which no pennies were dropping.

After a couple of moments, with the older man's brain clearly whirring so much Cam was convinced steam was about to break from his ears, he spoke. 'It'll probably be one of those things, where I've lost something and I only remember weeks later that it's gone.' Lassiter smiled, as if full of self-referential pride. 'I'm sort of like that.'

Cam didn't doubt it, but decided to play along. 'Me too,' he said.

'It might help to know what it is?'

Cam didn't want to give anything away unless it was really necessary. A bloody knife wasn't something you would generally misplace. Besides, if he told Lassiter about the knife, Lassiter might blab it to someone else who *did* know something about it.

And any potential investigation might be hindered, when discretion would surely give them time to pursue the right courses of action without outside pressure or interference.

'Oh, never mind,' Cam said. 'You have a think, and if anything comes up, you know how to call me.'

'Fair enough,' said Lassiter, although the disappointment at not being clued in was obvious in his petulant bottom lip, which jutted out for just a second. Then, 'Oh yes, of course!' he said and he ran back inside. Cam could hear jangling from inside the house, and the sound of rummaging.

While he waited, he let his mind drift once more to the knife and Doke End.

Cam had been the last person there, with Lassiter before that. Whether anyone had gone between those two visits was unknown – but Cam would have the chance to ask, because he still had the keys. If that Broads Trust guy, Forsyth, wanted them back, they would now come at the price of some information.

As for Lassiter, given the man's open-book personality, and his childlike way of going about things, Cam felt sure that Lassiter not only hadn't lost a knife, but didn't know a damn thing about it. Of course, Cam couldn't prove any of that, but he was an astute judge of character, or at least he felt he could be, when his own faculties were firing on all cylinders.

Abruptly, Lassiter emerged holding a tray upon which sat a couple of dozen bottles full of something deep red, with no label. Each lid had a date scrawled on them, in some kind of silver marker. They all said one week from now. Cam hadn't even put his arms out, when the entirety of the tray was thrust into his midsection.

'Your reward,' Lassiter said, with obvious pride.

'Oh, of course. I'd forgotten.' Cam had indeed failed to remember the bonus his client had promised him if he brought the lure back in one piece. He wanted to ask what on Earth he was holding, but found no words that would fit.

Lassiter looked at Cam, beaming, like he'd just given him a package of priceless gold bars. 'It's my own spiced breakfast sauce. Think brown sauce, but redder and spicier.'

Cam look down at the bottles. 'That's very… kind.'

'They go off next week, mind,' Lassiter continued, oblivious to the less-than-rapturous gratitude with which his reward had been received. 'So, I'd get cracking if I were you.'

'Thank you,' said Cam, stumped. 'I'll… get going then.'

He started to walk off, and one of the geese overhead hissed at him, as if reminding him that his time in their territory was up, and yes, he would do well to get out of there now. It was like being shooed away by a crap, feathered guard dog.

'See you Mr Diver,' Lassiter hollered to Cam's back. 'And remember, they all go off next week!'

As he left in bemusement, Cam felt suddenly sure of a lot of sausage sandwiches in his immediate future.

6

Cam wound his way back towards his home in Neatishead, wondering whether stopping for the day and calling it quits was a good idea. The trip to Doke End was his only work diary entry until later in the week, and he'd been paid for his work – *and then some*, he thought as he looked at the bottles of alleged breakfast relish on the passenger seat next to him. He had planned to spend the rest of the afternoon trying desperately to switch off and relax in the quiet barn conversion he called home. The reality being that he'd be fretting endlessly about his evening plans with Jess Tabernacle, she of the pink Crocs. They'd only known each other a few months, but a lot had happened in that short space of time. Two friends could just go out for a bite to eat, couldn't they?

Couldn't they?

Cam decided to take a detour to the petrol station in nearby Stalham, and top up the van. It didn't quite need fuel yet, but he wasn't ready to go back to Haven Cottage and bounce between those four walls waiting for something that was definitely, no way, categorically, not a date.

Pulling up in the forecourt, he hopped out by one of the pumps, and had to use a pair of needle-nosed pliers to get the petrol flap open, because the mechanism no longer worked after it was dented during the assault on the vehicle last year. Because it looked like he was trying to break into his own vehicle, the whole thing felt like more of an ordeal than it should be.

One to tell Pam, he thought, when he considered his next appointment with his therapist. She always ended each session by reminding him to keep a diary of things that provoked feelings of anxiety and panic. He could add the van's petrol flap and Charlie Lassiter to the conversation. He quickly pocketed the pliers and inserted the nozzle, and waited while the fuel filled the tank.

His mind drifted in an unhelpful way, as it was wont to do.

Cam hadn't been in any kind of a relationship for ten years plus, and he wasn't about to start calling this thing with Jess anything of the sort. But they'd been through a lot together, and it had undeniably bonded them in some way. They liked each other's company, enjoyed being in each other's lives to some extent or other, and Cam had stayed over at Jess's home soon after they first met, only to comfort her, and provide an emotional safety net. He was so out of practice, so thrown and so desperately awkward, everything that even approached something romantic had him on a quick burn to near-panic attack. He did believe, however, that they shared a degree of attraction.

Back in the van and paid up, he turned the air con up as high as it would go, to bring some cool to his cheeks. As he wound off the bend in the road that took him through the small village of Neatishead, he cursed himself for doing exactly what he'd sworn he wouldn't. Fretting and obsessing, churning in the quiet recesses of his mind.

Jess wouldn't be thinking like this. She was too strong.

Cam himself had seen what Jess Tabernacle could handle, could see just how much life could throw at her, only for her to throw it right back with venom and gall.

It was one of the reasons he liked her.

And he was very aware that something like her was missing in his life and it was strange to think that while he was in his early forties, his own biological clock was ticking. Did he want to be a father or a husband? He thought he might – but going off how glacially his romantic life had passed him by, the likelihood was a light growing dimmer.

Damn it, Cam, he chastised himself. He was a walking contradiction and cliché rolled into one. The soldier who quite fancied settling down; the tormented action man who needed a quiet life.

He turned off the main road down the narrow dirt track that led to Haven Cottage and the surrounding farmland he called home. Nala perked up in the back, as if smelling the homestead, readying herself to hop out.

Then Cam slowed. He did it without meaning to.

Did he really want to sit here for the remainder of the afternoon, beating himself up over his romantic failings? Or was he better off staying out and about?

What could he do?

As his mind hopped from one thing to another, his eyes caught that huge set of keys. They sat in the cup holder by his knee. He needed to give them back, but had agreed to return them later tonight in the exact same pub car park he'd been given them in.

Those keys were nagging at him from the cup holder, and as he thought about it, they gave him an opportunity he might not get again.

What if he returned them early? Purely as a very help-ful gesture, of course – but it meant he might catch that person unawares. Which would be the perfect time to get some information.

The person who disposed of the knife would have needed a boat for it to have found its way out into the middle of the water like that. It was too far to throw, too inconceivable to swim to. And those keys controlled access to the only way to get a boat into Doke End. So, whoever had put the knife there must've at some point had these keys. This was a firm line of enquiry.

Maybe there were multiple copies of the keys cut and in circulation, and his line of investigation might be at a dead end before it even got started – but he simply wouldn't know if he didn't ask.

He looked up again at his house. Nala looked up at him.

'Maybe later,' he said. And he reversed back down the track.

7

Cam had never been to the Broads Trust offices before, but a quick Google search took him straight to it. Nala had seemingly given up on her owner, and had retreated to sleep in the dog bed in the back, leaving just Cam and a job-lot of chutney in the front, as he pounded the tarmac yet again. The Broads Trust was based over in Norwich, so it was back into the city for the second time today.

This time he travelled into the complicated miasma of Norwich city centre via the A-roads and roundabouts from Coltishall, before entering the city past the Playhouse and crawling along the River Wensum, towards the train station. The afternoon traffic was sparse but carried the promise that things would soon change, as already people had started leaving the city prior to five o'clock quitting time. The river was a bruised ochre on his right, with reeds and bullrushes that clung to its bends like barnacles, as the water wound through the centre of the city like a huge eel. He saw his destination as he waited at the lights.

The Broads Trust was stationed in a glass riverside building, the likes of which, Cam thought dryly, the council never usually granted planning permission for. Though that observation might have been guided by Cam's cynicism for all the dealings he'd had with the governing body – which had been universally sticky, slow and utterly embroiled in bureaucratic treacle.

He parked the van at the twenty-minute drop-off spot at the railway station, leaving Nala asleep in the back, before jogging across the car park and squeezing through the railings to cross the road back to the riverbank. He crossed over the pedestrian bridge and quickly found the rear of the office building and its main entrance.

Cam planned his approach.

He didn't want to ring the bell. His aim was to disrupt and imbalance, and a cheery announcement would dent that. There were five car parking spaces, all of them filled, but he didn't see Forsyth's blue Volvo. The building was split-level, with one level on this higher roadside, and two levels on the other side overhanging the river. A wraparound deck seemed to service both sides, incorporating the alley around the right-hand side of the property, and Cam quickly vaulted its railing to go and get to gatecrashing.

As he walked around, he saw the river open out below him, and it was actually even more green than he'd anticipated. It looked like one of those kids' toxic slime toys – almost neon in places. An algae breakout, Cam assumed, and one that was probably choking out all the life underneath. Cam had some experience with sea-borne algae, but was less familiar with its freshwater counterpart – this bloom carried flecks and clumps of stringy, almost hair-like, clots of the stuff. The fact that it had decided to manifest itself right outside the Broads Trust offices wasn't lost on Cam at all – it was like the river was making its own feelings known about how much use they were.

Cam followed the deck around, and found himself in front of a long set of sliding glass doors, which clad the entirety of the building's rear aspect. Behind the glass, once Cam had shifted focus through the late-afternoon shadows and failing light, sat four confused faces in an open-plan office space that looked somewhat cluttered and disorganised. The faces belonged to two women and two men, and while the former looked at him with amused surprise, the latter seemed to view him with some outraged hostility, like their territory had been challenged. Cam found that amusing – and potentially significant – and simply waved.

The two men, one dressed in a jumper and jeans, the other in a power suit befitting a nineties courtroom drama, looked at each other in a wary agreement of mutual back up, and stood in unison to approach the door. It slid open with an expensive swish, and Cam greeted them with a smile.

'Sorry about that,' said Cam, doing what he always did when he felt unsure of how long his bravado would last, and simply pretending to be someone else. That someone was invariably the same each time. 'Your front bell doesn't seem to be working,' he said, with as much Roger Moore as he could muster.

One of the men glanced back in the direction of the front door, clearly disbelieving – quite rightly – Cam's excuse, but Cam pressed on regardless, with the pretence of friendly innocuousness.

'I've only got a few minutes left in the car park before I'll get ticketed, so I'm in a bit of a rush. Is Mr Forsyth about?'

At the mention of their colleague, the men eased the heat from their glares. One was shorter, with a smooth hairless crown, red-rimmed eyes, and a frosting of grey bristles around his chin from ear to ear, that looked like scraps of tinfoil from a hastily inhaled KitKat. He spoke, and Cam was surprised to note a depth and richness which suggested the man might actually be a capable baritone.

'He's not in today. And who are you?'

Cam glanced at the other man, whose clothes clung over a potbelly which, next to the slenderness of the rest of his frame, gave the impression of an abrupt pregnancy. He remained stone-faced.

'Are you sure he's not here?' Cam pushed. 'Is he not coming in at all today?'

Mr Tinfoil took the lead again. 'He isn't here. Who's asking for him?'

Cam looked at him, and noted a new pointedness to his gaze, and the fact that the capillaries in his eyeball looked like they might burst if he experienced any sudden excitement. 'Steady on, mate. I've just got a set of keys for him.'

'Keys? What keys?'

'These keys,' Cam said, as he pulled out the thick ring of metalwork. And as the keys came up in the afternoon light in front of the office workers' faces, Cam saw their eyes unmistakably widen. It was a tell. They knew the keys, Cam was convinced of it. And they knew he shouldn't have them.

'You didn't know he'd lent them to me?' He fished.

The men didn't answer. Cam thought a bit more information might open them up.

'He lent me the keys so I could go into Doke End and look for a fishing lure. I'm a salvage diver, you see, a customer of mine lost his favourite lure, asked me to go and look for it. Mr Forsyth was good enough to lend me the keys so I could go and have a look.'

The men stared at him in apparent incomprehension.

Cam glanced between the pair of them. 'I found it, if that makes any difference.'

Tinfoil held out his hand. 'I'll take them, I'll make sure they get to him.'

Cam wasn't going to let them go that easily. Having the keys kept him involved, and as long as he didn't have any answers, he wasn't going to part with them. Plus, he had the added sudden suspicious behaviour of these two middle-management muppets to factor in. 'Hold on. I thought by coming here it might save Mr Forsyth the job of coming out to meet me later as agreed. I think I'll just save the confusion and give them back myself.'

Potbelly stepped forward and smiled – but the smile looked fused in place and false.

'It's all right,' Potbelly said. 'We'll give them to him, save you the trouble.' The grin had become rictus in intensity.

Cam pocketed the keys once more and put his hands up. 'I'm just going to wait for the man himself,' he said with a smile as he backed away. The men watched him go, and he retreated back around the side of the building.

As exchanges went, that one had been curious, pointless and telling all at once.

The men were agitated about those keys; the very sight of them sending whispers of palpable nerves through them. Maybe it was as simple as a 'see nothing, know nothing' approach to impropriety being foiled (one thing that had become clear was that Forsyth shouldn't be lending the keys to anybody). Or…

What if they knew about the knife?

Either way, it was enough for Cam to want to draw this out longer, and speak to Forsyth again, this time with a real line of enquiry in mind. The bottom line was, as long as he still had the keys, he still had the chance to ask those questions.

As he left the decking and started up the road back to the train station and his van, his phone rang. He pulled it out and saw Rogers' name on the caller ID.

'Hello.'

'It's me,' said Rogers on the other end. 'Where are you?'

'In the city,' he replied.

'Good, can we meet?'

This was a summons he was not quite prepared for, nor used to. 'Yes sure, whereabouts?'

'Let's keep this off the books,' she said, before giving the name of a pub Cam was familiar with, and hung up.

Ordering him to the pub before clocking-off time? This was urgent. A spring hit his step and he got a march on – but not before he spotted a shop opposite offering something that could be very useful in the long run. Seeing it as an omen, he decided a quick detour couldn't hurt.

Some Time Ago

Lenny Drummond left the engine running and the SUV in neutral, but knew he'd got it wrong once again when he stepped out and his foot dropped into the freezing river. He was only soaked up to his shin before he hit the bottom of the concrete boating ramp, but still, this was a rookie error. He had a quick glance around, to make sure nobody had seen him, and quickly jumped back in the driver's seat. He pulled the car forward a few metres, and this time, looked down to check before he got out.

Perfect. Too late for now, one Nike utterly soaked, but, yeah, another time, perfect.

He hopped out for real this time, closed the front door, and walked around past the bonnet, to the bank. His foot squelched with every step, and the cold seeped straight into his toes, the weak early-spring sunshine having done nothing to mitigate the water's chill.

He'd used this particular boat ramp for months, ever since he'd started fishing the area in earnest, but he still couldn't get used to it. At least nobody had seen him. That would have been a real no-no. Image-conscious in the highest degree, Lenny was bedecked in the latest high-end angling suit, replete with the most sophisticated Gore-Tex layering. With his all-new electric four-by-four Range Rover, dragging a gleaming trailer, about to load up his pristine twelve-foot Seastrike fishing boat – itself bursting with all the high-tech bells and whistles – he looked every inch the modern, well-to-do fishing maestro.

The only thing he was missing, he thought glumly as he pulled the Seastrike gradually towards the trailer with a guideline, was a fish. He had blanked, again. He knew the fish were there – the reports were crystal-clear, and illustrated with sonar imagery – and he knew they were big. But tempting one was proving damn near impossible.

He hauled the rope tight and eased the boat's bottom between the rails and runners of the trailer, before walking back around to the trailer winch and feeding the guy rope through it.

It was with sudden but unsurprising disappointment Lenny realised that to reach it, he would have to get his feet wet again.

Bugger it, he thought, stepping directly into the river. Nobody was about, and Nike had brought a new colourway out. It would give him an excuse to upgrade these.

He sloshed his feet in thoroughly, grabbed the winch handle, and gave it a number of brisk turns, which sent a rhythmic staccato chatter across the water. A handful of ducks leapt from the water in a clatter of wing-beats, lifting for the heavens.

The rope tightened, and at last the boat itself started to climb up onto the trailer properly, inching forwards with every turn. It was soon thunking into place – another sound that rang out across the water.

His thoughts went back to the fish. They were there. But why hadn't he caught one?

He started to think about other baits he could be using. He favoured mackerel – always had – and always carried more of that than anything else. But what about herring? Or smelt? They had a cucumber smell that drifted beautifully in the water, leaving a scent trail that might lure the big predators right in.

Or maybe he should go for live baits, and stick a hook out there with a live roach attached? Statistically, he believed more big fish had been caught using this method than the others. But that meant he had to go and catch a bunch of live bait, or find someone willing to sell it on the side. Fishing for daft little fish like that wasn't Lenny's style, so it would have to be the latter. But he didn't know anyone who could provide such a thing.

Hang on – he was part of an illicit ring of anglers paying for a go at a particular forbidden fishing hole. Of course, one of those other anglers would know a live bait guy.

No, he thought. That might give away tactics for success, or worse – reveal that he wasn't catching at all, and was having to go back to the drawing board.

He couldn't admit that.

He couldn't be the guy that had all the gear but no idea.

He shuddered at the thought, as he jumped back up into the driver's seat, and eased the Range Rover silently forward, pulling the boat up and out of the water behind it.

Lenny Drummond would rather make up stories of monstrous catches and have to try to back them up, no matter how complicated that got, than have to admit that he wasn't getting anywhere.

Maybe I could use AI, he thought as he hopped back out. Picture of me with a huge pike, he could put in the instruction box. Yeah. He decided to give it a try when he got home.

Now fully on dry land, he walked back to the boat and started to strap it down properly to the trailer. He always felt better when it was out of the water. Easier to handle, and fewer chances to look like a dick.

Then he saw he had made an error, one he was really glad he'd noticed before pulling out of here onto one of the main roads. He'd left the engine lowered, like it would be in water, and the propellor was miraculously just off the cracked concrete of the ramp.

He breathed out in relief, then climbed up into the boat, and started to heave the engine back up. It was nightmarishly heavy, but he'd never come across an engine that wasn't.

He felt a pop in his back, like a muscle had gone abruptly. It took the breath away from him in a sudden gasp of outward air. He tried to straighten up but couldn't. He was desperate to stretch it out, and try to pop it back, but it felt strange, wrong. And his back felt hot, like the muscle pull had jarred an internal hot water pipe and caused it to burst.

He felt the muscle go again, an agonising relief, and more heat gushed down his back. Hunched over, unable to stand properly, he turned towards the middle of the boat – and saw a man holding a knife.

A knife that was caked in blood.

He didn't have time to think, when the arm holding the knife flicked out with practised ease and speed and rhythm, right into the centre of his chest. If the hot water pipe had burst before, this time the whole boiler imploded, deep inside his middle, and he dropped to his knees, the knife still stuck somewhere very important indeed.

He looked up at the man, the pain in his back suddenly an irrelevance, and his breath wouldn't come.

'No...' he gasped, a growing copper tang in his mouth. 'It can't be...'

The spectre was known to him. The long hair and beard were all new – but the eyes were the same.

He fell at the man's feet.

'No,' he said. 'No.'

And the last thing he thought of, as his blood began to pool into every well and crevice at the bottom of the boat, was that his Nikes would be properly ruined now.

8

It was just hitting five o'clock when Claire Rogers walked into the sticky-floored booze palace with the everlasting stairs, otherwise known as Wetherspoons. She'd managed to sneak out without getting collared, and even managed to finish off her reports on what they were now calling the Rackheath Robbery, which she thought betrayed a real lack of creative ingenuity.

As for this particular pub, Rogers liked stopping here on the way home for a number of reasons.

One? It was near the station – but not too close to be the shift-change booze haunt for the constabulary's workforce. She wouldn't say she was a regular, but then again, she wasn't exactly a rare sighting either. She knew the faces of some of the staff, but not their names.

Two? Wetherspoons was God's gift to people-watching and had charitably made sure the booze was appropriately cheap while you were at it.

She headed upstairs because the trek to the toilet would be a little shorter – but it was adrenaline making her take them two at a time.

There had been a break in the case. The knowledge glared like phosphorus in her head as she arrived at the discreet corner booth she was about to make her temporary war room for the next who-knew-how-long. She'd pushed, using her newfound weight and respect in the constabulary, and she'd been proven right.

The events of the previous winter, when she had been involved in a number of arrests that had solved the region's biggest and longest-standing cold case, had given her a certain weight and kudos, the kind she'd waited all her career to receive. Not just a senior detective, with years on the clock, she now had one hell of a major case in her professional history which cemented that status. She'd gone from has-been to revered, overnight – and she was making the most of it.

Cam Killick appeared almost immediately and sat opposite her. The mere sight of him triggered Rogers' gag reflex.

'Seriously?' she said. 'You're still in that bloody wetsuit?'

Killick looked down at himself, holding a pint of lemonade some joker had put a little brolly in, and the realisation seemed to kick in. 'I've had a busy day.'

'You're not the only one,' she said, and readied another verbal volley, before thinking better of it. Agitating him wasn't a good idea, because for all his quirks, real fragility was never far away.

'Never mind all that,' she said hurriedly. 'I've got one very quick question for you, Killick.'

He looked bemused, but open and willing, like a tired Labrador looking at a steak beyond a pane of glass.

'Is there anything at all about that knife or Doke End – or anything about the last few days for that matter – that you want to talk to me about? Anything you'd like to get off your chest?'

Killick looked back at her with zero change in his expression. She didn't doubt him one bit, but her own need to dot the i's and cross the t's had to be satisfied.

'Not a thing,' he said evenly.

'Good.' She took a neat pull of Sauvignon. 'You just found the knife, bagged it up, and brought it straight to me.'

'That really is it. I didn't even do anything stupid in between.' As he said this, a staff member came over and placed a bowl of fries in front of him. From the depths of his dryrobe, Killick pulled out a bottle of livid red sauce. Its colour was nuclear in intensity.

Rogers could only look at him in bemusement as Killick slathered the sauce all over the chips. He picked one up, popped it in his mouth, and his eyebrows flipped upwards.

'Do you know, it's not that bad,' he said, in apparent begrudging surprise.

'You were just telling me that you hadn't done anything stupid?' Rogers said.

Killick look down at the plate, shrugged and tucked in eagerly. 'What did you want to see me about?' he asked, as if his antics were perfectly normal.

Rogers found herself blinking a few times in quick succession, then gave a rapid shake of her head to clear the nonsense from her periphery. 'We've had some early results on those tests. We were treated to a little help from the gods of expediting.' Rogers paused for a moment to organise her own thoughts. This case, situation, whatever she wanted to call it, had only been with her a matter of hours as it was, and she hadn't had any real time to process it. The ball, now it was rolling, seemed to have found a momentum of its own volition and creation. 'That was blood on the blade you found. Your instincts were right. Now don't get ahead of yours—'

Killick looked up from his own claret-soaked meal. 'It's human?'

That had been one of Rogers' own primary questions. Maybe that knife had been used to fillet a fish or gut an animal out on Doke End, before clattering overboard. Killing catches was illegal on the Norfolk Broads, but it wasn't the freshly-fired smoking gun that they'd first imagined. The case wouldn't even be anything to do with them any more – it would be pushed down the police chain and end up an issue for the Environmental Protection Agency, at best.

'Yes, it is,' she said. 'This isn't a case of poaching. Nobody was filleting a bloody salmon up there.'

'There are no salmon on the Broads,' replied Killick. 'But there are a few trout if you know where to look.'

'Excuse me?' said Rogers.

'The Broads don't contain any salmon. There might be the odd one, thanks to spawn stuck on a duck's foot or something, but none are indigenous. But trout, someone's introduced them on the quiet somewhere along the line.'

Rogers simply shook this extra nonsense away again. 'Can we get back to the knife with the human blood on it, do you think? There's more. There was tissue found in the hilt. Embedded where steel blade meets wood handle.'

'Muscular tissue?'

'Organ. Carotid.'

Killick looked confused. 'An... artery?'

'Sorry, cardial.'

'Cardioid?' said Killick with a frown.

'That,' said Rogers, flustered. 'It's a piece of bloody *heart*, Killick.'

The word floated across the table and sat between them. Its weight grew by the second.

'Just to be very clear,' said Killick, the chips now forgotten in front of him. 'This knife was used to stab someone in the heart.'

Rogers sipped Sauvignon and nodded over the rim of the glass.

What Killick had found was a murder weapon – no more, no less.

Rogers swallowed and continued. 'The tissue had only just begun to rot, meaning that it got there recently. Unless the knife fell from a freezer, this attack had to have happened a matter of days ago.'

Killick caught on quicker than Rogers expected him too. 'Which means the chance of getting workable DNA from it just went up? I remember you said five days was the maximum amount of time.'

'The odds have certainly improved,' said Rogers.

'So, what are we going to do?' he asked. She saw that look in his eyes. The one that told her he was going to throw himself headlong at this, whether she told him to back off or not.

'We are going to have to play this very carefully, but obviously time is of the essence,' she replied. 'We have a murder weapon, but no body, which lends this matter a real air of the unique. We're looking at a much longer wait for a DNA profile, even if there is one – and only then can we try to match it to any profile on the relevant databases. But that doesn't mean we are going to pause in stasis until then.' She looked at Killick. 'We are going to have to interview you formally, as part of our due diligence, let's say.'

'But you know I had nothing to do with this?' said Killick.

'What balloon-headed killer takes their own murder weapon to the cop shop? You're a numpty Killick, but even you are above that. We have to make sure all the evidence and our workings are backed up and airtight. If this ever went to the Crown Prosecution Services and, you'd hope, a trial, even a defence team comprised of drunk babies would have a jamboree tying the prosecution in knots, because the investigators didn't consider the very person who brought the murder weapon in as a suspect.

'I've seen solid cases derailed by far less before. I don't want to give any excuse for reasonable doubt. Whoever tossed that knife into Doke End clearly thought it was the perfect place and the perfect way to get away with murder. We are going to prove them wrong.'

Killick nodded and reached for his plate. Put more toxic-looking fries into his mouth.

Rogers gave up and acknowledged the elephant in the room. 'Do you usually carry around your own pot of mental relish?'

'It goes off next week,' Cam replied.

Roger could only watch him collect the slivers of nuclear potato with a fork. 'Give it a few hours, and I'm sure your toilet will be really grateful. When can you come in?'

'I can be free whenever.'

'Be there for 9 a.m. in the morning,' said Rogers. 'I want to make sure I've got all my ducks in a row from the get-go. But before then, you've got to tell me something.'

The fork of mangled glowing chips hovered in front of Killick's face. The booth felt suddenly airless.

Rogers filled the void. 'Where did you get the keys from?'

Killick breathed easier, but still seemed flushed from the directness of Rogers' approach. 'A guy called Forsyth at the Broads Trust. He helped me out, lent them to me when

I needed to get in there this morning. I picked them up from him last night outside the Rising Sun in Coltishall. I've still got them.'

With that, Killick clunked the keys down onto the table, and finally scoffed the chips. There were so many offshoots that it was less a ring than a dense jagged jumble, like the fat metal carcass of a steel blackbird. 'I just went to the Broads Trust to try to give them back, but Forsyth wasn't there and his workmates, well, they acted all cagey about it. I'm hoping to give the keys back tonight, same pub car park. I'm aiming to sort it while I'm there meeting a lady friend.'

'Lady friend? I've got fifteen years on you Killick, and if you called me your lady friend, I'd dump you in a heartbeat.'

That caused Killick to go red again.

'Don't get any ideas, pond boy. Look, when you meet Forsyth, ask him who had the keys before you in the last five days. Let's cover that time frame to start with. Now, despite your obvious quirks, I believe you're a half-decent judge of character, Killick. Work out if he's lying. I don't think he is, because there is no way I'd lend you the keys to somewhere if I'd just dumped a knife there. Still, be vigilant, get a read off him.'

'Will do.'

'I left one of my new underlings checking in with the hospital services and all local mortuaries. See if they've got a John/Jane Doe with a hole in his/her heart. Living but most likely dead.'

'Hope someone turns up.'

She sighed, and sipped her wine deeply. 'It would be a big help if they did.'

She savoured the moment. A quick moment of respite before she knew that both their respective in-built urgencies would start firing at full capacity until there was a resolution to this mystery, one way or another.

'Quick word of advice,' she said. 'I'd take a shower before you meet your "lady friend".'

Killick looked down at himself. 'Point taken.'

'At last.'

'You'd been treated by Saint Expedite.' Killick was still examining himself.

'Who?'

'Earlier you mentioned help from the gods of expediting.' He finally looked up. 'Saint Expedite is the patron saint of urgent causes.'

Try as she might, Rogers couldn't hide a smile. Killick, as always, was full of surprises. 'In which case, I'll make sure I keep him on speed dial.'

9

The Rising Sun sat tight to an idyllic bend on the river Bure, on the shoulder of an expansive public green. On the other side of the drifting water, a mist-covered marsh sulked, over which Cam knew a barn owl regularly patrolled while the sun went down. He always hoped to catch a sight of the magnificent predator whenever he was passing, as it darted eerily and silently over the bullrushes before dropping down to end something's life. Tonight, it was simply too dark to see anything across the rippling surface of the water, save for the first few rows of hardy reeds before the black swallowed them up.

Cam pulled the van into the car park and drew it down tight to the water itself, his eyes scanning the waving reed tips opposite. Peeling his eyes away, he saw, by the pub's front door, the green VW Beetle that belonged to Jess Tabernacle. It was a classic edition, and Cam had no idea how she managed to keep it roadworthy. He hopped out and invited Nala to come with him with a nod of the head, and they headed to the front door of the pub.

With whitewashed walls and a grand, red and gold sign, the pub sat across three separate levels and was a constant popular spot during the summer months which the day's sun had hinted at. As they crossed the car park, Nala seemed to recognise the Beetle, suddenly picking up pace, and she trotted gamely towards the entrance. Cam opened the door for her like a butler, and she looked both left and right quickly before quickly settling on the former. Cam took one last look over the river before he went in, but couldn't see anything swooping with the right amount of grace.

Cam smiled, because while he was here to see his own companion, Nala was here to see hers. Following the L-shape of the bar, Cam found Jess sitting at a small, raised seating area that housed a couple of bookshelves, a crackling fire and two sofas facing each other. She couldn't have picked a better spot.

'Well, I'll be damned,' Jess said with a playful smile. 'You're on time and there's not a dryrobe or wetsuit in sight.'

Cam looked down at himself, and brushed away imaginary lint from the thick fisherman's jumper and jeans he'd thrown on after his shower. 'Contrary to popular belief, I do own real clothes.'

Nala took the small talk as her invitation to reintroduce herself to Wicket, a Shorkie just like herself – except he was the colour of freshly baked shortbread. They were thick as thieves.

Cam took the sofa opposite Jess, dropping onto the tired leather which swallowed him just a bit too far. Jess giggled, and Cam, surprised as the depth of the seat caught him off guard, found himself smiling too. Jess could do that to him sometimes – fill him with an ease and warmth that other people simply could not. They had met each other under the most trying and dramatic of circumstances, the effects of which were still lingering. They hadn't managed to get past their respective traumas, but there was an unspoken awareness between them that they needed each other in certain unexplainable ways.

Cam found everything about Jess Tabernacle beguiling and unpredictable in equal measure. Her appearance changed with the stubborn uncertainty of the English weather, but every result had the same effect on him. He'd been so shut off emotionally when he first met her that he hadn't known what those feelings were. He'd only recently started realising that the sudden imbalance and reddening of his cheeks when she was around wasn't anything to do with his PTSD.

Today her hair was a pixie cut in frozen blue, with purple eyeshadow and cyan lips. She looked like she could have survived the Titanic in a cartoon adaptation of the tragedy created for children, but it all simply worked.

'You know there's a Facebook group called "Dry Robe Wankers"?' she said. 'Where they post pictures of people in normal everyday situations in those robes?'

'I didn't,' said Cam, at last clawing himself out of his leather prison.

'I'm surprised you're not their celebrity.'

'How was your day?' asked Cam, shaking his head.

Jess took a mouthful of electric blue alcopop, presumably chosen for its aesthetic appeal in completing her look. Cam thought it might rot your insides with a single sip.

'Wild excitement at the supermarket today when an elderly lady dropped a bottle of red wine in the booze section,' she said. 'Then a toddler slipped in it, and became a booze-soaked geriatric within seconds. Little red footprints all around the store? Instant homage to a Chucky movie.'

She smiled. Cam loved to see it. After everything this woman had been through, every single smile was well deserved. 'How about yours?' she asked.

'Well, I went to a padlocked bit of the river where no one is supposed to go, looking for a lost fishing lure. I found it, but then I also found a knife that the police have already determined was used to kill someone.'

The blue bottle paused inches from Jess's lips. Honesty was the one thing that Cam Killick could give, and he always gave it plain – especially where Jess was concerned. Not only did he believe she deserved it, but he wasn't sure what else he could provide her in the emotional, grown-up stakes. He knew however, he could always tell the truth.

'You what?' she asked incredulously.

Cam knew she'd heard every word. 'Yeah, there was still blood on it, even though it's been underwater and they found a little piece of heart stuck in the hilt. Apparently, it means that it was used to go through someone's heart in the last five days tops.'

Jess's eyes were still wide and the drink still trapped in stasis. 'Well... do they know whose heart?'

'No, they don't, they're looking into that right now.'

She narrowed her eyes. 'Hmm...' She trailed off, but the look remained. It sent the message.

'I know, I know,' Cam said.

'Oh I know, I know – I know you too.'

'Just...' It was Cam's turn to trail off.

'Just what?'

Cam could feel the truth popping up again. It was a cornerstone of his being, but at the same time, so often his undoing.

'I've got the keys to this body of water on me, and the guy is coming here to pick them up. He's just coming into the car park, but you know, I thought I'd ask him a couple of questions about it while he's here.'

Jess's eyebrows unknotted and shot north. He felt compelled to fill the air between them with more words. 'The keys, you see, they're the only way to get in there. I need to know if there are any other copies, who's got them, and who's been in there recently. It could give the police a bit of a, bit of a leg up, if you know what I mean.'

Jess drank at last, then after she'd swallowed, said: 'You've not had enough excitement?'

Cam again didn't know what to say, and blundered about in his head for something to make things better. The last thing either of them needed was more unrest. They needed a period of fallow, to allow the seeds of recovery to take root.

Cam knew all too well, though, that you couldn't pick when drama came along.

'I couldn't help finding the knife,' he said. 'And if it was used to hurt somebody, then… isn't it worth helping to find out?' He looked at her with what he hoped was a hopeless grin.

Jess shook her head softly, and smiled – but did it contain a trace of sadness? 'You need these things, don't you?'

Cam stilled. She'd bull's-eyed him, not for the first time. For years, a reason and drive had been missing. And now, when they offered themselves to him once more, he found himself saved by taking them. 'Are you sure you're not a therapist yourself?'

Jess's smile became unmistakably warmer. 'How's it going with Pam?'

'She's brilliant. You were right.'

'I tend to be,' she said with a knowing wink. 'Well go on then. When is he coming?'

Cam glanced at his watch. 'Any minute now.'

'Great,' Jess said, rolling her eyes with a level of panto-mime you could see from the cheap seats. 'Just bloody great.'

10

A short while later, Cam and Jess took their drinks and dogs and decamped to a table by the river outside, overlooking the car park Forsyth was scheduled to arrive in. The dusk had dropped that bit tighter, and they'd had to wrap up warm to stave off the creeping chill, but, as if by magic, it had also brought that elusive barn owl out from its daytime hiding place. Now, they watched silently as it swooped with something akin to class, a feathered shard caught gliding in strobe wedges by the pub's floodlights.

The dogs cavorted by the water's edge, trying to reach geese that simply stared back at them from the river's surface below. An engine began to grow louder on the sloping road that led down into Coltishall village, and they both turned to look at it. A battered minivan came down the hill, in the kind of vibrant blue that wouldn't have looked out of place somewhere on Jess's outfit.

'This is him,' Cam said.

'Doesn't look like the getaway vehicle of the Zodiac killer,' murmured Jess. 'But then again, if he was one of those, it'd be kind of perfect, wouldn't it?'

Cam could see her point, but still couldn't quite square away the notion of this man – who he'd had the benefit of already meeting – being a killer.

That said, Cam didn't think that of himself either – despite having been one many times over.

The car slowed at the entrance of the car park, and turned in. It was travelling slightly too fast still, and had to screech to a sensible speed. For Cam, it belied agitation on the part of the driver. *Good*, he thought. *Rattled is good.*

Cam stepped forward and held the bunch of keys aloft in his right hand as he approached the parking vehicle, which came close enough to the picnic bench for them both to see the frazzled driver clearly through the windscreen.

Forsyth immediately emerged in a halo of swirling steam. He marched over, a short man who would be described by the children's books of Cam's youth as pudgy. He wore a tattered green windbreaker over office trousers and black shoes that were in dire need of either industrial-level polish or the tip. An unkempt scraggle of blond hair adorned his head like a low-budget straw crown.

'Well, that's the last time I lend you anything,' he said, clearly exasperated.

'Charming,' Cam replied. That switch had flipped in him again – the one where duty and its requirements guided his hand and his persona, and allowed him to find extra mettle when he needed it. It was fickle, and easily imbalanced, but pretending to be someone else was a tool that often worked for him just fine.

'Why couldn't you just give them the keys?' huffed Forsyth.

The fact that the keys had already caused this much trouble was bright red flag material to Cam, and left him with no qualms about questioning further. 'What's the big deal? I wanted to give the keys back to the right person,' he said. 'You weren't there, so I held onto them.'

'Yes, but I shouldn't even be lending them to you.'

'Why not? It's not like you were lending me the keys to a secret crime scene or anything.' Cam smiled as if it was a joke and not the bait it obviously was. He looked for a tell but didn't see one.

'The keys are secret, they're not supposed to be shared about. I thought… I thought that, you know, you'd be a useful guy to know.'

'Hang on, if it's dirty work you're after, you've got the wrong guy,' Cam said – although dirty work and Cam Killick weren't exactly foreign bedfellows in a historical sense. He moved on sharply. 'So, why shouldn't I have gone to your office?'

Forsyth looked like he was fifteen and stuck in the headmaster's office. 'If it was known that I'd been giving them out, the keys, I could get in loads of trouble.'

'How long have you been lending them about?'

'Well, a bit.'

Cam found himself frustrated by the man's inability to come clean. 'Bloody hell, Forsyth, just spit it out. How many people did you lend them to?'

The man only seemed to get more flustered, and was approaching the shade of a raw steak.

'Forsyth,' Cam said, trying to cut through his indecision. 'I'm not going to tell anyone. But sometimes I find things that might not be legal. When that happens, I've got a degree of discretion. But sometimes, the law comes knocking anyway.'

The man sighed, and flapped his arms once against his side like a penguin on the cusp of defeat. 'Seriously?'

'Look, if I have to answer questions about what I've seen when I'm diving, I'll just have to send them to you. I'm guessing you don't want that.'

Forsyth looked at him.

'Fine,' Forsyth hissed. 'Last year I got sight of an ecological survey of Doke End. It crossed my desk in its vetting phase, and I took a look, in the event it needed a second signature on sign-off. It didn't, but that's neither here nor there. The survey reported an abnormal migratory pattern of extremely large pike. There was a significant grouping of large specimens that had found their way there, somewhere they hadn't been in recent years. We'd found a preferred breeding ground for all the big mamas, but only during the specific months of January and February, when they are fattening up to spawn in March. It's a honey hole, where you know the biggest fish will be found. Guaranteed. And because they'd not been going there for long, no one else knew about it yet.'

'So… you let people have a go?'

'There's a group of people who I've come to trust, who keep it quiet, and pay me two hundred and fifty quid a go with the keys for a day.'

Cam couldn't stop himself from interrupting. 'Two hundred and fifty quid a go!' he said.

The man suddenly found eye contact very difficult, and decided his shoes were an easier option. 'It's five hundred for the first go, if I've never met you before.'

'Bloody hell, Forsyth. That's a nice little side earner.'

'Well it was, until you came along.'

'So that's why you didn't want me at the office. Did those guys know what you were up to?'

'Yes, *they* know. But the rest of the office has no idea. The original keys are in a box back at the office in Norwich.

I copied the one I needed – I've done it with loads, just none of the others are useful – and if anyone is spotted there using it, the rules are they've got to throw the key overboard, and swear ignorance.'

Cam found himself smiling in spite of himself at the extent of this very quaint ruse. It was a serious issue, of course, and tantamount to trespassing with a sprinkle of poaching thrown in. But he couldn't help but admire Forsyth's entrepreneurial opportunism.

'So… can I have those keys back now?'

Cam glanced back at Jess, and saw that she had been listening to the exchange intently – just as he'd hoped.

'I will,' he said. 'If you give me a list of everyone you've lent the key to.'

Forsyth threw his neck back and pleaded with the sky. 'Oh, come on.'

'Just give me this last week, then,' Cam said. Which would cover the five-day window if DNA was found on the knife.

Cam watched Forsyth's expression change from panicked inconvenience to suspicion.

'What are you up to?' he said. Panic then swam back in sharpish. 'You're not reporting this? Please say you're not reporting this.'

Cam chose to not quite answer the question. 'I'm a man of my word, Forsyth, and I promise you I won't mention a thing to anyone about your sideline. I'll even say I was diving there without permission, and I'll take the heat myself. Just write the names down on something, and then you can go on your way.'

Forsyth glanced from Cam across to Jess, who answered by shrugging and turning away to the barn owl's night-time activities. He even glanced down at the dogs as if they might help, but they appeared too interested in whatever was up each other's backsides to offer any guidance. Forsyth slowly shook his head, and went back to his car.

Cam and Jess swapped a glance. Cam's eyes went wide in exaggerated excitement, while Jess rolled hers in response – not for the first time.

A moment later, Forsyth was back with a receipt pad. What for, Cam didn't know, but the entrepreneur started writing. Cam glanced back at Jess again, whose lips at last found a tight smile. Cam returned the gesture broadly. He hoped, he was a little ashamed to admit, she was impressed.

It made him think about pushing it and asking Forsyth for phone numbers to go with those names – or addresses too.

No, I'm onto a good thing here, he thought.

Besides, of all the important phone numbers, he had Forsyth's. He could always come back and press for more info later.

A couple of moments went by with no sound but the scratching of the pen on thin paper, before Forsyth handed over the list, and blew out.

Cam did a quick count.

'There's seventeen names on this list!' he said.

Forsyth, not for the first time, glowed like a plum. 'So, I was charging by the hour, not the day.'

'Jesus, no wonder you didn't want to give this up.'

A little quick maths suggested that this scheme was worth tens of thousands of pounds in off-the-books cash. Cam checked again to make sure everything was legible. Seventeen names in clear ink.

He handed the keys to Forsyth who took them like a sulking teenager handed a bar of soap and marching orders to the bathroom. Without a word, he drove away, leaving Cam standing there – holding a list of seventeen suspects.

II

Moments later, over burgers and chips, the social aspect of the evening apparently having been revived somewhat, Cam and Jess pored over the list Forsyth had given them. Instead of sitting on opposite sofas, they sat shoulder to shoulder on the same two-seater, with the list between their plates.

'Anything stand out?' Cam asked.

Jess shook her head, and spoke between bites. 'Not really, other than the fact that the Broads Trust really does fancy itself quite a bit.'

She pointed a finger that had a dab of ketchup around the knuckle, the nail tapping on the letterhead of the receipt book. *The Broads Trust*, it read. *Saving the river, one bend at a time.*

Cam smirked and took a bite of burger as he scanned the list. Seventeen names was a hell of a gift. Rogers would be thrilled when he showed it to her. He reached for his jacket pocket, slung over the back of the sofa. Took out the breakfast relish, opened the bap, and slung thick dobs on the meat.

He tried it. It worked. God, that stuff was good.

Jess had paused to look at him, but then pointed down the list of names. She stopped on one. 'Tommy Jessup,' she said, as if trying out the vowels and consonants after a long absence since they were last used. 'That name rings a bell, but I can't think why?'

Cam spoke. 'School maybe?'

'No, I don't think...' She tailed off, as she mulled it over. 'Maybe that's it. I suppose that would explain why I'm finding it so hard to pinpoint.'

'Tommy Jessup. Tom Jessup. Thomas Jessup,' Cam said, in the hope different derivations of the name might jar something loose. All it got him was a look from Jess, so he stopped, and tried something different. 'Work maybe?'

'Yes. Yes, that feels a little more like it. I just can't think why.'

Cam used a couple of fries like floppy chopsticks to scoot that divine relish around the plate. 'Did he work with you? Maybe work in another area of the shop?' Jess worked in Roys department store, in Wroxham. The store, and its various categories of merchandise, straddled the main road through Wroxham and Hoveton. 'Maybe a name on a letter—'

Jess sprang to life. 'Yes! A bulletin. From management, we were all given it. It came with a CCTV picture, of some scrawny looking bloke with his hood up. He'd been banned from the store and we were told to look out for him. Give security the nod if he showed up.'

Cam thought about it. It was a start for sure. A murder weapon appears in a locked place, and one of the people who'd had the keys to it recently was someone who'd been banned from a local shopping complex.

Yep, definitely a start.

'Nice work,' he said. 'I'll get Rogers on it.'

'Is she working on this?'

'Yeah.'

'I should have known. A dog with a bone, the pair of you.'

Jess took a fry of her own, reached across, and dipped it in Cam's mystery relish. 'You know how mad the crime you lot are trying to solve is? You've got a murder weapon, you know it was used to kill someone – but you've got no body. That... is mad.'

'It is... atypical.'

'Do you have any more of that stuff?' she said. He looked at her quizzically.

Jess looked like she'd just found the key to immortality, when Cam realised she was talking about the relish.

'How much do you want, and how quickly can you get through it?' Cam asked.

12

The evening was over, for Cam at least, too soon, and he was on the road with Nala up on the front seat with him. They had parted with a hug, and eventually managed to separate the dogs who very clearly had other ideas. He would be melancholy, if it weren't for that little receipt with seventeen names that seemed to burn a hole straight through his pocket.

Despite the hour, he felt invigorated and recharged. He wanted to pull apart each name on that list, one by one. He was already planning next moves, but he didn't want to waste time making calls and combing through databases. That wasn't his forte, nor did he think it was the best use of his time. Cam, while never shy of getting stuck in, was also happy to delegate, so he found himself heading back into Norwich, after dropping a text to an infrequently used WhatsApp group called 'WE WANT TO BELIEVE', and found himself passing the journey by ruminating on his relationship with Jess.

Cam was big enough to admit – in his own head and heart at least – that he wanted more, but had no idea how to vocalise nor articulate it to Jess herself. When it came to feelings, especially big feelings, those were dealt with once a week by Pam, and their fledgling routine already had him in a dwindling reset mode until he got to see her again a week later. He felt things were going great, and he always left the sessions feeling bright and chipper, and thinking: 'Hmm, maybe we can start scheduling these sessions fortnightly instead of every week, because I feel so much stronger.' However, like clockwork, by the time he got back around to his allotted Friday morning slot, he felt in need of the comforting anchor point Pam gave him.

He talked about everything with her – everything. The vice-like symptoms of his PTSD were a big one, not to mention the ongoing panic attacks and the reasons as to why he only felt truly calm and at ease underwater. But they also talked about the dark points of his career, the moments when he had felt chunks break off his mental completeness for good. He talked about the betrayal he felt, when his orders and supervisors had failed him. About the misgivings he had where his career was concerned – and where the lines of right and wrong had been smudged so fiercely they'd damn near disappeared.

It seemed that his experiences in the forces, culminating in his time with the Sunken Skulls, still had a lot to answer for.

And with all that said, he still hadn't even mentioned Jess in therapy. Not once.

Which in turn, told him an awful lot.

As he wound around the dimmed bends on the outskirts of Norwich, he got a buzz on his phone which announced the arrival of a WhatsApp message, and since it was hooked up to his van's stereo unit, he simply tapped the button on the screen to open it. An electronic voice with all nuances of timing and intonation removed spoke.

'Message from "WE WANT TO BELIEVE". Meet at Funky's.'

Confused, Cam took a moment, before announcing: 'Repeat the message.'

The same words were played back to him.

'Siri,' he said, 'What is "Funky's"?'

The same voice came back through, this time a little more comfortable now it was using its own words. '"Funky's" refers to Funky's Norwich. It is a roller-skating rink. Would you like to navigate there now?'

'Yes,' Cam said, and the screen blinked across to a darkened road map. The time above said that it was nine in the evening, so not all that late yet – besides, Cam wasn't sure Gupta and Ferris actually slept. They certainly seemed to get by on little more than caffeine and paranoia.

The quickest way, the map was telling him, was to almost go back the way he'd come, so he took the next right, went down a pitch-black track, and with a quick left, emerged on the road he'd just travelled. He reached across to adjust the satnav, and as he pawed at the touch screen, he accidentally hit the radio button – which flooded the van with music. He didn't recognise the song, but the sudden crescendo of guitar chords, drums and a singer insistent *that* was not her name, took a scourer to his nerves. He quickly reached for the knob and turned the volume down.

'Bloody hell, Cam,' he said out loud. 'It's just music.'

Frustrated with himself, but unable to deny just how much the sudden barrage of sound had jolted his senses, he opened all the windows, let the cab of the van fill with chilled air, and practised a trusted breathing exercise.

In for three.

Hold for five.

Out for eight.

Funnelling that cold air into his lungs in such a regimented way pulled him back around in a matter of moments. He was getting better at this, he was sure of it. Things going sideways on him were never that far away, but he wasn't such a slave to these moments of heat and churn and discomfort, and even though they kept coming, he was amassing an array of tools that could help restore balance.

Nala stretched her body across so she could lay her head on his lap, and he stroked her ears in thanks. The radio presenter was blithering on about something to do with how their next song was a classic from tonight's chosen year for nostalgia hour.

A haunting, melancholic piano riff started, and it pierced through Cam like a very different knife through the heart. Adele started to sing in that once-in-a-generation mezzo-soprano, and soon she was crooning with affection about her hometown.

It caught Cam cold. He knew that song.

In Afghanistan, in 2008, it was a beloved song amongst the troops, and had become an anthem, a shared hope that, if they stuck together, they'd all be home soon.

Cam was suddenly back there. He wasn't on a darkened Norfolk back road. He was back in the dust and heat, on the flatbed of an old pick-up truck, bouncing through Lashkar Gar, praying that the next time the vehicle came back down, it wasn't on an IED.

As the song developed and swelled, his memory took him further, to a precise moment in that particular recollection – the moment when he found the song too difficult to hear, tainted for ever.

When the group of soldiers he was with decided, on one particular trip between sangars, which were essentially fortified watchtowers, to play what they called potluck potshot.

As they sped through the hustle and bustle of the busier settlements, they would take turns to fire a shot out of the back of the truck at the crowd – and see if anybody fell.

Cam was only twenty-five at the time, still a marine commando, but with no seniority to tackle it – but he did anyway.

The men were told not to do it again. That was all. But that hadn't stopped Cam from seeing at least three people drop in the crowd. Two men, and one child. A girl, who must have been about eight.

A battered radio had been playing 'Hometown Glory' when this happened, and Cam could no longer disassociate the song from the demented horror of that moment. It had become a symbol of all the things which should never have happened, things he'd witnessed, which were brushed under the carpet.

Finally, he turned off the radio.

His ghosts would always be with him, he thought. He just hoped he could eventually make peace with them, to the point they could coexist.

Frustrated with himself, Cam checked all around him, saw that the road was pitch-black, and empty, and hit the horn five times, a bit like an elephant might clear its sinuses.

In for three.

Hold for five.

Out for eight.

Onwards to Funky's.

13

Like any self-respecting roller rink, Funky's was housed in a warehouse on the edge of the city, a few turns down a blackened industrial estate.

Trust Gupta and Ferris, thought Cam. Only they would choose this on a chilly Friday Norfolk night.

Cam still had the van windows open and began to hear the throb of a wandering bass line. Sure enough, it got louder the more he followed the satnav, and was almost shaking the car by the time he arrived at the neon-lit box of the roller rink.

The car park was almost full, and there was even a ramshackle host of electric scooters and bikes parked by the glass doors to the establishment. Cam parked up at the back by a darkened hedge full of grit and litter, left Nala with a chew toy on the front seat, and walked across the pot-holed tarmac. The music began to carry a familiarity, those rolling bass notes punching and sassy, and when he opened the door, he instantly recognised Isaac Hayes' 'Theme From Shaft'.

The place was backlit, neon and hot. Cam could barely see anything other than some stairs and a reception desk.

Almost instantaneously, his blood vessels felt like they were breathing hot and heavy, open and closed, gasping then choking. It was a sensory punch in the temple, and his nerves knew it immediately. A sudden sweat popped again, and he started his breathing mantras right there in the doorway.

In for three.

Hold for five.

Out for eight.

It's just roller-skating, for crying out loud.

A young woman was looking at him from beyond the reception desk, her face adorned with black UV make-up of cat's whiskers and eyes. It was so bright and off-putting, Cam almost had to squint.

'One ticket for Roller Funk?' she asked, and even though Cam couldn't see the judgemental sneer, he could certainly detect it.

'I'm just here to speak to someone quickly,' Cam replied, putting his hands in his pockets and walking over. *Breathe, Cam, dammit.*

'Are you management? I've not seen you before.'

Cam's eyes had almost adjusted to the light, so he could see her expression now. *Yep, there was judgement, all right.* 'No, I'm here to see a couple of people who I think are skating here. It's just two minutes.'

The glowing cat pointed at the steps. 'You want up there, you've got to buy a ticket. Rules.'

'It's just two minutes,' Cam said.

The cat suddenly looked a little less sure. 'Are you someone's dad?'

Christ. 'No, I'm not someone's bloody dad – I just want to speak to someone for a couple of minutes, that's all!'

'Then it's ten quid.'

Cam sighed, and reached into his pocket. Only Gupta and Ferris could get him buying a ticket to a damn roller funk night.

'We're a cashless venue,' said the cat.

Cam found himself sighing again. 'Right,' he said, and flashed his contactless card at the proffered unit.

'Do you need skate hire?'

'No, I don't need bloody skate hire,' Cam huffed, as he went up the steps, his indignation at having to pay at last drowning out his lack of comfort.

Cam got to the top as the DJ segued neatly into 'Across 110th Street' by Bobby Womack, which, he had to grudgingly admit, was a serious jam. Across the warehouse roof swirled a dotted constellation of coloured neon lights choreographed by a disco ball somewhere out of sight. Below was a vast space that held a cafeteria and a two-tiered soft-play area on the left, and a skate hire desk with an arcade on the right. And in the middle of it all was a full-size roller rink, full of Day-Glo human shapes moving in a clockwise rotation.

After scoping out the cafeteria benches, and quickly ruling them out, he moved over to the rink. *Please don't make me go on there*, he begged inside. He was trying to make out individual people in the whirling lights, in an attempt to locate Gupta and Ferris. As he leaned against the railings, squinting across the boards, it wasn't long before one of the figures broke from the flow like a fish abandoning its shoal, and sped towards him. As whoever it was got closer, he clocked the trilby and ponytail.

'Fancy seeing you here,' said Anika Gupta, as she pulled to a neat stop on the other side of the wooden partitioning. She was late twenties, full of snap and drive, fully suited as usual, albeit one that looked like a neon ogre had sneezed all over it.

'A custom job?' Cam asked, pointing at the clothing.

'You wouldn't understand.'

'Damn right I wouldn't.'

'What have you got for us?'

Cam looked out to the rink again. 'Where's Ferris?'

'She's there,' pointed Gupta, to someone Cam couldn't make out. 'You will not be her favourite person for interrupting mid-song, though.'

Then Cam saw her, and he couldn't quite believe it. The usual clothing he had come to expect from Ferris was in place – the baggy jeans, obscure band T-shirt, dark hoodie, they were all there, as were the customary massive headphones around her neck – and she hadn't made any obvious colourful concession to the occasion. But she was moving. Cam felt his jaw slacken. Without meaning to be ungentlemanly, the robust form of Ferris was really *moving*. She had rhythm, and style, and grace. As he watched, she span 180 to skate backwards, but the forward motion of her feet gave the impression of moonwalking. It was mesmerising. Then she noticed Cam, span back to face forward, and broke away to arrow towards him.

'Impressive,' Cam said.

'You stick out like a narc at a marrow contest,' she said to him, as she made as neat a stop as Gupta.

'Not sure what that means, but never mind. I need your expertise.'

'Scale of one to ten on the weirdness scale?' asked Gupta.

'Anything less than a six and we're not interested,' said Ferris through a stout expression.

'It's definitely an eight,' said Cam, always ready to inflate the odds to intrigue the podcasting journalists from *Norfolk Unexplained* and the *Eastern Daily Gazette* respectively. Weird was their currency, and the more outlandish the better. But by the same token, they were news people, eager for a story, and they had the growing scope to blow it up. They had contacts on all sides of the journalism–conspiracy theory divide, and resources Cam simply couldn't reach. What they also had, however, was a tenacity that was hard to beat or break. When Cam blew the Brindley cold case wide open the previous year, Gupta and Ferris had not only helped, they'd told the true story – and attacked the exposed corruption with such venom that they had made an instant reputation for themselves beyond their previous fame as mere journalists with a penchant for the odd. The case was starting its rumble through the courts, but their determined reporting of the facts had earned them an instant notoriety. Bigger days were to come for them too when the case was concluded, and they could talk about all the lurid details that were currently under embargo.

'Churros,' Ferris said, and pointed at the café.

Moments later, the three were around a bench seat, the journalists with their legs stretched out to give their skates room, still on their feet as they were. Between them was a paper plate with what looked like freshly composed dog shit from a canine that needed quite a bit more natural fats in its diet. Cam watched Ferris and Gupta pull away chunks and scoff them away like it was their death row meal, sipping coffee as if the bitterness would stave off the revulsion.

'Talk,' Ferris said. Cam had noticed that, since their recent professional triumphs, she'd developed even more of a pronounced obtuseness.

'Same deal,' Cam said, determined to make eye contact and avoid the brown smears around her mouth. 'You'll get everything, but you don't report it until the official nod.'

'The nod coming from *Detective* Rogers?'

Cam pursed his lips. The podcasters and Rogers had a fractious relationship, no matter how much Cam himself trusted them equally. *Detective* was a thinly veiled dig at Rogers for reasons Cam didn't understand. Whether it was the fact that Rogers thought they were a pair of clowns, he didn't know, but guessed it might be. Then again, Cam could imagine the very timbre of someone's breathing irking Ferris, so it was not too much a stretch to think that they didn't get on. 'Yes,' he said. 'Rogers is involved, and if I remember rightly, that didn't work out too badly for you last time.'

'What is it?' Gupta said. Gupta was frankly less difficult, and far less bothered about any perceived injustices of status. Anika Gupta was all about the story: bright-eyed, idealistic and open.

They were both quite brilliant in their own ways, despite their oddness.

'Found a knife,' Cam said.

'I've got a wood block full of them at home,' said Ferris.

'This one has DNA on it, that has to be less than five days old.'

'How does that work?' Gupta asked.

'It was in water, and—'

'Got it,' said Ferris, dismissively.

Cam was finding her harder to deal with than usual. That heat on his arms again. Indignant tingles. 'All right, well, if you'd let me get my words out, there was also carotid tissue. Cardioid, sorry, cardioid.'

'A bit of heart?' asked Gupta. She was clearly mesmerised.

'Yes,' Cam said. 'This knife was used to stab a person in the heart, sometime in, at the most, the last five days.'

The two were silent. *At last*, Cam thought.

'To make matters more... along your forte,' Cam continued. 'The knife was found in a private chunk of water, very small, with very limited access through a locked gate. A locked gate that these seventeen people recently had access to.' He held up the note Forsyth had given him. Both podcasters' eyes locked on it.

He knew he had them. As much as he was socially defunct in other areas, hooking Gupta and Ferris was somewhat of a forte of Cam's own.

'Who are they?' Gupta asked.

'The people who had the keys to Doke End this week,' Cam replied.

'Doke End,' said Gupta. 'The Doke End near Upton?' She looked at Ferris as she spoke, and the two swapped an unmistakable glance.

'That's the one. You have to get to it through Upton Broad itself.'

Gupta nodded. 'We're in.'

'You've heard of it?' Cam asked, suspicious.

Gupta leaned back on the bench, and pursed her lips. She glanced at Ferris, who nodded in an apparent unspoken agreement.

Seemingly settled, Gupta leaned forward again. 'Upton has a history of disappearances that date back—'

'Abductions,' interrupted Ferris. 'She meant to say abductions.' She was pointing at the ceiling.

'I don't think aliens use knives,' said Cam.

'And how would you know?' replied Ferris.

Cam couldn't reply. She had him there.

'Do we have blood types?' Ferris continued.

'Jesus,' Cam hissed. 'No, we don't have blood types.'

'Protein coding sequences?'

'No.' Cam put his coffee down, and placed the list on the table. 'Look, I just need to know everything you can get on these names. The fruitier the better. You'll know what you're looking for—'

'You have no idea—'

Cam held his palms up. 'Just tell me who needs looking at. You help, you know what happens next.'

Gupta took the list, and cast a glance over the names. 'If we get something, can we interview you this time?'

Cam looked down. The podcasters dropped regular episodes of *Norfolk Unexplained*. Most of them were historical, drawn from the area's long Fortean history. Their four-parter on the Brindley cold case resolution was a sensation, but the one missing voice on the miniseries belonged to the man who had rolled a grenade under the mystery's foundations. Cam Killick himself.

He looked at them both. Gupta's eyes pled, while Ferris tried to make it look like she couldn't give two rats' arses and failed. 'Maybe a soundbite,' Cam eventually said.

'We're keeping this,' Ferris said, snatching the list.

'Then the deal's off,' Cam said at once. 'You can have a photo, by all means.'

Ferris's jaw squared, and she slapped the list down and took a photo with her smartphone. The flash caused Cam to squint for real this time.

'Leave it with us,' Gupta said, as Ferris flicked the receipt at him and stuffed another churro into her mouth.

Cam nodded his relief. 'How long, do you think?'

'You think we sleep?'

'Sleep is for the weak and weak-bladdered,' added Ferris, spraying crumbs of partially masticated dough.

'I honestly didn't expect anything different,' Cam said, standing.

Some Time Ago

Forrester noticed, in the tired, water-spattered mirror of the kennels bathroom, that he'd somehow caught the sun. He lifted his hair to check his hairline, and, sure enough, there was a pink glow to his forehead. There was also a soft panda-eyeing around his sockets, where his polarising glasses had sat for the morning. Not that they'd helped, of course. They were supposed to increase visibility below the surface by 50 per cent, by reducing the surface shine and reflection.

He hadn't seen anything, and had caught jack shit.

And now, he'd had to come back to the kennels he owned with his wife, who was now up in the old farm-house with the three kids, getting dinner ready. Forrester, on the other hand, now had his chores to catch up on. He'd promised Katie that he'd do her share if she let him go fishing for the day and, like the loving but toughened soul that she was, she had agreed – but only on the insist-ence that he'd get everything done before dinner, and he was also on washing up, bath and bedtime duty with the children too. He'd agreed at once, elated that he was going to have the chance to drop a line into the elusive and secretive Doke End.

Now, sweeping up endless servings of dog muck from the floor of each enclosure while making sure that its temporary resident didn't escape, it all felt a bit of an anticlimax. It had been beautiful out there though, he conceded. And the peace and quiet was a blissful tonic to the endless days of caring for the dogs, and the children. He didn't know which was more demanding, the kids or the dogs. He'd bet that for the most part, the kids were messier.

The dogs were bouncing today. They were excited, because there was a human in the kennel shed – which was two rows of thirty cages in uniform size – fifteen on one, fifteen on the other, facing each other like a tight-knit prison. And if a human was in there, it meant that some lucky canine soul was getting the gift of either going home or going for exercise, and each dog keened and pleaded in the hope it was going to be them next.

The truth was, Forrester didn't even hear the dogs any more. They were just added tinnitus to his everyday routine. They hollered at all times of the day or night but, because of their farmstead's isolation, they disturbed nobody. So, it was a strangely quiet and noisy life that he and Katie led.

The intercom system crackled in the overhead speakers. They had installed them to allow for easy communication between the main house and the kennels, and when Katie's voice cut through the howling, it was like pressing an immediate mute button. All the dogs hushed while they listened, and presumably looked for the owner of the voice that had spoken from everywhere all at once.

'Dinner in five, Ryan,' she said. 'If you aren't in, you're doing the kids' homework as well.'

Forrester huffed and the dogs started keening again – this time for the voice to return. He left one cage, locked it up again, then unlocked the next. He didn't open it yet, merely looked at the two dogs in the cage – a brother and sister pair of Basenjis who lived together, but couldn't be more dissimilar if they tried. One brown and white, the other with the black and white pattern of a Friesian cow; the former was agitated and jumpy, while the latter was a quiet, stealthy escape artist. As soon as the gate was open, the girl was always making a sleek break for it.

'Are we going to behave today?' he asked them both, before easing the gate open. The girl looked like she was about to burst into life, while the boy circled and hollered in excitement. 'That's it,' he said, as he opened the gate just enough to slide through. As he got his stomach through and into the cage, the female dog picked that exact moment to try to dart through Forrester's legs, but he quickly shuffled them closed, and slammed the door shut. 'Not today.'

He went to the back of the cage, to check the floor for muck there, but it appeared clear. He hoped that the boy hadn't been eating their own offerings again. Just the thought made him shut his eyes.

When he opened them, he realised something was different. The atmosphere was suddenly thick with tension, and it was silent. A small room with forty or so dogs in it, and there wasn't a peep.

Forrester looked at the two Basenjis. They were huddled next to each other. Their flanks tremored, their tails stiffened.

Gradually, their necks lowered, and they hunkered back and made themselves small. Their tails tucked right in – and Forrester saw that the dog in the cage opposite, a lone chocolate lab, had done the same. He was lowering himself to his bed, silent, with the whites of his eyes showing.

The dogs were terrified.

Forrester wanted to speak, to break the silence and at least ease the dogs' fears by showing that he was still there. But something stopped him. The abject, hardened terror was catching. He wanted to be like them, silent and small, withdrawn and in submission.

But he was in charge. And he needed to show it. Dogs are of course pack animals, and the human was usually regarded high in the chain of pack hierarchy. He'd read about it in those online forums. The ones he read when Katie wasn't around. You had to make yourself the alpha, if the pack was to respect you and obey, which was apparently one of the main principles of basic dog training – and human interaction, too. As the pack leader, it was important for Forrester to reestablish control.

He whistled once, long and loud, and walked out of the cage. 'I'm still here, it's all right – what's all this fuss?'

Then Forrester turned and saw what had just come into the kennel shed, and was now standing at the end of the row of cages, by the door. His blood froze to iced tar in his arteries. He couldn't move and, instead, could only look at the strangely featureless monster at the end of the shed.

The beast stood huge and immovable.

And suddenly, Forrester got it.

The pack – his pack – had a new alpha.

He turned around, dropping the scoop, and ran for his life towards the back door of the shed. He was midway along the row, which was enough of a head start, but he was nowhere near the size of that thing that was now in their midst.

He could hear its great pumping legs, and the impact of its feet. The dogs never made a sound as they both sprinted past.

Forrester hadn't made it close to the door when he felt as if he'd been ploughed in the back by a car. He went flying face first onto the concrete, and all wind left his body. He hoped Katie and the children would be spared. Something was lifting his head now, and rolling him over. He had no choice. He was helpless, cowed and submitting, just like the dogs all around him – who simply watched, as this new leader forcefully took his place at the top of the pecking order with bloodshed.

Lots, and lots, of bloodshed.

14

Back behind the wheel, Cam decided that perhaps for one night, enough was enough – but not before taking his own quick snap of the list and cueing it up to send to DS Rogers. He added the caption, 'the people who've had the keys to Doke End in the last few days' and pressed send. He put the phone on the dashboard charging mount, and let Nala out for a wee. She pottered to the edge of the car park, and disappeared out of sight for a couple of moments behind some half-dead shrubs.

As he waited, and the discomfort from being in that hellish funk disco place ebbed away, he couldn't prevent his mind from wandering to the knife.

Heart tissue. The strike that caused it had to have been deep, direct and so damn fierce. Something a ribcage couldn't argue with.

As someone who sadly had been involved in a close-quarters battle with a knife, Cam knew how hard it was to stab someone in the heart.

His nostrils flared, as if to clear them of the sight, sound, smell, all of it.

He whistled, and Nala pottered unhurriedly back out from the scuffed foliage. She watched him as she sauntered back up to the car, and hopped in beneath Cam's feet.

'Oh, take your time, by all means,' he said.

Nala huffed, seeming to clear her own nasal passages of the distaste of her owner's sarcasm, and stretched out on the front bench seat.

Cam didn't want to stop, but he felt that home time was the only option available to him. Night brought natural downtime to progress, even though Cam didn't want to tolerate it. Offices closed and people went home to lives outside whatever daily purpose had come to characterise them in the eyes of others. Rogers was a cop, and she was home for the night. Gupta and Ferris were journalist–podcasters, and they were enjoying travelling in rhythmic circles to classic seventies jams. Just because Cam didn't switch off easily didn't mean others couldn't.

He hit the ignition, and reluctantly turned the car around, home in mind.

He didn't see another car the entire twenty-minute journey back to Neatishead. No life of any kind. When dark hit Norfolk, everything switched off. Black nights here seemed blacker than everywhere else. It felt like he was a toddler changing positions under a giant weighted quilt. The corners, and light, were all so far away, and too heavy to lift.

He rounded the familiar chicane in the middle of Neatishead, past the White Horse and the village store, and up the farm track that led to Haven Cottage – the stone barn conversion that Cam Killick had bought with his military pension. It was simple, yet supremely effective as a home: modern features, but respecting the building's original character.

Cam eased the van up the gravel drive, and Nala sat up, knowing exactly where she was. He killed the ignition, and dropped down. It felt strange being at a place of rest, knowing that his heart and mind felt no desire for it.

He opened the door, and walked across the bare floor boards to the kitchen to fire up some camomile tea. He put two bags in the pot, and refilled Nala's water bowl at the sink. All the while, he didn't turn the lights on. Didn't need them, which was one reason, but he didn't really want to acknowledge being here, which was the other. He felt frustration grow.

Making a sodding tea, he thought.

There's a killer out there, and I'm making sodding camomile tea.

The kettle clicked on and it pissed him off even further. He put a third bag in the mug just to spite himself, and brewed the lot of them.

He walked back into the lounge, and lowered himself onto the beanbag. Nala didn't follow him, staying in the kitchen instead. He stared at the television. That was what people did to relax, wasn't it? Watched television.

He reached for the remote, and switched it on. The screen took a few seconds to come to life, and when it did, the colours seemed weird to him.

There were people on screen. It was the one with all the pretty people in the unfeasibly massive New York apartment. They were irritating in their unnecessary happiness. They were chatting about lobsters. Even Cam knew this one.

Could they *be* any more annoying?

He switched over. Repeats on every channel.

Some bollocks about cakes in a gazebo.

Bloody hell.

He switched over again.

Someone at a desk with a perma-tan and a part-melted face watching someone else on stage bend over and fart a dart at a balloon, to a screaming audience.

Bloody hell. He switched it all off. Being pissed off in darkness was preferable to any of that.

He got up, and walked into the kitchen. Nala, sensing his discombobulation, followed at his heels, and got doubly excited when he opened the fridge. He threw a slice of ham between two bits of sourdough from the bread basket – dropping a second slice to the floor which didn't even make it to terra firma before Nala had caught and inhaled it – grabbed that bloody relish from the huge tray he'd dumped on the sideboard earlier, and dobbed a fat dollop on the sliver of meat.

Cam chewed the lot sitting on the back step of the cottage, staring out at the cornfield. He let the cool night air deep into his nostrils and lungs, allowing it to cleanse and replenish him from within.

Why couldn't he just switch off? So often, he really wanted to be a normal person, but could he even be one if given the opportunity? He just didn't know.

Something unseen retched a yacking screech somewhere out amongst the stalks. A bird, large, announcing its presence. It hollered again. Bothered, reconfirming its territorial right.

A heron maybe, or bittern. But there was no water in the corn, only soil. And because of the height of the stalks, there'd be no real way for a large bird to take off.

Must be something else, he thought.

He looked out at the sea of corn, and the feeling grew from mere irritability to something more specific. Like he was horribly visible. Naked to all. Too exposed.

This therapy, opening him up too much, he thought.

Jess too, opening him up too much.

He needed to be on edge, balancing, mentally potent. Ready to track down a killer.

Bloody feelings, he chided himself.

He got up, and grabbed the 12 kg kettlebell he used as a back door stop. He'd perfected a twenty-minute work-out, what he called his gorilla complex. It worked all the main muscle groups with very small bouts of rest. It thrashed your heart rate into high gear, and worked you like a silverback. Just off the back step, on the grass, he got to work.

Within mere moments, he was sweating, heaving through a set of goblet squats, when that damn feeling of vulnerability caught him again. He felt like prey, that was it. It kicked something off in him that was protective, as if he wanted to shield those around him from threat and danger.

On his next scheduled rest break, he grabbed his phone, and drafted a text to Jess.

So much for keeping those feelings at bay, he thought.

He glanced through their recent messages.

It was chit-chat. Idle and warm. He tried not to scrutinise her column of replies, forced himself to remember that text on a tiny phone screen didn't include any of the nuances of inflexion or expression. He looked at his own column, and tried not to dwell on each word and turn of phrase. He had to put it down before he started to curse himself, because his side quickly looked too needy, too desperate, too direct.

He lowered the phone and went straight into alternating cleans and shoulder presses.

That bloody bird yelped again.

Probably seen a fox.

Dammit, he thought, and when it was time for his next brief rest, pulled the phone up again. He began to type.

Sorry I brought my work into it earlier. I should have just left the evening for us to catch up.

Then he remembered getting the list wasn't *work* – it was part of his stupid sense of duty, not employment. So, he changed the word *work* to *silly crusade*.

Then he looked at *catch up*. Chastised himself. It sounded so formal. Too formal. Too distant.

Ugh.

He changed *catch up* to *hang out*.

Then he berated himself for messing up his own workout.

While he was thinking, trying different platitudes in his head, the phone buzzed in his hand.

It was another WhatsApp message thread after his attention, and its name flashed at the top of the screen. 'WE WANT TO BELIEVE'. The UFO avatar stared at him, and he pressed it.

Gupta and Ferris. There was no idle chit-chat here. Just cold hard facts in inverted commas, a dearth of social skills on display by all present parties, and conspiracies galore.

Just now, Ferris had texted the group.

Here are the first five, she wrote.

Already?! thought Cam. He assumed they hadn't even left the funky roller disco thing yet.

But below that first message, one after the other, came a list of names. One at a time. It was indeed, as suggested, the first five names on the list. And next to each was an age, and a location.

God they were good, thought Cam by way of concession. Getting on their good side was even more of a master-stroke than he had anticipated.

He scanned the names eagerly; Nala picking up on his own elevated excitement and wagging her tail by his side.

Edward Thelonius, 56, Threehammer Common.
James Stockwell, 48, Reedham.
Ryan Forrester, 36, Crostwick.
Scott West, 69, Martham.
David Collier, 44, Wymondham.

He looked at the place names. All within thirty minutes' drive of Doke End. Striking distance.

In the reply box, he typed.

Addresses?

The addresses came through, one at a time.

Suddenly, all frustration was substituted out for the surge of excitement. The drive born only when there are leads to pursue.

He checked his watch. 10.50 p.m. 'You tired?' he asked Nala.

She looked at him with hopeful incomprehension.

'You can sleep on the road, girl.'

Suddenly invigorated, queries of the heart were all but forgotten, and he was out of the door in ninety seconds flat, reigniting the van's still-warm engine.

15

He'd start with the nearest, Edward Thelonius and Three-hammer Common.

What a pair of names, thought Cam, as he pulled off the dirt track onto the main road, careful not to obliterate a pheasant that had unwittingly wandered into the path of traffic. He always found that amazing. That so much British wildlife found the simple sight of two oncoming glowing orbs so near-religiously hypnotic that they would immediately martyr themselves to whichever horse-powered God was coming towards them with such a pace. Being disintegrated into feathers and fur appeared to be the desired outcome when navigating roads was considered.

The roads were somehow even deader than before, and he hadn't even seen anyone then. Cam felt the drive of progress force his foot harder onto the accelerator, and from his home on the outskirts of Neatishead, he made it to the hamlet of Threehammer Common in only four minutes.

The address led him to a ramshackle farm away from any other discernible human life. In other areas of the British Isles, its darkened countenance and cavernous barns could have been unnerving, but in this part of the country it was very normal. If anything, he found that the more shabby-looking and ancient the building, the more well-heeled the inhabitant. He parked up on the road, eased the door shut with the quietest click, and carefully headed down the muddy drive.

There was a car outside on the mud turning-track, an old red Fiesta whose flanks were caked in spattered dirt. The house, a red-brick square with green eaves, was dark. Cam checked his watch. It was half-eleven at night, so the inactivity was hardly a surprise.

So what was he here for? A blood-soaked boat – or at least one that had been recently cleaned. Whoever dropped that knife had been on the water – so they had to have used a craft of some description. And given that someone's heart had been skewered, there'd have been a lot of blood in that boat. If he found a suspicious-looking candidate, he'd tell Rogers, and she could get the Scene of Crime techs to give it a thorough once-over – and if they found DNA that matched the sample on the knife, then the case would be as good as solved.

It was a sound line of enquiry and it was better than sitting at home watching re-runs of televisual crap.

Get in the game, Cam.

Eyes open.

He was hoping to get round the first five names tonight, on the lookout for boats. Plus, you could tell a great deal about someone from where, and the manner, in which they lived. Sometimes, giveaways to something worth a closer look were sitting right there in plain sight. Going round all these dwellings tonight would give him more info than he otherwise had, and that was a start. He sneaked forward, down the track and glanced across the front of the property. There was a battered Land Rover Defender on the drive, at least fifteen years old – but no sign of a boat. The outbuildings loitered behind the modest farmhouse itself. It could easily be in one of them, resting on a trailer.

He tucked tight to the edge of the drive, and walked down to where it passed the property to curve around the back to the barns. He was keeping watch on the front of the house for any sign of life as he walked – when he saw, plain as day, a boat sitting proud on a trailer, in the front garden. It was a small vessel, maybe ten feet long, covered in a protective cover. His pulse sped. He retraced his steps and, at what he felt was a safe distance, he crossed the drive to approach the boat while tracing the large front hedge for cover.

The hedge smelled terrible, and as soon as he stepped onto the soft grass of the unkempt front garden, a light went on in the house.

Bugger, thought Cam.

With a clunk and an echoing squeak, one of the top windows opened, its ancient painted frame swinging outwards abruptly.

Cam held his breath.

'I'm holding my phone right now, ready to call the authorities,' said a voice across the chilled night air. The owner was merely a backlit silhouette against a softly glowing square.

Presumably this was Ed Thelonius, but what had Cam done to alert the man? He'd dropped the ball in some way, and it was a frustrating reminder of the skill set he had let blunt. Not once, on all his excursions around the globe with the SBS, had anyone cracked open a bathroom window and said: 'I can see you!'

'There's no point pretending you're not there,' said the voice. 'Motion-activated thermal cameras, chum. Only fifty quid from the big river website. Brilliant for catching sneaky perverts like you. Now come out. Or I'll fetch grandpa's old pea-shooter, and then you'll really have something to worry about.'

Motion-activated forward-looking infrared, or, as they called it in the military, FLIR. That was something the average civilian didn't think of, let alone possess.

Cam stepped from the shadows, his arms out wide and his hands in plain sight, and stood in the middle of the front lawn, like a six-foot mole caught in the act of night-time digging. He didn't think there was any point in pretending he wasn't there, the night vision assertion rendering doubt moot and mute. The subterfuge side of Cam's training, his ability to smoothly and efficiently get into position while factoring in all possible deterrents and outcomes, had clearly all gone sideways as his mental health had deteriorated. But FLIR? Off the internet? He suddenly felt like certain things, particularly aspects of his extensive training, were no longer entirely useful when it came to dealing with the unpredictable nature of members of the public and whatever they could get their hands on with a mere mouse click. He found the idea extremely disconcerting.

With that in mind, he put his hands up, not something again he was used to doing now he was a civilian, and stepped out from the hedgerow. 'I hope you're not going to shoot an unarmed man,' he said with a sigh, grumbling at the old Cam, who most definitely would not have ended up rumbled in a hedgerow packed with what had to be cat shit.

'You won't get shot,' came the reply from the window. 'But it does depend on what your answer is for being here. I could very easily take a sudden dislike to a bad answer.'

Something about this man's calm, not to mention his choice of burglar deterrent, told Cam that Thelonius may be ex-forces himself – or police, perhaps.

Either way, this represented a chance for Cam to find some common ground. 'How many cats is it then?' asked Cam as he stepped out into the middle of the lawn. 'If it's only one, you need to get it to the vet. Serious gut problems.'

'What are you doing here? Answer quickly now.'

Cam thought now was the time to play on any assumptions about the man's former career – plus, everyone, and that meant everyone, got FOMO when locked out of a big secret.

'If you're Ed Thelonius, yours is the first name on a list I've got,' Cam said.

'And that's not a list of people with cats with gut problems, is it?'

'No, it isn't,' said Cam. 'It's a list of people who were last seen at a murder scene.'

The man paused for a moment before answering. 'I'm assuming, given that you're pissing about in a hedge full of cat shit, your interest in the matter is unofficial?'

'Let's say half and half.' Which was true. He was an off-the-books guy through and through, and he didn't need to follow any traditional rules of service or policing, but anything he found out tonight would be making its way straight to Rogers – although he could picture the verbal evisceration she would give him when she found out about this.

He decided to take to a different tack. He'd found that simple conversation was a tool not often used in the armed forces. Words and an open mind were often as useful as – and preferable to – a stick of dynamite stuffed in the door jamb. 'Perhaps I could pick your brains, over a cup of coffee?'

'Perhaps you could piss right off.'

Cam thought now was the time to do a little fishing of his own. 'Iraq? Afghanistan?'

Thelonius paused. 'Both.'

'Same here.'

Silence again. Cam knew the door was open, and that rare brotherhood was about to grease all wheels. 'First Battalion.'

Thelonius answered immediately. 'Black Watch.'

'Panther's Claw?'

'I was there in Lashkar Gar.'

'Me too.'

There was a pause between the two retired soldiers, as the weight of their combined histories settled between them.

'And all these years later,' said Thelonius, 'you're in my garden in the middle of the night covered in cat shit.'

Cam shrugged. The man he assumed was Ed Thelonius sighed audibly and started to close the sash window. 'You'll get the coffee how I make it, and we're talking on the back step, Mr Cat Shit.'

16

While Cam waited on the back step like a kid asking if his mate could play out, he established a plan of attack. If he hadn't just been caught rummaging about in this guy's garden, he might have played hardball. He wasn't bothered about authority, past or present. He was long past playing nice with any force's top brass. But the fact was the power in this exchange was with Thelonius. If Cam didn't play nice, Thelonius could call the police, and Rogers would probably kick him out of any investigation, including withholding all the details that Cam craved so much. Worse, she might find herself in trouble with her superiors for involving him at all. That sense of duty was back again, and overwhelming just like it always was.

The back door opened a few moments later, and the silhouette from upstairs graduated to full form – now holding two mugs. Ed Thelonius handed one to Cam, and pulled the other closer to his chest like he was drawing life force from it. Steam drifted up to his face.

'Speak,' Thelonius said.

'Thank you,' said Cam, taking the mug. Cam took the man in properly for the first time. He was in a checked dressing gown, with striped pyjama bottoms poking out beneath the hem, presenting a lordly figure of geometric yet garish lines. It appeared he'd stamped on a pair of walking boots before coming out, which gave him the air of an extremely committed sleepwalker. His short hair was mussed, while his goatee was pin sharp and set-square precise. A pair of reading glasses hung off the bridge of his nose, and he looked at Cam with the sort of assessment a head teacher might grant a particularly scrotey student. Unmistakably, there was also the keen air of past authority that the man still exuded in waves.

'First Battalion where you learned to creep about in people's hedges, then?' Thelonius asked, before taking a swig of coffee so black it could well have been a ceramic ink well. It caused Cam to look at his own. Cam's had a dash of milk in it, so it just looked like hot mud in the light cast from the kitchen instead. Thelonius hadn't invited him in, and merely stood in the door frame, occupying most of it with his impressive bulk.

'No, I got most of that from the SBS,' Cam said.

Then Thelonius's demeanour changed in a quiet instant, and he looked at Cam with a bit more curiosity. 'It really messed you up, didn't it?' he said.

At other times, under different night skies in his life, such a blunt assessment and instant judgment would have really upset Cam – but now he felt the best thing to do was simply to own it. And with that ownership came a growing measure of empowerment. Yes, it was a problem, but it was *his* problem, and he was doing what he could to make it better. Not that it worked all the time, of course, but every now and then he felt like real inroads were being made, and he credited his self-imposed ownership of his condition for making those inroads permanent.

'Yes it did,' said Cam. 'A lot. Look, I'm sorry for this obvious inconvenience, I'm sometimes not the best judge of what the best course of action is.'

'I can see that,' said Thelonius, looking him up and down, as if Cam was an exhibit at a museum of oddities. 'So, go on then, who's dead?'

'Well, this is the thing,' said Cam. 'We don't know.'

Thelonius sipped coffee, and grimaced gleefully at its obvious bitterness. 'Who's we?'

'I'm working with the police on this, you could say, but yeah, it is all pretty unofficial.'

A hard stare invited him to clarify.

'I help them out from time to time,' Cam said. 'I'm a diver, and they sometimes find me useful. And every now and then I sort of can't help myself and end up mucking about in gardens in the middle of the night where I shouldn't be.'

Whether it was because the older man could see a bit of himself in Cam, or because of Cam's general plight as a discarded soldier with no outlet for his skills and dutiful urges, Thelonius seemed, if not to get it, at least to be willing to humour it. There was a frown, but a wry smile buried somewhere within it.

'So how have I ended up on that list?' he asked, and Cam couldn't detect any slight tendril of bluff.

'It seems you're part of an elite invitation-only club, so to speak,' said Cam. 'All the names on this list have recently fished at a place called Doke End, after borrowing, in inverted commas, the keys from a guy at the Broads Trust.'

'I take it that's where your murder weapon was found?'

Cam simply nodded.

'This list, do they have a time frame?'

'Five days.' Cam wasn't about to go into the specifics of the cardioid tissue, and the five-day ticking clock specifics of the DNA signature, because he didn't want to obscure the facts. He just wanted to know what Thelonius knew. 'Were you there?'

Thelonius answered as if it was obvious. 'Of course I was. You're not a fisherman, are you? If you were, you'd know about the importance of what hides there.'

'The pike?'

'Yes, the pike. The Holy Grail might be on Doke End. Of course when I heard about it I had a go.'

'And the Holy Grail is?'

'A thirty. Maybe even a forty.'

'Pounds?'

'Pounds.'

'Did you catch anything?'

'Nothing. Not a sniff.'

Cam noticed something else creeping through Thelonius's demeanour. A hint of embarrassment. For a man who clearly saw himself as an upstanding member of the community, this was a blot on the copybook. Especially in light of the fact that he was paying for his involvement. He finally broke eye contact with Cam and glanced off into the dark night in a slightly vacant way. 'So,' said Cam, 'if you wanted to confess to any murders, that would be really helpful, and I won't have to spend all night garden-hopping.'

'If that's the question, I'd invite you to go and fornicate with yourself,' he said.

'So, if you're right and I can scratch you off this list, maybe you'd give me a hand…' Cam said. He pulled the piece of paper out of his pocket, which was already looking more and more ragtag with every trip into his jeans. 'There are seventeen names on this thing, and anything you can tell me about any one of them would be very helpful.'

Cam wasn't in the habit of showing crucial pieces of evidence to potential suspects, even if he didn't himself think they'd done anything untoward. But he wanted to invoke the brotherhood of their earlier lives, and hoped Thelonius still carried the same dutiful urges as he did and felt like sharing. Luckily for Cam, it seemed that Thelonius had as much of a hang-up for justice – real justice – as he did.

He took the scrap, and pulled his glasses up his nose to squint through the lenses.

'Just so we're very clear, I've got nothing to do with any of your murder business,' said the veteran, casting a steely glare. 'So, scrub that out of your mind right this instant. I'm a keen angler given a shot at the impossible – that's all. Doke End has been on everyone's radar for years, ever since it supposedly did a twenty-nine-pound fish almost ten years ago. Some lad sneaked on, caught the fish in the middle of the night, took a few snaps, and blabbed after one too many pints of Southwold Bitter. So, it's a well-known hotspot, and one of those places where people are desperate to get on and have a go themselves. There is nothing in the law about me being able, or not able, to fish there. Not really. If that turnip Forsyth wants to make a few quid, it's his neck that's on the line, not mine. Don't you go around making me out to be a criminal, young man.'

Cam thought this betrayed that Thelonius actually did feel guilty about taking Forsyth up on the offer, and decided to use it immediately. 'Look, you can save your moral gripes for another time – I'm really not interested in who paid who what. Just have a proper look at that list,' said Cam, 'and tell me if there's anyone on there that rings any alarm bells? Seriously, Thelonius, a murder weapon was found out there that had to have been used five days ago and there are only seventeen names here. You say it's not you, and I get that. Fine. Combat brotherhood and all that. But you've still got more info than I've got.'

Finally, Thelonius settled enough to check over the scrap of paper. As he did, he made a few snorting sounds, as if clearing his passages of phlegm was crucial to the proper working of his brain. Cam nearly jumped out of his skin when he felt something brush his lower calf, and he looked down to see a cat, poised delicately above his right shoe. His nose suddenly full of the hedgerow, he gently scooted the tabby away with his toes.

'As it happens, there is a name on there I think you should look into,' said Thelonius, causing Cam's heart to race. 'Not because he's been done for murder or anything, but the family is well known round here for always being into something. If I were you, I'd check out Tommy Jessup.'

Tommy Jessup.

Jessup was the name that had jumped out for Jess, too. That there, in itself, was a connection worth looking into.

'Thank you,' Cam said, offering his hand.

Thelonius, after a moment, took it. 'I bet you were a real stubborn bugger in your day.'

They shook.

'I wish I'd never done any of it,' said Cam, before turning away and walking down the blackened drive.

He assumed Thelonius watched him go, but he didn't care. Another circle had been drawn around one particular name – a name he wasn't going to forget in a hurry.

He checked his watch. Midnight.

A familiar feeling washed over Cam, and to his relief, it wasn't a negative one.

It was momentum.

That moment where his teeth set in his jaw, as his body willed itself forward to follow a mysterious invisible power.

And when he was in this mindset, there was no way in hell he would sleep.

He looked at the list again.

Tommy Jessup.

He wasn't going to bed yet.

17

Cam made it back to his van, and fed Nala a dog treat from the glove box that was a kind of twisted cheese and ham tube, which he thought looked kind of appetising himself. He grabbed his phone, and flicked it on. He needed an address for Tommy Jessup, and the podcasters hadn't got one for him yet, considering he was much further down the list.

Cam's diving recovery business had a Facebook page, to which he posted the same promotional messages on repeat. The idea of sharing anything more on there made him spasm with discomfort, but it did mean that he had a foot helpfully in the social media door for when, for instance, he needed to track down a potential murder suspect. So, after making sure, four times, he wasn't typing in the status-update bar, he typed in the search box 'Tommy Jessup'.

The algorithms immediately did their job, and pulled together a list of Thomas Jessups, Tommy Jessups, Tom Jessups and one rather fabulously named Thomason Bartholomew Jessup III who had a picture of a bald eagle against a flaming Stars and Stripes as a profile picture.

He adjusted the search parameters to nearest first, generating the immediate top result of a Tommo Jessup who stated his home town as Ludham.

Bingo. Cam had two jigsaw pieces dropping together at last.

He clicked through to the profile, and found that Tommo appeared to be somewhere in his early thirties with a bit of a Rasputin look going on, with those same eerie, hyper-focused pupils.

It made Cam think immediately of the knife, and the chunk of heart that had been stuck in it.

A quick scroll down the profile revealed that Tommo Jessup was an alumni of Ludham Primary and Broadland High. He'd been good enough to add certain employment highlights as well, in an act of transparency so many Facebook users seemed happy to commit. A few pub jobs followed by a couple of gardening jobs, then it confirmed his current employers as Jessup and Son Landscaping.

The name of the business was in blue, underlined. A hyperlink. Cam clicked it.

This took Cam to the business's own Facebook page – which boasted an address.

Eight, Middlewater, Ludham.

Cam closed the door, and popped the key in the ignition.

Middlewater sounded idyllic. It sounded like the kind of place you could just drive up to for a peek. Which, despite his better judgement, he decided to do right now.

18

It had become one of those deep Norfolk nights where the atmosphere sat pregnant and oppressive, when cloud pressed heavily and forced the issue, the promise of the unseen and hidden forcing itself just as obstinately. It was a beguiling mix, and one that had always intoxicated Cam, right from his very first visits to the region with his old military dive recovery unit. Now, the closer he got to Ludham, the more anticipation he felt, the more weight accumulated in his gut and the tighter it began to swirl.

The middle of Ludham consisted of a pub, church and small convenience store tight to a chicane snaking through the town. The King's Arms pub itself lay blackened and dormant.

The satnav told him that soon after the dual bends was a left-hand turn, which would take him a mile down another road to Middlewater. That track, when it eventually emerged, was without signs or maintenance, and looked more of a woodland throat leading directly into the guts of the overgrown darkness.

Cam took it, no stranger to heading face-first into dark places with no clue what he'd find when he got there.

There was no other illumination aside from his head-lights, which showed that the track into the woodland was deeply furrowed, and therefore frequently used. The tyre treads were fresh, and deep. Nala stood paws up on the dash, staring out into the ink.

For a place that sounded as inviting as Middlewater, Cam expected some lights to guide him in, but there was nothing. This was either so high-end as to be unadvertised, available only to the invited and super wealthy, or some-where purposefully kept from the light.

When they arrived at the end of the tunnel, Cam saw it was the latter.

The place was so dim, he doused his own headlights so as not to alert anyone, stopped the van, and simply stared. For a moment he thought he'd stumbled upon a nest of sleeping static caravans, only they were all hovering above water. It was a floating trailer park, about a dozen tin resi-dences on stilts over a moonlit marsh.

In its own way, it was really quite beautiful. Peaceful.

Some of the caravans were tight to the edges of what appeared to be an overgrown lagoon, whose surface was broken by reeds and bullrushes. These were accessible by land, although their foundations were clearly in the water. Other dwellings were right out in the water itself, pylons reaching from the murky depths to support them, with small dinghies moored next to their floating decks. Thin moonlit tentacles of power cables reached between the caravan roofs in a patchwork of hasty engineering, increas-ing his impression of some giant multilobed organism growing out into the lake. This wasn't so much a develop-ment as an ecosystem.

And Cam wanted one on sight. Idyllic, functional, and quiet. While close to that water he so loved.

He turned off the engine, unsure of how to proceed. Cam had encountered communities like this before, back when he was with special forces. They were usually tight, protective and vigilant. If they were awake, they'd already know he was here.

He turned the ignition key once, to allow the battery to activate the onboard electronics, then clicked the front passenger windows down. Miming a finger to his lips with one hand, he stroked Nala's ear with the other.

He listened for a few long, drawn-out moments, his eyes scanning the trailers.

Nothing.

Which one was eight?

Without warning, a door opened somewhere, out in front of him. A telltale click, and the soft moan of a hinge.

Nala looked up, and Cam shushed her again, listening intently.

No other sound came.

Maybe someone having a smoke?

Maybe someone trying to see who had come down the track and shut off their engine.

Cam didn't wait. He hit the ignition, and smoothly yet speedily span the grass turning-circle that led to the track, and powered back down the lane.

He was fascinated. Transfixed.

And when he got to the roadway, and saw the lights of more familiar civilisation, he knew yet again that he still wasn't done for the night.

19

The van safely parked down at the now-darkened pub, with Nala curled up with both water and food bowl on the knackered dog bed in the back between racks of scuba gear, Cam marched back down the track. He'd thrown his trusty dryrobe on to stave off the chill, but he realised he must have looked quite the sight stomping down the muddy track like the villain from *I Know What You Did Last Summer*. Sans hook of course.

The night was a blissfully deep quiet, no sound from any corner, as if a vast empty circus tent had been erected over everything, and swaddled the lot. It was close and dank, his trainers sticking and sliding in the tyre tracks. If anyone saw him, he'd announce he was lost and plead ignorance, but luckily, nothing else lit the track. Mizzle had descended, half drizzle, half mist, and he was glad for the extra layer of cover. The end of the tunnel began to yawn wide with a barely perceptible glow of sodium bulbs as he emerged once again into Middlewater.

Like before, he was immediately taken with the place. The quiet and mist spoke to him invitingly, implored him to stay, sought his understanding.

It calmed him like no other place on earth had – that is, aside from Doke End itself, which, despite being mere hours before, felt like days prior. A place like this, hooded and tight, could only carry secrets.

He listened, but there was no sound. No cracking doors, or distant voices. So, he decided to walk the entire perimeter. The lagoon existed in a loosely formed clearing. The edges of the surrounding woodland appeared frayed and ragged, as the meeting of clearing and trees appeared patchy in some places and suddenly thick and engulfing in others. But the overall impression was that of a crude circle.

As he walked, he noticed that some of the hovering structures did indeed have numbers on them, albeit in random places. One had a little halo with the number two over the door. Another had a plant pot with four etched into the mucky terracotta at the top of its deck steps. And eight, the one where Tommo Jessup lived, held its identifying digit scrawled on the side of an orange buoy that floated by one of its support turrets. He studied it only briefly, taking in its faded green walls, wraparound deck that was the unlikely parking spot for a mountain bike, and a bistro set replete with an abandoned mug.

It took him only ten minutes to walk fully around the site's circumference, and he learned much about the place as he took in Middlewater's varying perspectives.

For a start, it seemed almost entirely enclosed, with power coming from its own generators rather than the grid. It looked doomsday-ready, as if everything outside of this lagoon was an unnecessary afterthought anyway. The caravans and trailers were all different sizes and models, and had clearly been arranged together piecemeal, rather than there being an overarching aesthetic for the settlement, which was definitely the correct word as opposed to development. It was gone midnight now, and some of the trailers' windows still glowed and buzzed with late-night television, but he couldn't make out any figures beyond the panes. It was strange – he hadn't seen a soul since he had come down the track. The only noise in the air was the soft buzz of the power lines, which sounded like a huge bug zapper. For all the evidence at hand, this place could have been a mock-up for a *Twin Peaks* theme park.

But Cam had definitely heard that door creak. There was certainly life here.

Having gone all the way around now, he walked carefully to the water's edge. In the dim light, he had no idea what the bank integrity might be, and while he wasn't worried about falling in per se, he didn't want to crash into the water and alert the residents of Middlewater to his presence.

The edges of the lagoon were just as indistinct as the separation between the lagoon's clearing and the forest. In some places there was a definite bank carved out of dirt that stood a foot or so over the murmuring surface; in others, the grass simply sloped into the dark water.

There was a part-submerged post that played host to a huge bunch of small rope loops with carabiner clips dangling from them. Clipped underneath were a couple of dinghies. It was either the village car park, for residents to tie up their own dinghies, or the taxi rank, where they were kept for communal use. Another quirk to add to the litany of quirks in this deeply quirky place.

'Who the fuck are you?'

The voice came from the lagoon, as if the clearing itself had demanded who the intruder was. Cam span to look, and it seemed that he'd been sneaked right up on.

There was a woman behind him in a long green wax jacket and a trucker cap, and her expression left him in no doubt that she meant all the venom that her words came out with.

'Oh, I got a bit lost. Sorry, I've been on my way to Potter Heigham and thought this was a shortcut.'

'Oh, shut your gob hole,' she ordered. 'I've watched you walk all around, and you didn't look for a way out once.'

Cam was bang to rights and he knew it.

She pointed at him with a finger like a lump of coal, the digit stuffed in a black ski glove. 'You're a liar. And you know who else are liars? Thieves. Is that what you are? A thief?'

No amount of cool air could chill the heat that burned through Cam's whole body now. It was a horrible, sickly, tidal heat that swept and dragged him to deep mental waters. He couldn't think of anything to say. The truth of his lying rang in his ribs, sweat beading immediately in his hairline.

'I'm looking for someone,' he managed at last, his voice coming out thick like it had attained a physical form too big for his throat.

'Who, go on, give me a name, blow my mind?' The woman leaned forward, goading him.

'Tommy Jessup,' he said.

The reaction was immediate. Her eyes widened, then narrowed instantly with intensity.

'What do you know about him?'

'I just want to speak to him, that's all. I've been guessing where he lives. I've got the rough address but this place...' Cam pointed at the small homes hovering about the waterline.

'Do you know him?'

'A bit, you could say.' It was rubbish, but what else could he say?

'So where is he?'

That threw him. He pointed weakly at the homes, which simply stared back at him.

The woman looked behind her, following his finger, then looked at the dirt at her feet. 'He's been missing for four days now,' she eventually said. 'And then you come along.'

Cam's mind seemed to burst and broaden.

One of the names on the list had been missing? This whole time?

As Cam's mind took another trip through the murk of possibilities, the night air was punctured by a new sound. Soft and sonorous.

Sirens.

Getting closer.

He looked at the woman, who smiled wide and crooked.

'You hear them?' she said. 'They're here for you, sunshine.'

20

Fight or flight kicked in hard and fast.

Turn and sprint straight into the trees?

Or stand and face the music?

Under the watchful eye of Middlewater's trucker hat-wearing security matriarch, a third option presented itself.

Cam immediately dashed to the water and threw himself in. The dryrobe was totally unfit for the job, and immediately swamped his torso. The inside layer of the cloak was thick towelling, and it seemed to drag him to the bottom with an impossible grip.

Cam had prepared himself for the cold, but when it hit, it was fierce. At this time of year the water temperature would be around six degrees Celsius. Most people moseyed along completely unaware that falling into water that was between ten and fifteen degrees could kill you in around a minute – that is, without a wet or drysuit. Anything under ten degrees would be life threatening within seconds.

First comes cold shock – an intense, debilitating pain that renders you agonised and gasping. Then your muscles lose function as they shut down through lack of blood flow. You end up almost literally frozen. Then, you become hypothermic, as the temperature of your vital organs drops and you lose the ability to continue fulfilling any of the essential requirements to stay alive. Perhaps the unluckiest effect is circum-rescue collapse. When you're pulled up out of the water – just when you think you're safe – the abrupt change in temperature can cause immediate crashing blood pressure. Sudden low blood pressure on a hypothermic heart? Instant cardiac arrest.

Cold water could kill you in a lot of different ways – and Cam was up against all of them now.

He opened his eyes, and saw nothing at all. Just black, overwhelming and pressing.

He treaded water, and shrugged out of the dryrobe with a grimace. They weren't cheap, but it was either that or drowning in comfort. It would sink, he was sure of it, so he let it drift off below him, consoling himself that at least it wouldn't give away his location.

Cam started to swim in long, deep strokes, off into what he hoped was the middle of the lagoon, his shoulders protesting strongly thanks to the punishing workout only a couple of hours prior.

He ignored it. Ironically, he could focus on mind over matter just fine – it was when mind butted against mind he became unstuck. It was a temporary fix, though. He was still made of matter, and if he stayed in this water for too long, science would overrule all and kill him regardless.

Those sirens sounded a couple of miles away, which he reasoned would give him maybe five minutes tops before the responding vehicles arrived in Middlewater. He had to act fast if he was going to pull off the daft notion he'd yanked from thin air.

Speaking of air, he needed some. He eased his speed as he came back up to the surface, so as to break it with minimum fuss. He eased his forehead through the meniscus, and opened his eyes.

The quiet of the clearing was gone, and in its place was a mish-mash of competing voices, doors screeching and footsteps clanking.

This was going, in military parlance, full CF in the blink of an eye.

Clusterfuck.

Cam took his bearings. A career under water meant he'd got himself some distance out into the belly of the pool in very little time, and as he looked back to where he'd come from, he could see figures on the bank looking for him. He couldn't decipher what they were saying, swamped by the growing sirens, but they were agitated. He turned back to the surrounding caravans, and looked for the one he was after.

There, north-east of his position. He could see its floating orange buoy, now at eye level in the distance.

Number eight.

Another strong couple of underwater pushes, just like the first one, should do it. He got his head down, and forged on.

He was immediately relieved to be moving again, such was the speed with which being stationary had allowed the cold into his bones, joints and very blood vessels.

He surged on, and when he needed air again, he only broke the surface enough to gulp oxygen.

When he came up again, he was at the tall legs of the Jessup caravan – and its flanks were washed in blue rolling lights, and the sirens had stopped.

The cops had arrived.

Cam made no sudden movements but clung to the caravan support struts, and slowly, inch by inch, pulled himself beneath the overhead decking. He listened hard. Voices called to each other in the distance, three in total he could clearly detect, the loudest belonging unmistakably to the woman he'd left just moments earlier. He wouldn't forget those dulcet tones in a hurry.

He peered out from beneath the vaulted dwelling, watching, with his mouth only just above the waterline. He couldn't quite see the bank in the darkness, but time wasn't on his side. They'd surely have a look for him in a boat, once that woman told the attending police that he'd fled into the water, and that he was showing an interest in the Jessup caravan.

Cam had to act now. All that training, all those years of diving in the harshest pressures, had to come into play now.

He listened, made sure that nobody was watching him from the other caravans, paying particular attention to the home directly over his head. There was no movement, and it sounded especially dead. He couldn't remember any lights on inside either, when he was checking the whole place out.

He had to strike while the going was good. He emerged from underneath the overhead veranda, and span in the water so that he faced the caravan. He sank slowly, then pushed himself upwards with a strong kick. With his left arm, he pulled himself upward, reaching as high up the platform as he could.

His hand grasped wood, and he brought his other hand up to join it.

Dangling now half out of the water, he pulled himself up and used the railing slats as a ladder – but the warmer air, with the temperature differential, felt like burning oil thrown onto his body. He gritted his teeth, tried to keep going, heaved himself upwards even though the pain throughout his body was now monstrous. All the while, his soaked clothing tried to yank him back to the depths. His core screamed, until he was able to hook a foot onto the wood.

That gave him all the assistance he needed to reach up and over the barrier, and grab for the mug on the small bistro table. He grabbed the handle with outstretched fingers, and immediately began lowering himself back into the water – staying careful not to drop the mug or let it get submerged. The frigid water, strangely, was a relief after the scalding sensations a moment earlier. But he knew it was a false relief: he couldn't stay in here much longer.

He retreated back under caravan eight.

He had it.

Now to get out of here.

He watched, and listened again.

The voices had dimmed in volume.

And he could hear the familiar clank and swing of oars in rowlocks.

Really, definitively, time to go.

He checked his dive watch, which he used as his everyday watch merely because it was convenient. In the top corner of the dial was a small two-letter reading of the compass direction he was heading in – and when he'd checked the time while walking up the track, he'd seen he was heading NE. North-east. Which meant that the way out, and his car, was in the opposite direction. South-west.

But he didn't want to go down the track, in case a backup vehicle was en route and caught him soaked, frozen and wandering, holding a mug. Instead, he faced west, and aimed to enter the surrounding woods heading that way. Then, when he was entrenched in the vegetation, he would walk through the woods south to the road, and freedom.

First things first though. He needed to get out of the freezing lagoon. Fast.

Hypothermia was surely only moments away.

Training could only prepare you for so much. Soon, this wouldn't be a question of mental resilience. It would just be a matter of human tissue doing what it naturally does under extreme duress.

Break apart and crumble.

Focus, Cam.

There was a ten metre gap between caravan eight and the next one west.

With the coast still clear, he swam, the mug still aloft. Every stroke was agony, a million hypodermic needles puncturing every inch of his skin, then pushing as deep as they could go.

Come on, Cam.

It sounded as if the boat was somewhere south, and he couldn't see anything yet.

He just made it under the balcony of the next caravan when suddenly the van's door opened overhead and heavy footsteps clattered the deck. Cam's blood chilled somehow further, and his anxiety flourished with near-flammable intent. He retreated into the shadows, praying that he hadn't been seen.

The owner of the footsteps boomed across the water. 'What the hell are you lot doing here?'

Cam didn't know who he was talking to, but he was clearly unhappy with the intended recipient.

A voice shouted back, scratched and high-pitched. Cam couldn't decipher the words, as he found himself retreating as far back as he could without emerging into the open on the rear side of the caravan.

'You called the police? You brought them here? Seriously?' The owner of the voice above now had Cam's attention in more ways than one.

Another response. His breathing was rapid now, each gulp indistinct from the one just before it.

'Oh, you fucking idiot,' came the shout back from above. The man stomped quickly back into the caravan, and Cam could hear footsteps moving this way and that overhead. He'd remember this caravan, if he ever came back. Someone clearly had something to hide.

Then something else came to his attention: a rowboat came into view. Cam held his breath, and retreated to the back corner, as far from the steps up to the deck as he could. Two police officers sat in the boat, a woman and a man, the former rowing while the latter waved a torch through the misted tendrils that danced across the lagoon surface. Checking behind him, he saw that the caravan stationed to the rear of his hiding spot was darkened and quiet, and he gambled that it was unoccupied. He pulled himself behind the rear stanchion, held the mug tight, and tried to keep from drifting.

The police drew closer, and the officer with the torch mercifully didn't check beneath the overhead home. He was directing the light at the deck, and the door the gobby complainant had just closed.

'Sir?' The officer shouted.

Cam was relieved and grateful, despite the excruciating pulses throughout his body. Every moment was now crucial, every second vital. He needed small respite fast, or shutdown was imminent.

Then he remembered there was a way he could help himself. An inbuilt heat source that would immediately warm his core.

He had to concentrate and allow his seizing muscles the chance to relax enough for it to work.

He breathed, and focused on it, counted the seconds with each breath – and it happened.

A gentle warmth spread gradually across his midriff, and then across his core. He brought his legs up into the growing cloud of warm urine. It was like experiencing the touch of an angel sent to soothe him, if, of course, you discounted the fact that he was huddled in his own piss.

Immersion diuresis was the scientific term for it. He'd beaten science with science, and it made him smile – or it would have if his face still worked.

The agitated antics of the caravan's owner above had distracted the officers from looking for what they had come for. With no answer, the officers looked at each other, and the woman nodded. She angled the boat at the bottom steps to the deck, six inches from the waterline, and the man grabbed the railings as soon as he was within reach. Within moments, they were both climbing the deck steps, ascending out of sight.

Cam sprang into action and, staying at the back of the caravan, swam carefully, albeit one-handedly, out and across the open water to the western bank.

He pulled himself out, his juddering skin on fire, and had a last pained look at Middlewater before he darted for the trees, their cover, and their safety – still clutching the dirty mug, and all the potential Tommy Jessup DNA it contained.

If only he could survive long enough to get it to Rogers.

Now

I don't know who he is.

That's twice now, he's shown up in places he shouldn't. He's brought the police here. It's no good at all. All I wanted to do was get a few things from the empty place. Mementos. Reminders. Good memories. What does he want? He's going about this all wrong. You want something, you stay quiet, stay close, stay in the dark parts.

Only then do you take it.

I heard him on the track, coming up to the trailer park. I was on my way up myself, buried in the trees. He didn't see me when he walked past. I was interested. They are all interesting, men like that. They're going somewhere only they know. He's spent his whole life going there. Like there's always been a goal he's aiming for, and every time he gets near it, the goal moves. Those people are always interesting.

As he walked around the trailer park, I decided to stay put. It's a good job really, because it brought out that woman. The mouth woman. You don't cross her. And then the sirens and blue lights came. I've been sat watching ever since.

What's he doing? I find myself feeling sick as I watch him swim to that caravan. The same caravan I want to go to.

No.

He's not supposed to be doing that.

I feel like I'm going to be sick, but it will all be red and angry. I'm so angry. I have to swallow it back down, but it tastes of all the black. It's a familiar taste. It's how I used to feel. How I used to feel all the time, thanks to those things. It's fear.

This man.

He makes me feel how all those things did.

He makes me feel in the ways that made all of this start.

He's taken a mug from the deck.

The bastard.

The *bastard*.

The police are moving towards him now. No, don't see him. Whoever you are, hide. Yes, that's it, retreat. Go deeper. I'm tempted to make a sound, throw something, distract the police, do anything to make sure that the man isn't caught. I know why he's got the mug. He's holding it above the water. He's a clever boy.

Damn him.

Who is he? The police are inside another caravan now. He's swimming to the bank. I surely can't go now. I hate him.

Like all things that made me this way, the same result should come. The same price should find him. I could kill him in here. My knife is gone, so I can't do it. Unless I do it with my hands? I can't. He's in the woods. Away from the police. Safe for now. I'll follow him. I need that mug. I have to follow him. He's careful. Quiet.

There's method to what he's doing now. He's taken his clothes off, rubbing his chest furiously. His arms too. And legs.

144

He's done this before. He's fascinating.

I love him.

I hate him.

I need to kill him.

Crack.

I look down, at the twig I just stepped on. The great betrayer. It echoes through the woods. The man has frozen. He's slowly beginning to turn towards me.

No.

21

Cam froze.

Moments like this invoked either senses you didn't even know you had, or made all your senses join forces to create a state of hyper-perception.

It was like hitting a switch into immediate prey mode.

The snapping twig had rung out directly behind him, and although he was still, indecision was short-lived.

Suddenly sure he was being watched, he span on the spot, the dirt beneath his feet softly scraping as he did so.

Anyone could be behind him. But this felt different to dealing with a human. Cam had been all over the world in direct combat cat-and-mouse moments with hundreds of people, highly trained, civilian, and everywhere in between.

This felt like none of those occasions.

This felt animal. Unpredictable. A different kind of danger.

As he stared hard into the trees, he saw nothing.

But something was there. He knew it. Could feel it.

Moonlight broke the trees, and gave the trunks a blue-ish hue. The leaves were black brush-strokes in the dark, the occasional frond offering refracted moonshine with its surface dew.

And it all stared back at him: nothing amiss. 'Hello?' he whispered carefully, although the police were now arguing quietly with the obnoxious man in Middlewater, and Cam didn't think he'd disturb them.

He listened for any kind of response, or movement that might give away his voyeur's position.

Yes, that was what it felt like. That he was being watched with fascination, and something touching excitement. He was suddenly extremely aware that he was almost naked.

'Is anyone here?' he hissed.

The woods kept their countenance.

All life seemed sucked out, all birds silenced and woodland mammals gagged.

He tried to fit the whole strangeness of the moment with what he was here for – to make headway into the story (and apparent disappearance, he now knew) of Tommy Jessup – but he couldn't see the joins or links, if there even were any.

He tried a different tack.

'I know you're there,' he said, with as much dismissive bite as he could muster, 'and I know who you are.'

The silence that replied seemed to grow fat, loaded with unspoken answers, becoming so bloated with unfulfilled promise, Cam almost pleaded aloud with it to be broken.

But nothing came.

Maybe this is one of those moments, he thought. One of those moments where I'll look back and think *yep, there were signs I was losing it.*

Perhaps this was the first brick dropping loose from the wall of his mind.

No. He tried to give himself the benefit of the doubt, tried to be kind to himself. It had been a tumultuous last half hour, which he'd have had no clue how to explain if he'd been caught.

He went to his breathing crutch, and closed his eyes.

In for three.

Hold for five.

Out for eight.

Rubbed his chest furiously the whole time to keep the blood flowing.

Three repetitions, and he was already feeling more balanced, controlled, and rooted.

He opened his eyes, and the woods felt different.

The threat seemed to have lifted. Or moved on.

'Maybe next time,' he said out loud, and turned quietly. He marched on into the woods, and tried to forget what had happened.

Even the tiniest creature could make a sound in the woods, especially those as densely packed as this one. If it weren't for Cam's training and experience, he'd be crashing through like a lost elephant. The simplest explanation was always the most likely, he liked to think.

His clothes and trainers in one hand, he looked at the mug in the other. If Tommy's DNA was on it, and if it proved a match with the genetic material on the knife from Doke End, it would be nothing short of game-changing. Their victim would be identified, even if the body was still nowhere to be found.

And having a name would turbo-charge the investigation and give it focus. For all the floundering Cam felt he'd been doing, if this was the breakthrough, it would all be worth it.

The sounds of the police search had been left behind, and the night began to take on a more normal character. The sights were as expected, with dim shafts of blueish moonlight spearing through the overhead canopies and intersecting branches, and now the birdlife had come back. The usual sounds of breeze and rustle had returned.

And it made him think again of the odd feelings only moments earlier. He couldn't shake it.

Those moments of stillness were often attributed to the near-supernatural impact of a predator being in the vicinity, and the prey animals' desperate attempts to stay quiet and out of sight.

But Cam had a slightly different take on the phenomenon, or thought that it was six of one and half a dozen of the other – the other being that, when you were in these situations, and you felt a presence with no answer, your senses heightened, and adopted their own sense of almost automated self-preservation. They filtered out external unhelpful sound, to give you the best chance of locking on to your unknown target and identifying it. Result: an impression of eerie silence, even if that wasn't the case.

The side effect, however, was the sheer discomfort and nerve-jangling state that usually came with it.

Our human brains are prewired with tools that keep us alive. A genetic imprint that certain things are to be avoided for reasons of self-preservation. These instincts manifested themselves in all manner of ways, but one of those was fear, in situations just like this one. And Cam's instincts had left him very sure of at least one thing.

That there was something very fucking dangerous in these woods.

Dicking about in a predator's territory was a stupid move whatever day of the week it was, so Cam was pleased to see the trees give way to a field up ahead. It was fallow, and the way its uncut grass rolled in the breeze almost had Cam thinking it was yet another body of water – not that that would have surprised him given the characteristics of the entire region.

He jogged across the bobbled turf to a thick black hedgerow, which he traced around a bend to a fence. He carefully climbed its wooden slats, and took one last glance at the forest he'd left only moments earlier – and felt the predatory presence crackle through his nerves once more.

Just who or *what* the hell was in there?

22

Rogers ran down the stairs, dragging the dressing gown over her shoulders. She would have sent Martin down, but that time had long gone – even if he had still been here, that sad-sack would have been as much use in defending her honour as a neon sign shouting 'after you'.

At the front door, she tried to snatch a glance through the glass at whoever was ringing her doorbell. The dawn light threw soft blue at her front door, and only served to highlight her visitor in royal shadows.

The shape was one she didn't recognise but, intrigued, she threw caution to the breeze and opened the door anyway.

She felt dual waves of predictability and surprise, as she recognised Cam Killick without his ridiculous giant overcoat but still oddly in shorts and a T-shirt.

'Where's the dryrobe?' she said, as she swung the door open. 'I thought it was like your blanky when you're not in the water.'

'Lost it,' he replied with a chatter of teeth. Killick looked frozen, and she almost felt bad.

Well, not bad, but marginally regretful enough to invite him in. 'You best get inside before anyone thinks I'm kicking you out after a disappointing performance.'

As he crossed the threshold, she saw he was soaked and muddy, and carrying a white mug.

'Do you do anything normal?' she asked. He looked at her as he stood on the mat by the front door. She realised she quite liked giving him a hard time, in what she begrudgingly recognised was an affectionate way – a bit like when you keep on telling a particularly daft dog how thick it is.

'I'm sorry to get you up—' Cam said, but Rogers waved him off.

'Did you think getting up four times a night is only an ageing male thing?' she said, as she took the mug from his hand and walked down the hall. 'If only all life's problems were explained away by something so simple as an enlarged prostate.'

She put the mug on the kitchen counter, and hit the button on the side of the kettle. Grabbed a jar of instant, and fixed to pour.

'Don't!' Killick said, with more urgency than she was used to from him. It paused her hand. 'It's not mine.'

She lowered the jar, couldn't work out what the idiot was up to now. 'Then why are you carrying around someone else's mug? And can you stop hovering by the bloody door?'

Cam entered the kitchen, still shivering. She threw a paisley tea towel at him, and he draped it pathetically across his shoulders. 'It's Tommy Jessup's. I got it from his place earlier tonight.'

That stumped Rogers.

'He's one of the names on that list, isn't he?' she asked, and dammit, she couldn't help herself from wondering where this aquatic cretin was going.

'Yeah,' Killick replied. 'It seems he lives in some floating trailer park – I don't know how else to put it – near

Ludham. The mug was on a little table outside his front door.'

Rogers could only stare at him and found it hard not to let her jaw sag. 'You went off the reservation here, didn't you…'

He looked at the tile flooring.

'Oh, no. That was you. Middlewater.' Rogers had heard the radio earlier, the call-out late the previous night just as she was clocking off.

'Yeah,' Killick said. 'I didn't mean—'

'Burglars never mean to trip the alarm, but the thick ones always do. I assume they didn't catch you?'

He shook his head.

She rubbed a weary hand across her eyes. 'A fugitive in the kitchen, just magic.'

'I figured it was for the greater good. A woman there told me Jessup has been missing for four days – that's what made me want to grab the mug.'

'The DNA.'

'Yes, the DNA. Even if it's not his, it could prove a familial relation, and mean we're on the right track.'

'Bloody hell,' Rogers said. She opened a drawer by the oven. 'We've got to stop putting vital evidence in sandwich bags.'

She put the mug into a small clear bag and tied the handles. 'These ridiculous requests are going to get me a reputation. What else did you find?'

'Not much. But it's a weird set-up out there. Seems very tight. Protect their own.' He looked away, preoccupied.

Rogers looked at Killick, and could see that there was something eating at him. Something that he wasn't totally comfortable bringing up, and hadn't made his mind up about. 'What else?'

He didn't answer.

'Come on Killick, if you're dragging me up and out of bed at Christ knows when, you're morally obliged to offer everything you've got.'

He glanced up at her, then twisted his features like he was physically chewing something over. 'Something about it wasn't right. There was someone there.'

Rogers crossed her arms. 'Embellish.'

Killick mirrored her, but she noticed when he folded his arms, his hands cradled his upper arms – as if he was subconsciously comforting himself.

A man of Cam Killick's background and experience didn't often spook. And that got her attention, loud and clear.

'I ended up leaving Middlewater via the surrounding woods and walking out,' he said. He was staring into the middle distance now, his eyebrows slightly tilted down in a perplexed scrunch. 'And I had feelings that I've only had a handful of times before.'

Rogers couldn't give a frosty shit about the smoke and mirrors. 'I'm about to start a countdown, before I kick you out.'

'In the service, you'd find yourself mixing with all sorts of different enemies. Some who clearly didn't want to be there, some who felt they were born to do it, some who were drugged up, or drunk or whatever... But every now and then, you'd be up against someone who was just completely different. Someone who was more animal, in the way he behaved. Someone who absolutely couldn't give a damn about anyone or anything, and was all the more dangerous for it.'

He turned to look at Rogers, and the honesty in his eyes gave her a chill along her own forearms.

'Whoever was in those woods around Middlewater, they gave me that feeling.'

'Do you think,' she suggested, 'that you ended up in the deep dark woods and, if you'll forgive me, shat yourself?' Even as she said it she didn't believe it.

But Killick's expression didn't waiver. 'You never forget that. It doesn't come around often, but it leaves an impression.'

They stood in silence, as the kettle began to bubble noisily. Rogers clicked it off before it had the chance to reach boiling point. 'I'm heading into work,' she said.

'What's the plan?'

'I'm going to make sure this mug is the first thing forensics finds when they come in tomorrow morning. Then, if they confirm Tommy Jessup as our victim, I'm going to pull each one of those seventeen names apart.'

23

Cam decided at last that it might be acceptable to get some sleep. He was in Norwich, however, a good twenty-five minutes or so to home – another half-hour lost on top of the time he'd be asleep. But he was nothing if not resourceful.

He decided instead to climb into the back of his van and curl up on the bare boards, using Nala's dog bed as a pillow (and most likely a bit of Nala herself), and a selection of towels as a duvet. The back of his van was windowless, so he could probably get a few hours back there without being disturbed. He was flat out exhausted, and drained by his near-brush with hypothermia. The tension and pressures of the visit to Middlewater would usually have his mind in a PTSD tailspin, but the effects of the cold had rendered his very brain sluggish.

He drove out of Norwich towards Sprowston, the heat on full blast, and picked a layby ten minutes out of town by Sprowston Golf Club, where the cracking of tee shots by dawn golfers would be the only disturbing sound. He eased into a gap between a lorry and a sandwich van and flicked his phone off silent, because he wanted to be alerted if anyone came to him with more information.

As he climbed into the back, Nala looked confused, suggesting even *her* body clock was beginning to spin. He got into position, then took out the Tupperware he kept in the van which contained reserves of all his medication. He was a bit late, but the adrenaline had been masking the very slight withdrawal. He counted out each chalky morsel, all the different types, and threw the lot in his mouth, washing it down with a slug from his insulated water bottle.

A good sleep, nice and warm, would do him the power of good.

Nala crawled next to him, trying to lie alongside his torso, before clambering up onto his chest to stare down into his eyes.

'Ease off, love,' Cam said, pushing her back.

But she came back with more force. She seemed worried about him, not working out that she was actually preventing him from getting some much-needed shut-eye.

He stroked her back and left her there.

His eyes began to sag, losing focus of the roof of the van overhead with every passing breath.

He felt that fuzzy loosening of his muscles, the one that usually happened just before sleep. Nala yawned in his face, and he was gone.

It felt like only seconds later his peace was shattered by a crashing rumble which wobbled the walls of the van, causing the air tanks to rattle in their cage. A huge lorry had gone past on the road outside. And then another.

The rest of the world was going to work.

Nala was on him, and he put his hands to her flanks. She was shaking. The lorries had scared her, too.

'Sorry, girl,' Cam said, trying to soothe her with a flurry of strokes.

He tried to close his eyes again, but if anything, he felt worse.

He blitzed them back open. The throaty rumble of morning lorries was going past them at a constant rate. The cruelly ended sleep had utterly confused his system, and his mind seemed to abandon exhaustion and detach into an electrical storm, floating this way and that, exploded by warring currents. It felt as if his senses had been poured into a macerator. Once his eyes were open, he found he couldn't shut them again, not anything more than a blink, and Nala, yet again, seemed to sense his unease. She shimmied up under his chin and licked at his stubble until he had to get up. The dog, again, seemed to know more about him than he did. She looked at him as if to say *less of this nonsense*.

He checked his watch and saw that somehow, despite everything, he'd managed to get a grand total of six minutes sleep. Worse than that, the battering, jarring drop in and out of consciousness, had multiplied his tiredness exponentially. Rather than feeling like he'd slept on the side of the road, he felt like he'd slept in it, lorries and everything.

Then he got to thinking about the very reason he'd been so active the last twenty-four hours. Visions of knives, and killings, and blood from a heart danced behind his eyes.

It was doing his head in, all this waiting around while the clock was ticking. There was a murderer on the loose, and it frustrated him endlessly that he couldn't do anything further about it. He had to wait for other wheels to turn.

He sat in the dark and tried to convince himself he had done enough for the time being, but all it did was make him want to get out more.

And worse still, his head was shredded in half by a piss-poor attempt at sleep.

He lay back, and tried something else. Pam had described it to him, but it had never worked for him before. He knew that his meds usually needed about fifteen minutes to kick in – maybe trying this new technique would coincide with the first flows of those calming chemicals, and work.

It's better than nothing, he thought.

He started to breathe, heavy and deep. As far in as he could, then as far out as he could. Forcing the air in as far as it would go, and then purging every last cubic centimetre of it on release.

Then he focused his mind on the tips of his toes. Forced all the muscles in those distant digits to still, and loosen.

When he felt slack in his toes, he moved his focus up to the tops of his feet. Commanded all the sinew across both sets of metatarsals to slacken.

Then onto the ankles. He focused all his energy on making them unclench, uncoil, and still.

A lorry thundered past, but his feet remained motionless, and lost in an almost zen-like state of float. *Breathe.*

It was working.

Encouraged, he moved up to his calves, forced them to unknot.

Then his knees.

He stayed slow and methodical with each stage of his body, as he came up higher.

His hips and groin. Stomach. That was hard, and took longer, butterflies still racing as they were, but he managed it.

Fingers by his side, forearms, and biceps, suddenly all floppy and at ease.

His chest followed. Then his shoulders.

By then, his head felt like it was lying atop a cloud of floating candyfloss. He willed his jaw to unclench, and then focused on his temples.

Everything felt slack. Everything felt peaceful.

He couldn't hear what was going on around him, and it didn't bother him.

At last, mercifully, he drifted off, to real perfect slumber – for the first time in a long time.

24

Cam was dragged awake by the ringing of his phone. He rummaged for it in a groggy state of semi-animation. He didn't know how long he'd slept, but God, it had been good.

He eventually found the handset swaddled in the pile of towels he'd been sleeping in, its glowing screen in the darkness of the van ending the brief hide-and-seek. He answered.

'Hello, I'm here.'

'I should have bloody thought you are, and where is here?' It was Rogers, her tone direct and acerbic as per her norm and apparent custom.

'I'm near Sprowston.'

'Well, I need you to come in. What's that, fifteen minutes?'

Cam's head wasn't anywhere close to cleared. 'What's happening?'

'They got a sample off the mug. DNA tests need time, but they come through piecemeal, so we've got some early feedback.'

'This early?'

'The sample from the mug was apparently in mint condition. It enabled extraction and purification, PCR and sequencing, according to the email in front of me.'

'Was it Jessup?'

'They can't confirm identification yet, but they can show a familial link – in this case, a direct link through the paternal side, a generation upwards.'

'So that is… ?'

Rogers sighed down the phone but it was half-hearted, her trademark sarcasm being brushed to one side by the excitement of what she was about to say. 'The DNA on the mug belongs to the father of whoever's DNA was on that knife.'

'So, the mug had been used by the victim's dad?'

'Yes. That trailer is the registered address of Tommy Jessup, and Jessup and Son Landscaping. He lives in that trailer with his father. Right?'

'Stands to reason.'

'So if you follow that reason, Tommy Jessup is our missing murder victim.'

'Wow,' said Cam. He wasn't prone to overt acts of celebration, but the vindication of his hunch being right felt *damn* good.

Rogers just sighed, but he could hear her words escape her mouth through a smile. 'It's a bit of a jackpot.'

Within the hour, Cam was at Norwich Police Station, sitting in yet another meeting room kitted out with selections from the Beige World Office Supplies catalogue. This time, however, he'd been treated to a double espresso – his choice, because staying alert was becoming ever more troublesome.

Rogers looked like she'd ingested several such beverages already. She seemed incapable of sitting still, and was pinging from seat to computer screen to television to whiteboard – all with a glowing iPad in hand. This particular office had apparently become the investigation's incident room, and it now comprised other officers who had been seconded to assist. It all added to the heat and congestion of a situation now injected with momentum.

Cam sat at the large central table, watched them work, and waited for instruction.

Rogers had been busy wrestling a mass of paperwork, ruffling the sheets into an order undecipherable to the naked eye, while simultaneously connected to her phone in an umbilical way. It lay on the tabletop between her and Cam, screen up, and she kept refreshing it, as if waiting for a text.

'What is clear,' said Rogers, her voice a clipped staccato with excitement, 'is we've had a staggering stroke of luck.'

'Can you tell me what's going on?' asked Cam. The tiredness was now bone-deep, but he didn't feel like he could relinquish himself at the altar of exhaustion again just yet.

'I'm waiting for the green light from higher up,' said Rogers. 'As soon as I get word, we can put out an all-points bulletin on Tommy Jessup. While it's not going to turn him up, not alive, with a piece of his heart stuck in that knife, it'll get information coming in as to his recent movements and we can establish a pattern. Work out the last people to see him. Start to put this thing under the microscope.'

'Do think they'll go for it? Your higher-ups, I mean.'

'I think they should. A senior detective presenting this amount of incontrovertible DNA evidence pertaining to a murder victim? I'd be frankly amazed if they didn't. Even for that shower of nonsense.' She pointed at the ceiling, suggesting said nonsense was all in higher corridors of power. 'But the reason I pulled you in here wasn't just to tell you that.'

'OK...' said Cam warily.

Rogers was cueing something up on the iPad, but managed to keep on speaking uninterruptedly in a show of multitasking that Cam felt would be beyond him if he tried.

'I've been going through your list of suspects, using Jessup as the centre point of the Venn diagram,' she said. 'You know two of the other people on that list have been reported missing?'

'You're kidding?'

Rogers tapped the tablet's screen, which somehow prompted the wall-mounted flatscreen to blink to life. It showed a Facebook feed. 'Leonard Drummond and Ryan Forrester,' she said.

'I remember the names.'

'And guess what?'

'What?'

'When you cycle back through their Facebook posts, you can quickly see they're in a number of the same photographs together.' The picture on the screen showed the two men sat by a pool somewhere hot, holidaying with short, fat tins of lager in hand.

'Shit,' said Cam.

'Shit indeed,' said Rogers.

That changed a lot. If these men were friends, then the pattern just solidified, and flipped on its head. The seventeen men who had accessed Doke End weren't just suspects. They might be fellow victims.

'Any idea how long they might have known each other? Roughly?'

'As far as I can tell,' Rogers said, 'these two go back to at least 2009 – maybe earlier. They were old friends. Fishing, golf, nightclubs, you name it.'

'It's coming together,' Cam said. 'Three missing friends.' Another layer was unravelling.

'We need to get this information out there, and have this friendship group examined in full. What is so special about these three that means they've ended up missing and/or dead? And what does it have to do with Doke End?'

Cam leaned forward and spoke quietly. 'It probably stands to reason we are looking for three bodies now.'

'The thought had occurred to me. So, a plan. We need to recreate Jessup's most recent movements, prior to Doke End and the knife. Establish last seen contacts, and pin down a pattern and his activity before he went missing. Hopefully then we can work out who he's been with and draw up a list of suspects.'

'A second list of suspects,' piped up Cam. 'I've still got the podcasters on the original one.'

'Then we'll reserve all reference to alien abduction to them, OK?'

Cam reddened. Time to move the discussion on. 'Forgive me for being thick,' he began.

'It's OK, it wouldn't be the first time,' said Rogers.

'But how do we find out who's in Jessup's social circle, so to speak?'

'Well, when we put out the APB, we should be inundated with responses. Some will be pure bollocks, some will swear down they've seen him down the Co-op which, considering he's got a somewhat weepy heart at present, we know he wasn't. Some will swear he's been abducted by ET and he's playing Dungeons and sodding Dragons with him – I'm thinking of your podcast reprobates here,

Killick. But for every umpteen of those, there will be nuggets of truth. We just have to sift through it all and find those genuine morsels that connect. That's what these lot will be doing, the lucky sods.'

A few of the attending officers turned to look at Rogers.

'Yes, you lot.' All eyes looked away quickly. 'And Killick, you're going to need to do two things. One, take a long hot shower, the kind that actually ends up boring. I've never known a man to carry so many wildly discordant smells. And two, bring in Forsyth. You were the last to see him, and I need you to bring him in. We need to find out when Jessup was on Doke End.'

'That just might give us a date of death at least?' Cam said. In truth, he thought he'd quite relish putting the squeeze on that weasel Forsyth again, so as tasks went, he was up for this one. 'Are you going to have a chat with him, too? Is he a suspect?'

'Now we know it's Jessup that's missing, presumed dead, that makes Forsyth a last known. So you don't ask him anything, just bring him in. Don't need you blundering about getting details from him when he's not on record.'

Cam put his hands up. 'I'll play dumb.'

'Something you're very good at,' said Rogers. 'And don't make me get second thoughts about keeping you involved, Killick. We're doing you a favour, not the other way round, so don't get too big for your boots – you're still floundering about in the dark getting lucky, as usual.'

But Cam could see that she didn't really mean it. Sarcasm and cynicism were her currency, her armour which protected her from the world's darkest corners.

'By your good grace alone,' he said, but he was confused. 'Why me?' Anything official like this should really be handled properly by uniforms, and both Cam and Rogers knew that.

'Because we are going to do this part off the books. Who knows who Forsyth has been farming that list out to – the last thing I want to do is spook him. If that man sees uniforms, off the back of the announcement of a murder enquiry, he's going to go full turtlehead and bury himself.'

Cam wasn't sure she was using the right metaphor, but didn't want to point it out. 'So where shall I take him?'

'I'll think of somewhere. Watch for my text. When you've got him in your sights, let me know. We'll get a proper welcome sorted, and sweat him.'

'OK,' Cam said.

Rogers looked at him for a moment. One moment became two, then three. 'Now, Killick. I want you to go find him now.'

'Oh, right,' Cam said, standing with an obnoxious scrape of wooden chair leg on vinyl floor.

Rogers spoke again, her eyes back on the screen. 'Well, there we go. It's up on the intranet.'

'What is?'

'The appeal for info on Tommy Jessup. Press release.' Rogers pointed at the ceiling again. 'They've gone for it.'

'Full steam ahead, then.'

'Full steam ahead – whether we are ready or not.'

25

When it came to the hunt for Forsyth, Cam knew exactly where to start – and, having remembered the parking debacle of the last time, he decided to walk. He knew the way, only fifteen minutes from the police station, past Anglia Square, through Tombland, around the back of Castle Meadow under the watchful gaze of the towering ramparts, and back towards the inner-city banks of the River Wensum. The day was up and warming itself, and the city centre had come to life with the shops lively and street vendors out in growing force. Buskers too – one with a preposterous ability on the classical guitar, making notes that sounded like a glittering flow of water. The melody gave Cam the sensation of having slipped through time back to the city's medieval days. Music, smells and bustle, they were always present. They just altered through different prisms of time.

Nala ambled along at his heels. She too was enthralled with this human soup, and cocked her head at almost everything she saw, before delivering a verdict on it with a huff or snuffle.

When they arrived at the Broads Trust, it was clearly just another day at the office. The usual Tetris mêlée of cars was in place in the car park and Cam immediately thought how awful it would be to be that little blue Citroën at the back, who had obviously been the first in the office and by sheer force of poor parking would have to be the last to leave. He decided he'd keep them all on the hop and go via the riverside entrances again, forgoing any announcement.

He walked round on the wraparound decking, Nala delighted at the sight of an array of ducks on the river that emerged below. They all made instant bids for freedom, unaware that Nala didn't have a murderous bone in her little fur-clad body. The smell of the river this morning was earthen, and a couple of boats sat moored off-centre in the water, where rod tips sat stooped ready to bend under the weight of whatever might be coming next. The algal bloom had receded slightly, it seemed. As for the rear deck, it was empty, no early morning cigarette smokers grabbing a quick nicotine hit before the day really got going. Although a lone ashtray sat clean, ready to receive action. Cam walked along the glass windows, and knocked on the door.

There was an instant response on the other side of the panes, as Pot Belly James Dean stood up, his eyes angrier than ever.

Cam put his hands up in surrender, although it was a mocking submission. All the other eyes in the office looked to him. Cam decided the wind was now in his sails and growing in knots. He felt bold enough to open the door, which he did with a soft swish of expensive carpentry.

'Sorry to pop in unannounced,' he said. 'Just wanted to see if Mr Forsyth had shown up for work yet.'

James Dean went almost volcanic, while Tinfoil was now up and coming over for a second go. In the meantime,

Nala darted between Cam's legs into the office through Pot Belly James Dean's legs. Cam could only smile, watch and say: 'oops.'

Dog forgotten in a raging instant, Pot Belly James Dean was at the door, blocking his way in. He was one of those men that puffed and reddened, but the more they puffed and reddened, the more pathetic they came across. Cam found it very hard to take such a man seriously.

'Ever since you showed up,' said Pot Belly James Dean, 'Forsyth has buggered off. He's not been in at all.'

That was interesting.

'What have you done with him?' said the enraged man, jabbing a sausage-like finger at Cam.

Cam waved it away. 'I saw him last night. You mean he's not been seen since?'

Tinfoil had arrived to back up his rouged colleague. 'You start showing up, and he goes missing – coincidence?' he said.

'God,' murmured Cam. The man was trying to match his colleague's attempted threat, but neither could conjure up a thimbleful of actual intimidation. 'Bless you guys. Do you have an address?'

'I'm not giving out his address,' said Pot Belly James Dean. 'For all we know his disappearance is your fault.'

Cam smiled. 'You stick on that line and see if it brings your mate back.'

The three men simply looked at each other, each party waiting for the other to break. Cam's stubborn streak would allow him no such thing, and even his anxiety was being kept in check by how much he was revelling in this moment of bully-baiting. He hated bullies – would never let them win.

The silence was broken, and the standoff shattered, when a woman walked in between Cam and the two posturing office workers. She was holding Nala and offered her out like a totem. 'Oh, look at these silly boys,' she said to Nala. 'Boys are never far from showing themselves to be true boneheads, are they? Please take this lovely dog of yours, Mr Killick.' Cam took Nala, muted himself now in quiet surprise. He'd never given these people his name. 'Now, take your unannounced visitor and get going.' And when Cam looked at her to gauge her seriousness, the left side of her face, the side that was away from her two colleagues, twitched.

It wasn't a twitch though.

It was a wink.

So he went along with it, wondering where it might take him.

She closed the door on him and Nala, sequestering both parties on opposite sides of the glass, and neatly diffusing the situation in a belittling instant.

He looked at Nala. 'What did you tell her?' he asked, before looking back through the glass. The woman who handed him Nala was all but back at her desk, but when she saw him, she shooed him away with an outward sweep of her hand.

He glanced across the room and saw Pot Belly James Dean give him an angry middle finger. Cam gave a cheery little wave and laughed.

With that, he walked back around to the front of the building. He half-expected the front door to open when he got there, and that same woman to pop out to give some more information away from the prying ears in the office.

But no one opened the door. Cam stood, flummoxed, and clueless, and looked down at Nala.

'Well, that didn't work,' he told her. And then he saw, wedged in her tattered red collar, a scrap of paper.

He pulled it out. On it was written an address.

26

The address was in a place called Wymondham, some twenty-five minutes away. Cam hightailed it back to the police station to fetch his van.

He eased the grumbling behemoth out into the road, guiding it through the criss-cross of small yet busy streets, between buildings old and new, and out onto the A-roads which snaked and funnelled off into the surrounding countryside. Nala still seemed excited and charged, her paws up on the dash, watching the road ahead with a keenness that suggested, knowing her interests, that she was seeing sausages instead of cars. It was amazing how animals picked up on vibes and atmosphere at times, and now Nala, sensing her master's excitement and urgency, was responding with her own – even if she had no idea what it was about. But that was the joy of dogs, in a nutshell. Unwavering doting and loyalty and empathy, even when reasons are short at hand.

Cam hit the A11. Newbuild projects seemed to sprout everywhere, on either side of the ribbon of tarmac, as red brick boxes began to litter the farmland like discarded building blocks. It was eating into the area's unique character, and that saddened Cam to a degree. He wasn't against progress, far from it. But he loved this area for what it was, for its look and feel, and how history and time seemed to pour out of both of those things. He supposed that new histories would have to be created in these developments. New characters to be forged.

Cam soon found himself in the quiet market town of Wymondham. He'd never been there before, and he was immediately taken with the place. He drove through, following the directions on screen, while taking in the sights. There was a square on his right, upon which market traders were set up with neat rows of stalls, bustling customers flitting between them, many of them dragging those wheeled bag things that so often came in checkered colours. Cam had often thought they looked like perfect carry-on holdalls for flights, but since he now hated flying, there hadn't been many occasions to give his theory a try.

A large square building overlooked the market. It looked like a municipal building. Cam was fascinated, therefore, to see that it was actually a bookshop. Kett's, it was called. Under different circumstances, he'd go in.

At the end of the square was what appeared to be a large Victorian gatehouse, proud yet unique in its overhanging shape and stature. This was a town that clearly clung to its history and values, while embracing the progress that would ensure its relevance.

Cam, simply put, liked it, and it was another place in Norfolk that, now he'd visited, he'd remember affectionately.

The satnav yanked him from his misty-eyed interlude, with a command to turn left beneath an archway, into a sloped car park that boasted a set of public toilets that were – shock horror – actually open. It pushed him straight through the rows of cars and out to the rear access, where another road wrapped back towards the market square.

The satnav proudly announced that he had reached his destination, and should stop. Cam did as he was bidden, and looked out of the window at the row of houses on the side of the road. It appeared to be a block of flats, in a fairly nondescript brown building that Cam would forget the moment he left here.

He parked up, and left Nala to watch from the dashboard. He turned and gave her a wave before walking up the path to the establishment. The cracked concrete and overgrown lawn that leaned over it on both sides gave the impression of a management company that couldn't give a good god damn what their rental property looked like. They were providing four walls and a roof, weren't they?

The street was quiet, but the hubbub from the market and the road next to it all filtered up to Cam in an oddly muted way, twinned with the bleating demands of seagulls. As for humans, there was nobody about, but Cam knew that small towns had eyes everywhere, particularly where residences were concerned. He walked with purpose, but caution. If you look like you're supposed to be there, most casual observers think you are.

He walked up to the door, hit the bell for number four. Stood back, watched for the shapes behind the locked frosted glass door to move, but nothing did.

He hit the bell again, then took a couple of steps back while the electronic chime faded within. Nothing.

Try the others? He mused for a moment.

No. He didn't want to raise any kind of alarm. He wanted to see the whites of Forsyth's eyes when he realised he was going to have to come in and talk all about his little side-earner under an official eye.

Nobody else came to the door. No nosy neighbour. Cam backed down the path, and walked around the back of the building.

There was a small communal garden that carried the distinct air of the forgotten, with wheelie bins stood in a haphazard clutch. He paused to take in the rear aspect of the building, and remembered how the buttons were organised at the front door. In two columns: one and two on the first, three and four on the second.

He looked at the back windows, flipped the doorbell layout in his head, which would make the bottom left number four – or at least had a half chance of being so. He went to the window and peered inside. Beyond the mucky streaked glass was a small living room that looked as tired and unloved as the rest of the place. The fixtures and fittings were faded and ragged, yet there was no rubbish about to suggest recent occupation.

Cam couldn't be sure that anyone lived there at all.

It was like a tomb.

But he had to be sure.

Every now and then during his time in the armed forces, he'd had to perform inventive ways of getting into places, and now he looked around for anything that might be useful to someone with a certain breaking and entering persuasion. As he looked, he remarked in his own mind how easy it had been for him to decide that he was just going to break in. The police would have to wait for a reason or some official backing to enter someone's property, but Cam himself was a civilian with, as a popular movie character put it, a particular set of skills.

Is this right? he asked himself. And then he remembered the ticking time bomb of the knife and the DNA embedded in its steel. Every hour that went by took them further from finding whoever had used it with ill will. With those facts in mind, breaking into this place was an option not far out of his self-perceived remit.

Suddenly he thought of his van's busted petrol cap. And, more pertinently, the needle-nosed pliers he used to jimmy it open. Those pliers were in his pocket right now, and should be all he needed to get inside.

He took them out, and slid one of the prongs into the gap, forcing it as high up as he possibly could into the white plastic casing of the frame and heaving as he forced it. As soon as he could, he twisted the prongs sideways, and in the opening, closed the pliers. He then twisted them upright again so that the entire nose of the pliers was in the window jamb.

Having spent so much time in situations where bad tools could cost you your life meant that his particular set of pliers had a 20,000-lb breaking strain – which should make them too much for this window. With all his might, he tried to open those pliers once again while they were wedged in the frame.

They didn't pop the entirety of the frame open, but they did give some, and it meant that Cam could lift his right leg and squeeze the end of his shoe into the gap, immediately thankful it was made of what seemed indestructible rubber. While the toe of his pink Croc was keeping the window ajar, he took the pliers, closed them and, still on one leg, reached towards the corner of the frame and pushed the nose up and inside the gap. He was looking for the locking bolt that slid across when the handle was engaged. If he could just find it, he could knock it open.

He had it.

Two little knocks on the bolt and it clunked upwards, and the window yawned open.

He was in.

Cam climbed through the window, and landed on a mint-green carpet that looked like it had been installed in 1987 and had been hoovered only four times since. Perhaps only on Royal milestones.

Immediately an airborne staleness hit him, and he knew straight away, without making any leaping prejudicial assessments, that the man lived alone. Simply, there was no way that any self-respecting woman would live in a house that smelled like this.

Boys, he thought to himself. The living room was swamped by an oversized sofa bedecked in a tired brown leather that in no way complimented the pistachio colour of the carpet. It looked like it had been fashioned out of orangutan droppings and was only half as comfortable.

Opposite was a TV and an Xbox. Both old models, next to a handful of glasses and plates Jenga-stacked on a coffee table that looked like if he so much as blew on it, it would collapse.

But there was no sign of Forsyth himself.

When he was working with the military, breaking and entering was usually followed by having to shoot someone. Instead, in this instance, he was just looking for someone – and the fact that he wasn't going to immediately blow them to bits when he found them was strangely jarring.

He decided to attack things with a bit more transparency. 'Hello? Forsyth are you here?' He edged closer into the room – tentative, yet deliberate. He subconsciously adopted the room-clearing techniques that had become second nature in the forces. Take corners wide. Follow clear walls that are already in sight. Eyes on the spaces you can't see.

He felt dust come up with every footstep. Grime loosening wherever he placed his feet. He found his way to the living room door, cleared the corridor and spoke again. 'Anybody about?'

'Can't you just leave me alone?' came a voice from the back bedroom.

Got him, thought Cam. 'Your window was open,' he said. 'I was worried about you.' He started looking for Forsyth's hiding place. 'I need you to come down to the nick to answer a few questions.' He didn't know whether any of these were the right things to say, but he said them anyway and it seemed he was right when Forsyth answered with an exasperated: 'Fine.'

Cam went into the bedroom, and found him slumped across the bed. The first thing he thought he'd seen was a vast sack of mayonnaise, covered with tufts of grey hair. It was Forsyth's torso.

The smell in this room was worse.

'Bloody hell, Forsyth.'

'I'm getting up,' he said, and rolled off the bed. 'Is this what facing the music feels like?'

'It might be,' said Cam, averting his eyes. 'Probably best to face the music with some clothes on, I would have thought.'

He could only imagine what Rogers might say, and Cam would remind her later of the bullet he'd dodged on her behalf.

'You decided you're done with work?' Cam asked.

'I decided I was going to try to lay low—' Forsyth stopped sharply, as if suddenly aware of what he'd just said, and how it could be taken. 'I've got nothing to hide, don't start jumping to conclusions. I just don't like the attention, you see.'

Cam thought if Forsyth didn't like the heat now, he really wasn't going to like it when the bulletin about Tommy Jessup went out. He saw a pair of jeans, with a belt in the loops, on the desk chair opposite the bed, and he picked them up with a jangle of the loose change still in the pockets, and tossed them to Forsyth – who was now sat on the edge of the bed in his pants.

'They're about to announce that they are looking for Tommy Jessup. And it turns out that two of the other names on that list of seventeen you gave me, they're missing too.'

'What?' Forsyth looked up wide-eyed, his features shorn of pretence or composure.

Cam continued. 'And if you find that uncomfortable, it's about to get worse. Come with me, I can get you in under the radar. Get you out of harm's way, see if we can keep your name out of the press.'

Forsyth looked up at Cam with pleading pupils. 'They'd release my name?'

'I've no idea what they'd do,' Cam said, honestly. 'But this murder weapon has to belong to someone, and the only name they've got is yours. Wouldn't it be better to get ahead of this, tackle it head-on?'

With about as much enthusiasm as Daniel Craig faced with playing James Bond just one more time, Forsyth pulled on his jeans – and as he wrestled with the belt, Cam's phone burred in his pocket.

He checked, while keeping half an eye on the dressing man.

A decisive instruction on the 'WE WANT TO BELIEVE' WhatsApp group:

WE NEED TO MEET.

Cam pocketed the phone. The podcasters wanted to talk – and when they were that direct, it was rarely for nothing.

27

After Cam delivered Forsyth to the back door of Norwich Police Station, with a nod to Rogers and a word in her ear to catch her up on his skipping work, he got back to the van and pulled out his phone. Rogers had got authorisation for a full dive team to search Doke End in full, which was scheduled to start momentarily. Cam was pleased, but run through by a shard of jealousy that quickly abated. He'd opened the door, and flippers in the water was what they needed now. The day was barely hitting lunchtime, but so much had happened, in a flip book of progress that had whizzed straight on from the previous day. His exhaustion had abated, though, chased away by the thrum of his blood.

He sat in his van driving seat and texted the podcasters, to see where they wanted to meet. It worked for him too – he also wanted to keep them updated and to set them off bloodhound-keen to tear through Tommy Jessup's movements and contacts.

Nala hopped up on his lap, and started panting directly into his face.

'Ease off, love,' he said, pushing her down. As much as he loved her, there was no cure for dog breath. He ruffled her ears by way of a peace gesture.

Forsyth would spill everything he knew, Cam was convinced. But in the meantime, he'd run out of instructions, so would have to occupy himself. He let his mind dance through other avenues of enquiry, trying to think both laterally and outside the box simultaneously.

What could he do, that the police couldn't?

He checked the phone. It hadn't buzzed. And with every ten seconds that went by, Cam found that odder and odder. They were glued to their phones, those podcasters. They text back, day or night, within seconds. Two minutes, which was where it had got to now, was downright unusual.

What do I do know? thought Cam, sitting there lemon-like.

After four frustrating minutes, the phone buzzed, and Cam couldn't grab it quickly enough.

WE'RE ON THE SOUTHERN COMFORT. COME OVER.

That stunned Cam. Last time he'd been on the *Southern Comfort*, the faux-Mississippi paddle steamer that ferried tourists around the River Bure, he'd had to dive off it – because it was on fire. And he'd left it burning, pilotless, floating into the marshes off South Walsham Broad. What on earth were Gupta and Ferris doing on it?

He knew where it was moored up – or where he assumed it was still moored up.

He could get there in thirty minutes.

He hit the ignition.

This he had to see.

Horning Main Street looked the same. The newsagent was on the left, just after the fish restaurant. The Heron's

Reach pub sat opposite, facing the river, just like always. The village green sat peppered with fat geese. But the village was overrun with white trucks, and in the public car park by the footbridge to the sailing club sat a couple of trailers. One said 'catering' on its side in an unapologetic font.

Cam's hackles rose. This was more activity than he'd ever seen in Horning, ever. A dozen or so people were milling about in purposeful patterns.

Oh no, he thought.

And then he saw the spools of cabling, running to and from a generator unit hunkered down beneath a tree, and he knew his fears were justified.

This was a TV crew. Whenever there were white vans, wires and food, the cameras would be nearby. And it was so far from Cam's comfort zone, he'd need a passport to get back.

And there was the *Southern Comfort* – or what was left of it. What had been a two-decked vessel was now one. On that grim night not all that long ago, the boat's top deck had been entirely burnt off and out, chunks broken off, and wood disintegrated. The memory of it always saddened him, not just because of the events of that night themselves but because that boat was almost fifty years old, a quiet yet beloved mainstay of the region, and hadn't deserved such a fate. To see it paraded corpse-like, evidently under the gaze of the as-yet-unseen cameras, caused him to grimace. He wanted to turn around and go, but no. He wouldn't. He'd go and see those podcasters on the remains of that boat.

Cam had to park the van a short distance further up the road, past the post office and, in a strange quirk of God knew what, a flight simulator shop, and hopped out, Nala overjoyed to be allowed with him on this one.

He turned left down the access road to the village green and the dinghy launch, and walked along past the Willow Staithe café and the souvenir shop. That was when he saw two large cameras atop tripods, pointed at the *Southern Comfort's* remains.

The sight of it immediately prickled his nerves. That boat had been the stage for a life-or-death battle. He breathed out, trying to discard the memories of his previous visit, soothing himself by focusing not on what happened but on what came of it all. Jess's safety. Bad people caught. A new hope for him. And friends.

As he arrived at the commotion outside the boat, he found that not only couldn't he see the podcasters, but he couldn't see anyone obviously in charge. The gangplank was there, the same one he had used to climb aboard in the dark last time. Pretending he knew exactly what he was doing, he strolled aboard. The bottom deck of the boat had survived surprisingly well, and the remaining soot and muck had been cleaned away. The main cabin door opened to the lower deck, and a couple of people emerged. Yet again, nobody questioned him. If anything, they gave him a couple of smiles.

He took the doors to the main deck, holding it open to allow Nala in first. She'd never been on the *Southern Comfort*, having been left in Cam's van while the drama unfolded, so this was suddenly a new playground for her, with new people. And these new people were huddled at the small but perfectly formed bar down at the far end of the room, near the bow of the boat.

It was also where heavy lighting rigs were pointed, which made the bar look like it was a quaint little drinking hole on the surface of the sun. Sat on bar-stools next to each other, facing another high chair which was occupied by a man in a baseball cap, sat Gupta and Ferris. They saw Cam immediately, and Gupta waved him over, while Ferris was the picture of smugness. Like she was in her utter element in the (literal) spotlight.

As Cam got closer, he passed a couple of monitors, and got a look at what they were filming. It was an interview set-up, a couple of talking heads, and those two talking heads were Gupta and Ferris.

'Is this what I think it is?'

Gupta swivelled in her seat to face him. 'You told us you didn't want any part of any future media appearances,' she said. There wasn't apology in her voice.

Opposite her, the director, or the baseball cap-wearing person Cam took to be the director, let his hands waft between his interviewees and their sudden visitor. 'Do we need a short break?' he asked. He seemed agitated, as if filming wasn't going quite as well as he'd hoped.

As someone who had experience with working alongside the podcasters and their quirks, Cam sympathised. And if that was the case, Cam's interruption couldn't be helping either. He decided to keep it brief, but the director stood and moved away, not before offering Cam his chair with an open palm. Cam nodded his thanks and took it, then caught, from the corner of his eye, the director looking at him. A soft realisation chimed in his chest.

He looked at the podcasters. 'You told him who I was, didn't you?'

Gupta at least had the good grace to look sheepish, while Ferris just smiled.

'That explains how simple it was to get on board. Nice and easy to get on set. Do I really need to explain to you that you can't talk about any of the Brindley matter while the attempted prosecution is ongoing?'

This was an extension of the rewards Cam offered the podcasters for helping him out on the Brindley matter. He gave them the exclusivity of the real story behind the mystery, and the inside track. Gupta and Ferris, like proper conspiracy theorists, but even better journalists, were sitting on the powder keg of a story that would eventually garner national attention, once the court's proceedings were out of the way.

'We're not thick,' said Ferris flatly.

'It's a prelim,' said Gupta. 'Deal's done with a big streamer, but it's not been announced yet. They know the embargo, and so do we. Don't worry. This is footage to be screened when it's all done and dusted.'

'And I'm not involved?' Per the terms of their agreement, Cam's name was to be kept out of it. So was Rogers'.

'You're not,' Gupta said. 'But the director would really like to talk with you, if you'd be up for it. Just saying.'

Cam rolled his eyes but paused them on their surroundings. 'So, what are you telling them, considering you can't tell them anything?' he asked, risking a quick glance at the director, who glanced away quickly.

'It's a three-parter, filmed in chunks. Pre-trial, during trial, post-trial,' said Gupta.

Cam turned to the director. 'I was never here,' he said. 'And can we have some privacy?'

The director stood up, with his script. 'By all means,' he said, heading for the door. 'Any thoughts before I go?'

The director took one look at Cam's expression, was hopeful for a total of three seconds, then thought better of it, ushering the camera crew away with him.

Then they were alone under the lights, the cabin abruptly quiet save for the hum of stage lighting filaments. 'Thank you,' Cam said, 'before we get on to, you know…

thank you for what you did pulling in that list. You did an amazing job. Attention now is on Tommy Jessup.'

Gupta nodded.

'I've not found him,' said Cam, 'but we found a DNA link to him on a mug from the address in Middlewater. The link is to the DNA on that knife from Doke End.

'This means it's looking very much like Tommy is our victim, and we now need to look at all his known associates. The police are trying to establish Jessup's movements, all of that stuff – but I thought you could maybe reach places that official channels won't, if you get my drift? Time really is of the essence here.'

'Can do – as long as the same deal between us applies,' said Gupta.

'Exactly like last time.'

Ferris did a circular motion with her finger at the set-up. 'And our terms have changed.' Cam could have rolled his eyes. The last thing Planet Earth needed was Ferris going big time.

'Plus,' Gupta said. 'You haven't heard what we've got for you yet.'

Cam was ready for it. 'I'm all ears.'

'So, you know how we mentioned that there are a lot of funny disappearances connected to Doke End?'

'I recall.'

'So we've got the other two missing. Forrester and Drummond. It's on social media, their families looking out for them, asking if anyone's seen them. But we switched things up in our investigation, because we knew something else.'

'What was that?'

Ferris jumped in. 'That disappearances associated with the Upton area aren't limited solely to Homo sapiens.'

'Could you just spit it out?'

'Animals,' said Gupta. 'A lot of strange disappearances of animals. Usually livestock. We've had reports of sheep, pigs, goats, even a couple of alpacas from a farm not far from there.'

'So, what do you think it is?'

Gupta drew herself up. 'We have it on good authority that a puma is loose on the Broads.'

Because this came from Gupta, not Ferris, Cam looked up. 'Really?'

'Yes. It's not talked about widely, but it's there. Escaped from a zoo, or maybe released on purpose. Either way, it's legitimate. Those that know, know. And one of those could certainly account for what we're talking about.'

'But pumas don't use knives,' Cam said.

'It was just a suggestion.'

Consternation wafted through Cam's thoughts. If the area had a disappearance problem, then the move up from animals to humans was a significant jump. If, of course, they were connected.

'You've got evidence on this?' he asked.

'Actual data. There's a spike, right in the Upton area.'

'Whether it's something human, beast, or those aliens again,' said Ferris, 'something has been happening in the vicinity of Doke End for years.'

And for once, Cam couldn't argue with something Ferris had said.

28

Back at Norfolk Constabulary, the interview room was starting to smell very much like a human under pressure, and while the strip lights were cold and unforgiving, the glare they gave disseminated an unforgiving heat of a different kind.

The blaze of scrutiny.

Rogers knew that, under duress, some people crumbled quicker than a communion wafer in a cup of builder's tea – but those people, it turned out, had nothing on Ken Forsyth. That man had gone from mute shell to open book in a hummingbird's heartbeat.

Whatever Cam Killick had said to him when he picked him up had cracked him wide like a mollusc, desperate for its pearl to be stolen.

'I'll tell you anything you want to know,' said Forsyth, before Rogers had even switched on the tape.

'That's very kind of you,' said Rogers, as she took a seat, wrinkling her nose.

Forsyth nodded eagerly, offering BO and compliance in abundance.

Rogers began the formalities with the tape recorder, and hit the red button. A junior detective, DC Fliss Bronson, stood at the back of the room, playing the heavy muscle in an apparent good-cop bad-cop formation. She was a five-foot nothing bulldozer, curly copper hair in a bird's nest jumble on her head, and a set jaw which suggested compromise was nothing more than a quaint theory. Given the easy start Forsyth had given them, she briefly considered letting the DC take the reins and get some valuable interviewing experience – but she thought better of it. Murder cases needed the most senior cop available, and that meant the buck stopped with Rogers herself.

'How long have you been working for the Broads Trust, Mr Forsyth?' she asked.

He quickly replied. 'Twelve years.'

'And have you been running this little side project of yours all that time?'

'Only for the last two,' said Forsyth, pulling the requisite mug of tea closer, and giving it a polite sniff as if he was some kind of brew aficionado.

'When did you start realising that you could make a few quid on the side, let's say?'

'It wouldn't be long before then. When the environmental authorities wanted to establish fish migration, particularly in relation to spawning places. It was about when they started planning that new bridge in Yarmouth.'

'Can you elaborate, Mr Forsyth?'

'The planning bods were modelling what the bridge would do to the surrounding waterways, and wanted to cover every base. One of the hoops they had to jump through was all manner of surveys. Everything you could think of. Silt levels, salinisation points, fish stock and so on. The wildlife population and its movements were a big one.'

'And during this period, you noticed a change?'

'Yeah, there was a big discrepancy in pike movements. Their spawning ground had changed. They were no longer using a couple of the boatyards, the ones they'd used for years. They'd obviously moved on, but then we got the data for Doke End, and there they all were.'

'And you saw pound signs, right?'

Forsyth looked at the swirling surface of his tea. 'It was so we could protect them, but yes, I thought I could, you know, get something out of it on the quiet.'

'So, you found out where all the big girls were ending up, and charged people to head on over and have a private go at them.'

That caused Forsyth to look up. Rogers thought it might be because he assumed she didn't know anything about why this new pattern would be important to anglers.

'Spawning time, right?' Rogers added. 'October, they're feeding up, before releasing eggs in March when they are at their biggest.'

'Right.'

'And with it being March now, it's a busy month for you. Hence seventeen people visiting in five days.'

'That's right.'

Unlike that fool Killick, who somehow got things right despite fumbling about in the dark so often and stubbing his toe on something useful, Rogers had done her research. She knew that all large pike, particularly specimen-weight pike, were female and that their weight fluctuated by as much as ten pounds during spawning time, putting on chunks every week. By learning this, it had helped her understand why Doke End was suddenly so popular, even though Rogers herself couldn't think of anything ghastlier than hauling in one of those slimy things.

'So were the Broads Trust aware of what you were doing? Any of your colleagues, perhaps Mike Flowers, or Sean Blantyre? They work with you at your Norwich office, I believe.'

Forsyth went purple. No sound left his lips.

Rogers could have smiled. 'The shagging habits of fish wasn't the only thing I researched this morning, Mr Forsyth. Do they know?'

Forsyth's face faded to another unlikely colour – now a sort of yellow.

'I thought you said you were going to be compliant?' said Rogers.

Forsyth cleared his throat. 'I give those two a bit of the spoils once a month. To keep quiet. They also fish there from time to time. I'm going to lose my job over this, aren't I?'

'I don't know how the Broads Trust treats traitorous employees, Mr Forsyth,' said Rogers. 'Let's just get you off the list of murder suspects, shall we?'

'Yes, please,' said Forsyth.

'How did you advertise the fact that you had these keys?'

'There are a number of pike angling groups online on Facebook, I simply sent a few a message when I started, asking who wanted to pay for the chance to fish on a private water. It's amazing how many people put their hands up. I put a couple of sonar images up, showing them sitting there, all lined up like they were at a buffet.'

'So how much money has this made you? Where is it going? You weren't living in any high-class accommodation, so I'm told – no offence – but you're not pumping it back in to the ecology in a philanthropic way are you?'

'No,' said Forsyth. 'I like to go fishing abroad. Giant Trevally in Oman, things like that. It's not cheap to go out there, and the kit is mad.'

Rogers found herself smiling, despite herself. Committed anglers were something else. Nothing stopped them from going after that one prize catch they had their eyes on.

'What about the kind of people you were lending these keys to?'

'Well, I've got to be honest, I wasn't the most critical of them. I sort of checked them out via Facebook and that was it really.'

'So, if they weren't an obvious psychopath, they'd be on the shortlist?'

'Something like that.'

Rogers looked at him judgementally. It seemed fairly likely to her that Forsyth's less-than-stringent application policy might have allowed a killer to slip the proverbial net.

'How many keys are there?'

'When I got involved in the environmental studies, and started collating the evidence, I offered to grant access for the surveyors. So, I was given the main set. That's when I made my copy.'

'Yours is a copy?' asked Rogers.

'Yes.'

'So, who has the original right now?'

'It's at the office.'

'But the land is owned by... ?'

'Well, we own it. That's how I thought it wasn't, you know, the worst thing in the world that I could—'

'Make secret money from it?'

'Well... yes.'

'So what you're saying is that the key isn't really that important. Anyone who had the key could make a copy and get on there. Because if you can copy them, anyone can copy them, can't they?'

'I suppose – but it was a provision I made clear. If you've been found to copy it, the lock gets changed and you're banned.'

Rogers gave that some thought. It still seemed to her that the water, and access to it, held the key, no pun intended.

She turned and looked at DC Fliss Bronson. Gave her a little wink, as if to say *here we go and pay attention.* 'Three people are missing. At least one is most likely dead. Can you give me a full rundown of your whereabouts these last five days?' She asked, hands on the table.

'Yes. That's very easy,' said Forsyth.

'Why is it easy?'

'Because I was away for the first three – only came back here a couple of days ago. I'd gone to Cambridge on a conference.'

'So, it could be verified?'

'Yes, I was there for a whole week.'

Rogers could at least cross Forsyth from the list. The DNA and the five-day timeline meant he couldn't have been the one to drop the knife into Doke End.

'Well at least that's something,' Rogers said. 'How did the keys get passed about while you were away?'

'Before I left, I gave them to Ed Thelonius, with instruction to pass them on. I let them know on Messenger who they have to pass it to next. It's never gone wrong before.'

'But you were the one to hand them to Killick?'

'Yes, I was. I didn't want bloody Lassiter to hire a diver, but he was insistent.'

'So, you can vouch for all those people on that list?'

'Yes, very easily. It's a closed group now. I'll tell you everything I know about each one of them, if it helps – but I've got to tell you, I can't see anyone of them as a murderer. They're just a bunch of fishing geeks and a couple of know-it-alls.'

Rogers nodded. That would certainly help, having each name eliminated. It kept coming back to that list, and the growing conviction that someone from the list had murdered Tommy Jessup on Doke End.

In which case his body might well still be there.

She hoped those divers of hers would strike it lucky.

'I'm going to have to keep that key I'm afraid,' said Rogers.

Forsyth shrugged. 'I never want to see it again.'

Roger's phone rang then, and she checked the caller ID. It was Cam Killick. She ignored the call, and pulled an assembly of photographs from the folder in front of her. The missing men, in various photographs pulled from social media, all looked up from the tabletop, as if pleading to go back to the happier times depicted.

Her phone went again, this time with a text. Killick again. She gave it a quick glance.

What do we know about livestock going missing near Doke End?

She wanted to sigh, but the tape was still running. What was he on about now?

29

Cam's brain, as it so often did, sparked tangentially to something – and it happened when he left the remains of the *Southern Comfort*. He always enjoyed following the logic of geography when he was planning, because bare facts never lied. It was following this exact line of thought that had helped him solve the mystery of the Brindley family, not all that long ago.

He found the tattered *Norfolk A-Z* under the driver's seat of the van, the one that he'd stopped using as soon as familiarity set in. Sometimes there was no substitute for spreading a map out and tracking routes with a fingertip. The three people who were missing were all from different places, none of which were all that far apart, but still not identical. Now, because Upton Broad and the surrounding areas were so isolated and off the beaten track, there weren't many roads leading to it – which meant their routes had to have converged at some point.

Cam laid the map out on the dash, and mentally drew the reference points. All routes eventually converged on the A1064 close to Acle – which meant that there was a good chance they had all travelled that road at some particular point or other.

He pulled up Google and searched for that same stretch of byway, and as he zoomed in, business names appeared. He was looking for something like a petrol station or café, something where all the missing men might have stopped on the way through Upton Broad and Doke End. He scanned across – there was a Thai restaurant of all things, in the comparative middle of nowhere. Then he saw it.

Martin's Bait & Tackle.

Cam felt the static charge of certainty.

Forrester, Drummond and Jessup. Three men going fishing. And a bait shop less than three miles from Doke End, on the only main road in.

'Come on Nala,' he said, more for his own benefit than hers, since she was already curled on the front seat. 'Let's go and buy some maggots.'

The journey was brief, mainly because Cam found it especially hard not to jam the accelerator in anticipation. He was going to learn something valuable, he was sure, not least because of angling stores' reputations for being good places to learn absolutely anything, useful or otherwise. If you wanted to know the gossip in a given area, particularly water-related, you'd head to the local tackle shop, and someone in there, employed or otherwise, would give you the skinny.

Pulling up outside the destination, in another spring spurt of sunshine, Cam parked in one of the handful of bays that stood in front of the shop. The wraparound glass display windows were filled with fishing accoutrements and assorted rods, reels, green tent things, even some sleeping bags and survival gear. On one of the chairs propped open around a faux-campfire sat a large stuffed toy pike.

He hopped out, and beckoned Nala to follow him – with no disrespect to bait shops the world over, it was hardly a spotless Fifth Avenue bridal boutique. They walked in, and Cam was suddenly in a darkened, funny-smelling world packed to the rafters with stock. On the left were racks of angling greens of all sizes, folding chairs and bivvy bags. On the right was row after row of densely packed shelves, the contents of which he had extremely little understanding of, but the pricing of which suggested they had to be crucial in some way. In the middle was a square island of counters with tills on one side, and trays of maggots on the other. The rest of the shop receded into darkness and the iridescence of a back wall made up almost entirely of patterned fishing lures of all types, whose hooks and patterns glowed like a distant constellation.

In the middle of the island was a chap of maybe sixty or so, whose face was carved with abundant laughter lines. His left hand jabbed at the thick numbered keys on the decades-old till, while his right cradled, incongruously, a plastic beaker of red wine, which sloshed jauntily as he moved. He looked immediately like the favourite uncle at every family cookout, and his tanned wrinkles suggested a full life beyond these four walls. 'One pint of mixed,' he said, handing a small plastic box over the counter to a young man dressed in the omnipresent dark green. 'Two maggots should do it. Three might overface them, and nobody wants a meal that'll make you choke. Look for the quay heading, pop the float maybe a foot from the bank, and over-depth it by six inches or so. It's gently-gently at this time of year, until it's much warmer. They're skittish, but they're there. Bit of patience, you'll find them.'

Cam found his presence immediately warm and comforting, and he seemed like one of those sports commentators who they pick because you don't mind listening to them even when nothing is happening. His eyes wandered upwards to a hand-painted driftwood sign hanging from the ceiling over the counter.

'Dead bait don't move,' it read.

Cam liked that. For some reason, it resonated with him deeply.

Nala trotted off between the shelves, her nose presumably abuzz with all the new smells, which Cam realised had to be coming from the big tubs of maggots squirming in some kind of sandy aggregate. As he approached the counter, he saw the wriggling larvae in all their writhing glory. Different tubs, for different colours of maggot, in an open-topped refrigerator, with a stack of empty pots next to it.

'How can I help you mate?' the man asked.

'Hi,' replied Cam, somehow immediately at ease with the guy. 'I'm after a little local know-how. Are you Martin?'

'That's me,' the man replied, easing back to rest a hip on the counter to the right, folding his arms and resting the bottom of the plastic cup on the top of his stomach. His manner was easy-going, but a touch of reserve had entered his voice. That was the other thing about fishing shops – information was to be had, sure, but it was coveted. You didn't necessarily give things out like the location of a red-hot fishing spot for example – exactly like Doke End.

'Don't worry,' Cam said. 'It's not fishing know-how.'

The man immediately eased. 'In that case, I'm all ears. What can I help you with?'

'I'm sort of privately investigating something. I'm a diver, and I've got a bit of a conundrum.'

The man's brow furrowed but his smile remained. 'That's a strange combination, mate. Diver and private investigator.'

'Yeah, well, I'm trying to track the movements of a group of guys who fish out this way, and I wondered if they'd been through here. Maybe if you'd seen them recently.'

Martin cocked his head. 'Well, I'm not always in the habit of talking about other people.'

Cam looked at him earnestly. 'Their families are worried about them.'

The man straightened. 'You have pictures of them with you?'

'On my phone.'

'OK, best to do this in private. Loose lips being bad for ships and all that.'

He came out from behind the counter, and started for the back, before he shouted into the depths of the shop. 'Give us a shout if you need anything, mate.'

A tall man with long, lank hair nodded by the humming fridges in the far corner. He wore a branded T-shirt with the same slogan: 'Dead bait don't move'. Cam fancied one of those T-shirts. Cam followed Martin to the back, while Nala yapped at the customer as if to remind him not to nick anything. Cam shushed her, beckoning her to follow him with a curt whistle.

Martin led them into a jammed stock-room that had no evident inventory system. A row had been cleared between the boxes the length of an oche, with a dartboard hung up on the wall.

'Let's have a look,' he said, turning and putting his hands on his hips.

'As far as I can tell,' Cam said, lifting his phone from his pocket, the photos already cued up, 'they're old mates. All gone missing in the last few weeks.'

Martin looked at the phone, and didn't take long. It was a picture of Leonard Drummond. 'He's definitely been in. All the gear and no idea. You spot them a mile off. A lesser owner of a fishing shop would consider them an easy target for an upsell…' He gave Cam a conspiratorial sideways look.

'Did he tell you where he was fishing?'

'He was very secretive – said a private syndicate water was where he was headed.'

'That checks out.' Cam thumbed across to the next one. This was Tommy Jessup. 'How about this one?'

'Not so sure on him.'

Dammit, thought Cam. He thought about asking again, but wanted to keep the exchange as relaxed as he could. 'OK, what about this one?'

The third one was another easy one. 'Yeah, I saw him. Forrester. Um… Ryan, that's it. Knew him already, mind, because he's got the kennels over near Crostwick.'

'Did he give you any idea what he was up to?'

'No idea. Just didn't expect to see him out this way, because it's a bit of a trek from the kennels. Usually means they've come out this way for a reason.'

'Maybe the same syndicate water?'

'Would stand to reason.'

'These guys, what were they after?'

'Getting the usual pike stuff. End tackle, treble hooks, dead bait, you get the picture.'

Cam didn't, but pretended he did. 'Did these guys usually come in? Were they regulars?'

'No, definitely not part of the usual crowd.'

'Thank you. Was there anything about them that seemed odd? Anything in particular that you remember?'

Martin thought about it for a moment. 'No, would be the answer. Then again, if you think about, the idea of three mates who are all that chummy and heading to the same place not coming in here together seems a bit strange. But then again, they might have been in their cars, or sharing the same day ticket between them or whatever. But still. Three of them coming out here, and three of them going missing? Even I think that's no coincidence.'

Cam pocketed the phone. He was on their trail. With Gupta and Ferris echoing in his mind, he gave it one last shot. 'Are there any, you know, reports of animals going missing round here?'

Martin looked at Cam, and his gaze seemed overcast by unhappiness. 'Well... nobody talks about this, not least business owners. But there's been rumours of animals going missing for years. Every now and then, you get a whisper of something. You just dismiss it, usually.'

'Would any of the owners – would they talk to me?'

Martin snickered. 'You must be joking, aren't you?'

'I'm really not the joking type.'

'Fair enough. That's a no. But, now... three strapping fellows go missing out here?'

Cam watched him carefully. 'What?'

Martin sighed. 'That doesn't happen unless someone made it happen. You understand that, don't you?'

Cam felt his words drop into his skull like a lead weight sinking to the bottom, displacing sediment and burrowing in. 'I think I do,' he said.

He decided to try Rogers again, as he left the back room and stood around the tents.

This time, she picked up. 'You make interviewing a timed activity, you know that?'

'Sorry about that,' Cam said. 'Did Forsyth talk?'

'If he had any guts, he'd have spilled them too. He gave us everything. What's this about animal disappearances?'

'It's the next thing to look into. Turns out that animals have been going missing out Upton way for years. Lots of examples, but nobody reporting them, let alone talking.'

'OK, I'll check it out.'

'So our three missing – they've all been to the same fishing shop out here on the A1064. I've just been chatting with the owner. He remembers a couple of them.'

'Tell me everything when I see you. I've got to go.'

'Oh?' Cam knew that Rogers was under no obligation to share anything with him, but he hoped she would.

'I've got to call Saj, the dive team leader. Turns out Doke End is empty. Nothing there.'

'Damn.'

'Damn indeed.'

Cam was gutted. Doke End held the key, he was sure of it. It had to.

And it was only ten minutes away, if that.

'I might have a little look myself.' He had his own key, after all. When he'd been to the Broads Trust offices the first time, he'd noticed a locksmith on the other side of the street. Still in possession of the fabled Doke End key, a eureka lightbulb had pinged on.

'Don't be an idiot,' protested Rogers.

'Oh… you're breaking up…'

'If you hang up on me, you're for it, you didn't even do the hissing and crackling—'

'Gotta go.'

Cam hung up.

If he found something out there, something that the dive team had missed, he'd be forgiven. Maybe.

He pocketed the phone – and saw a dryrobe on a rack behind him.

Cam Killick wasn't sure he believed in fate, but if he was to start, now would be the time.

30

The day had taken a foreboding character and that was reflected in the mood on Doke End. Gone were the shafts of spring sunlight, replaced now entirely by the moody eeriness of a place that seemed to know that it was the centre of a real storm.

Cam was once again in his dinghy, stood at the helm with Nala by his side, floating gently out into the middle. Beneath the dryrobe, his wetsuit was fully zipped up already to stave off the chill, and the scuba tank sat at his feet ready to be hoisted onto his back.

He was walking with the electric motor towards the exact spot he'd found the knife – or to the nearest approximation. Because of drift and the ever-changing shape of trees in breeze, it wasn't going to be completely accurate – but if he could get underwater while visibility wasn't so bad, he'd be able to make a half-decent go of a half-decent search of his own. Thoroughness meant that he'd pretend no team had been here, and that no prior search had taken place. He'd start again.

When he thought he'd found the correct spot, he lowered the mud weight, which entered the water with a soft plop. He turned to take the rear mud weight rope too, and lowered the second anchor to the bottom so that the boat wouldn't spin in the flow.

Safely pinned in place, he ran over the last checks of his gear – and noticed that Nala was staring at him. It was like even she had successfully assessed he was an idiot.

The breeze was up, the water was rolling, and the temperature was dipping as the day grew longer. 'I'm afraid the clock's ticking, my chum,' he said. 'Now go on, curl up.' With a point, he commanded her to sit on the rear seat. She span a couple of times on the spot, before deigning to lower herself to the tired wood, and then Cam eased himself over the side, rolling backwards.

He landed with a lung-tightening splash in the water and took a few seconds to orient himself and find a temperature equilibrium. Once the sun had started to tip earthward, and it just about already had, it would go dark quickly here, which was why he had his dive torch with him, strapped onto his left wrist. He resurfaced and checked his surroundings, trying to keep as much of a grip on his positioning as he could, then slowly lowered beneath the surface. He was grateful for the neoprene hood he was wearing because even with it on, his ears seem to make a damn good go of shrivelling up and dying, while his extremities, particularly those between his legs, could have simply fallen off for all he knew.

The water was entirely different now, thick with colour, and swirling with portentous intent. Visibility was a couple of feet, if that, and he had to drop right down to the bottom and stick his nose almost flush to it. He spotted a few underwater features that let him know he was roughly where he thought the knife had been, and got ready to search. When in open water, he was a fan of spiral searches and started to do the same here – although this time he lowered a pointed finger into the silt at the bottom, tracing a line as he wound in outward circles. The intention was to create a marker indicating where he'd already searched, so he didn't accidentally go over it again in such poor visibility.

As he span outwards from a central spot, going wider by a couple of feet each time, he started to trace the shape of a huge snail shell on Doke End's bed. He took his time, didn't rush, and meticulously performed one ten-metre spiral around where he thought the knife had been found.

He knew the police dive team had been here only a matter of hours earlier, and felt bad to doubt them and their efforts. But Doke End spoke to Cam in a way that few other places did, and the offer of answers was loud in Cam's metaphorical ears.

He stopped, moved across a handful of metres, then started another spiral shape. He kept going until the two large circles crossed like a very tentative Venn diagram.

A second concentrated search yielded the same results. Nothing.

Cam glanced above at the surface, and saw the sky over-head rendered a deepening purple like a vast hematoma.

Time was short.

He pressed on. That familiar tug of duty and obligation, even though no one was really expecting a damn thing of him, pressed him forward. He made a third search spiral. And a fourth.

The fifth took him until it was well past dark, and he was navigating solely by the cone of torch glare. He'd covered an approximate fifty-metre radius from where he thought the knife was found, which he reasoned wasn't a bad effort considering the late hour he arrived. He considered continuing. Dark had fallen, so it wasn't like visibility could get any worse. It would if poor weather came in, but the Met Office weather app said there was nothing severe incoming.

His main concern was Nala. She was as understanding and hard-wearing as a beloved pair of boots. She'd been fed and would be completely fine, but he still wanted just simply to make sure, and check in with her. As he headed back to the boat, he considered how much longer he could give it tonight. If he did another five such search spirals, he'd cover 100 m², which would help him feel like he'd done a more complete job. As he broke the surface by the dinghy, the soft splashing he made caused Nala to immediately look over the side of the boat, her ears cocked.

'I'm still here, love,' he said.

She huffed dismissively, letting him know he was a troublesome idiot.

'I know, I know. You've got your blanket, and water. And I promise a sausage when we get back, OK? A real one.'

Cam fancied one himself. Preferably coated in that relish. He checked his airways, and the dials.

If he wanted to do another five circles, he'd better start with a fresh tank. He unlinked his present tank, freed it from its harness and heaved it over the side into the belly of the boat with a clunk, before reaching over and hauling the next one out into the water with him. Changing air tanks in the water was a useful skill: it stopped him from having to get out and get frozen all over again. 'Just a bit longer,' he shouted to Nala, as he coupled everything back up.

He lowered himself back under the surface, and even in that short time, visibility had turned to what felt like less than nothing. It was like slipping into a glove when you were one of the fingers, as he dropped to the bottom and found the swirl markings of his previous searches by torchlight. He went to an outer edge and started again.

And again.

And again.

Warming again to the task, he thought he could go on all night if he had to – if it weren't for Nala and the fact he had no more air tanks.

He realised with his third search with the new tank (and the eighth overall) that the bank was inclining upwards. It was getting shallower, not by much, but certainly enough to both sense and notice.

Hang on. *I can see*, he thought.

That meant that suddenly, and without too much warning, the water clarity was changing again. It was the moveable bridge, miles away, surely, but down here, it felt like another one of those mystical quirks that only under-water life on the Norfolk Broads could possess.

It began to reveal more and more to him, including the fact that the shallowing levelled off at about four feet deep before it hit the firm bank. His searching had obviously dragged him closer to one of the walls and he'd lost track of time, which was a regular cost of this kind of dedication.

This had to be the nearest bank to the discovery site of the knife.

He popped up to the surface, an idea having blossomed. He emerged to darkness, his torchlight the only illumination. But out here, the lack of light pollution meant that the sky was alive and buoyant. Galactic clusters winked at him, looked at him from afar, rendering him tiny, small, speck-like. At the end of it all, he was just one tiny organism trying to connect an equally tiny knife to another organism, and it made him briefly question whether any of it was worth it. He glanced at the boat, and the light immediately reflected off Nala's eyes.

'Hello,' he called across to her. She barked in response. She'd be in a proper sulk with him when he got back.

He turned and looked towards the bank he'd arrived at and saw that the vegetation was thick with marshland, covered in reeds five feet high – and God knew what underfoot. On the marshes in Broadland you had to be careful where you set your foot, always aware that, beneath your very toes, the ground could give way in an easy instant. It wasn't just treacherous, it was scheming.

He swam towards that edge, intent on getting out to see if there was a route through the trees and reeds, even if he did have to be extremely careful, and there was no way anyone out here was walking through *that*. There didn't seem to be an obvious pathway through, nor a trail, but that didn't mean it wasn't there. He got to the edge or what felt like it, and tried to step up and over – but he couldn't get a footing. There wasn't anywhere really to place his weight and push off. The clumps of reeds weren't going to support him and there was no firm bank to grab on to.

He peered through the stalks, half-expecting his torch beam to land on the errant, squealing form of Stephen Spielberg's ET. He would have a full heart attack if that happened. He hated that little shit.

Eventually, however, he caught the sight of ground in the distance. It looked firm enough to stand on, so he pushed towards it and flattened his hands on the suspended bank. The strange thing, however, was that his feet didn't touch anything solid in front of him, and as he eased his legs forward, he was confused to find that he couldn't touch anything at all.

His feet were poking into nothingness, but they shouldn't be.

Could this chunk in front of him actually be one of those floating islands of reeds? The ones that look like a solid island, but are just a drifting ecosystem all by itself?

No, it was tight to the bank – it couldn't be.

He slipped back under the surface – but when he trained his torch on where the bank wall should be, he was stunned to find that the bank had been carved out.

The entirety of the bank was undercut and, at some point or other, some unseen pressures in the water had forced the sides to scoop out, creating a steep overhang. He ran his torch along the recessed wall. It was set further back in some places than others, ranging from one foot underneath the overhang to three feet, maybe even more.

It was a marvel – an underwater curiosity he'd never seen before. No wonder his feet couldn't find purchase.

And that was when he saw what looked like a curtain of weed, drifting down from the reeds above, and hanging over the overhang like a skirt. But...

No, this didn't look right.

Weed grows upwards, from the bottom, their roots buried in the river bed.

This seemed to come down from the top. How?

Cam moved closer, and parted the fronds.

To reveal a gaping tunnel, yawning in the bank wall.

31

Cam came back up to the surface with a gasp.

Never mind the boat needing an anchor, *he* needed one. Desperately.

Had he really seen that?

Was there really a dug-out tunnel hidden underneath this beautiful place?

He shone his torch at the dinghy, and saw Nala's eyes glow back it him in the glare. She barked once, and he could see the steam from her breath lift from her mouth. It grounded him, rooted him once more. He treaded water for a moment, letting the cool water do its trick on him again.

Yes, he really had seen that.

And he needed to call it in.

But… the other part of him was desperate to get down there and see it for himself. Because the tunnel had looked man-made. They were deep, inch-wide rakings in the mud and dirt that formed the walls. They looked like they'd been made by…

Fingers.

Cam started to paddle slowly back to the boat, nice and gentle, a queasy mix of dread and excitement sloshing inside him.

When he got to the boat, threw his tank over and then hoisted himself up, Nala greeted him with an attack flurry of licks.

'It's a weird one, sweetheart,' he said. 'A really weird one.'

He didn't want to leave the site, not with the water clarity playing ball for the time being. He didn't know how quickly that might change here on Doke End, but during both his visits so far, the conditions had been very fickle. Maybe he'd just seen the last two periods of real clear water in as many days.

Bottom line, if he was going to search the tunnel, he wanted to search it while the going was extremely good. But going down there, into that, alone, was almost suicidal.

But who could he get out here to help him out?

He checked his watch.

Gupta and Ferris – would they be able to get out here? They'd come to his aid in a dinghy only last year, but the way they'd handled the craft left him not totally convinced they'd be the right people for this job. And Rogers was still in Norwich, dealing with Forsyth.

That left Jess Tabernacle, who was still at work, but with no way to get here – especially considering he knew for sure Jess didn't have access to a boat.

So, who did have a boat? In a flash of memory, he remembered and placed a call.

'Hello,' came the answer down the handset.

'Thelonius?' Cam said, his voice coming out more breathless than he expected. 'It's Mr Catshit.'

'I wasn't expecting to hear from you again,' the retired warhorse replied stiffly.

'I'm full of surprises. Listen, I've got a situation here, and I think a man of your prowess might suit. Can you get to Doke End as quick as possible?'

'May I ask why?'

'I'm about to do something very stupid, and I need someone to watch my back.'

'I feel honour-bound not to miss you make a fool of yourself,' came the immediate reply.

'Good. Get out here ASAP. Oh… you don't have a wetsuit, do you?'

'Since my slide into the sedentary, I'm afraid not one that fits.'

'Don't worry about that then. A good set of hands on deck here will do just fine.'

'Give me half an hour.'

Thirty minutes later, having split an old cheese butty with Nala – with an extra, almost liquid, banana for himself – Cam met Thelonius at the padlocked gate. He heard the sputter of the fellow veteran's engine before he saw it, and then saw the shape of a man at the helm.

'Thelonius?' shouted Cam.

'Mr Catshit,' replied the shape. As the boat drifted closer, Thelonius held up a hand by way of greeting. 'You're a bloody nightmare when the sun goes down, aren't you? Always showing up where you shouldn't.'

Cam wordlessly guided him through the gate, then swung his own boat to close it again. 'I'm going to lash us together,' said Cam, 'and then you hop on board, and we'll get going.'

Cam caught Thelonius take one look at Cam's wetsuit and raise his eyebrows. 'Yep,' he said. 'A proper nuisance bugger you are.'

After Cam had secured the boats together with knots at the bow and stern, they drifted the joined vessels out from the steel gate, allowing the flow and breeze to take them from the surrounding trees. When they were in open water, Cam hit the trolling motor and ever so gently eased them through, back to the bank across the water.

He turned to Thelonius. The man spread his arms in a 'so now are you going to tell me?' gesture.

'The bank under the reeds here has a hollow in it. Looks like a man-made tunnel. I'm gonna clip this rope to my dive belt,' Cam said, holding up a thin length of cord with the dog-lead carabiner looped on the end. He handed the other to Thelonius. 'There's one hundred feet on this thing. I don't expect I'll need to use all of it. But I don't know how far in it goes.'

Can pointed to the reed bed.

'You're going underwater,' said Thelonius. 'In a tunnel. Made by God knows who. In the dark. Oh goodie.'

Cam nodded. He knew how stupid this was – but the urgency outweighed it.

'Yes,' said Thelonius. 'A proper nuisance bugger.' He looked at Nala, who just yawned as if to say, 'Welcome to the circus, pal.' He lowered on to the seat at the bow of the dinghy, clipped the carabiner around one of the cleats, and looped the rope around his hand and elbow, ready to belay slack out to Cam. Cam was relieved to see he'd clearly called the right person.

'Have fun,' said Thelonius. 'And do try not to die.' Cam took a deep breath, nodded at the other man, then his beloved dog, and dropped backwards into the murk.

Now

I've been out and fed the animals, even the sick one. They're all behaving, all looking well. With chores done, I can roam. My territory is fixed. Mine again.

The challengers have been beaten, their blood used to label the ground with my claim. The claim I inherited, the claim that was always mine. I walk through the trees, following the path in my head. The one I know is safe. The darkness is my ally and home.

Yes, a really good night to patrol.

Wait.

I tense. *What's that?*

It's a clunk, in the dark. It's wood on wood, echoing off water.

I know that sound. Everyone around here would most likely know that sound. It's an oar dropping into a boat. Nobody should be here. Not at this time. But what if they are? What if the man with the keys changed the rules?

There. There is the water. There is a moon up there, so I'll be able to see enough. Two boats. Lashed together. Why is he...? *No.*

The diver. He's there, with someone else. Another man I don't know. They're pointing. The diver is pointing at the reeds.

No.

They can't do this. It isn't theirs. This is a claim. He's taking what isn't his. He is in the water now. The diver. He shouldn't be here. Not him.

I'm conflicted. I almost want him to see. I see myself in him. He too carries a wildness. The proximity to blood. He might understand it. No. He's underwater now.

Get away from there. It's not yours. None of this is.

I should intervene. Put a stop to it. But they might get me arrested, and that will be it for the animals, the sick one in particular.

No, all I can do is watch this happen. For now.

32

Cam approached the tunnel with extreme caution, the swaying fronds of the camouflage curtain wafting in the gentlest flow. The underwater world in pure night was an entirely different kettle of fish, the latter of which there were suddenly many. They were everywhere, littering his field of vision, shoals of roach whirling like a tight murmuration of diamond starlings.

His heart thumped so heavily each beat hurt.

Focus.

Breathe, and focus.

Readied, calmer, Cam slowly approached the bank with subtle flicks of his flippers.

His torch beam hit the curved, irregular wall of the recessed bank and, once again, he marvelled at its creation. A long time ago – a damn long time ago, he thought – there must have been a consistent flow along this bank, and erosion must have done its job as the water passed by. Doke End must have been part of the actual river at some point, before eventually getting cut off. But even with that being said, these features were associated with much faster rivers. He'd never seen it here, on the Broads. Cam would have to go back to the library, and hit the books and maps, to try to find out exactly how this place had transformed all those years ago. It was, in itself, a fascinating quirk of geography. But that was for another time. Now, he had to spin his attention away and back to the hole he'd found, because those undercut bank walls might have been created naturally but this damn hole surely wasn't.

No wonder the police dive team had missed it. In the murky conditions earlier, it would have been impossible to see unless you swam straight into it.

He shone his torch beam along the wall of the recessed bank until it abruptly disappeared down the tunnel, as if he'd turned it off. With no small degree of nerves, he approached.

As he looked at the walls, he thought he could make out, not just finger imprints, but tool shapes and scrapes, presumably from when it had been dug out.

Who did this?

When was it dug out?

The river and history clung to each other like mating serpents, so the answer could be anyone and anytime through the region's rich past.

The walls of the tunnel were perhaps three feet apart. It was an oval, upright, maybe four feet tall. Definitely big enough for him to get in. He inched closer. Fish were cruising in and around the entrance, darting this way and that out of the torch beam. He made sure the carabiner was still clipped to his belt, and that the rope was drifting unhindered, before swimming into the entrance.

As soon as he was over the threshold, he looked up. The last thing he wanted was the roof to suddenly give way. But the soil beneath the reed bed was compact, tight like clay, the same as the walls.

He had only got a couple of metres in when the tunnel seemed to take a right turn. Cam edged to the bend. Four huge shapes darted at him. Long green slabs of muscle, they arrowed at him with eyes of dying embers, before powering past him and out into the main body of water.

They were pike. Huge ones.

The massive hidden pike of Doke End. They were here all right.

And they were massive. Four of the biggest specimens he'd ever seen. Crocs.

Mercifully, they wanted no part of him. He breathed in relief, reset, and pressed slowly on. Adrenaline was good; crippling nerves, bad. If he was buzzing with the intrigue of discovery, that was fine by him.

Cam went around the corner, edging slowly ever further, until the smooth walls bent away and opened out, and his torch beam gradually crept into another opening – revealing a small, underwater cavern.

And a sight that confounded and horrified him.

In this heinous underwater chamber, three bodies listlessly drifted.

33

Cam had seen some things that were so scarred in his memory, it was like they had been chiselled on the interior walls of his head.

This would be another addition to that horrible cavalcade of parading grotesqueries.

No amount of therapy was going to scratch this – but duty, as always, would take priority. If he had to carry the mental can for this, he knew he would.

Steeling himself, he paddled into the chamber at the bottom of Doke End.

With a hand that was shaking far more than he would have liked, he pulled out his phone in its waterproof case from his trusty dive pouch, and took a video of the scene.

He tried not to dwell on the horrible images in front of him, hoping instead merely to document the scene as dispassionately, yet comprehensively, as possible. Instead of the bits and pieces that were missing, chewed or scrambled, he focused instead on the back of the phone screen and getting everything into frame.

There were three bodies, each in various states of decomposition.

All were still dressed, clothes drifting gently in the flow, in jeans, check shirts, fishing greens.

All had clearly died fairly recently. They were, for sure, men, judging from their overall size and shape – and what was left of their hair. Their flesh, however, was mottled and picked apart, natural predation by small omnivores almost disestablishing any clear facial features.

Most macabre of all was the feeling that he was looking at something staged: like a modern art installation on the decay of the human condition.

Speaking of the human condition, Cam felt it laid bare once again in so many ways. The obvious reminder that we were all, at the end of the day, flesh and blood that withers and crumbles and reduces to nothing in the face of pressure and nature – but also something else.

It spoke of the shocking level of depravity and degradation and warped sense of all things right and wrong that could have created this.

A shocking display of what it meant to be human and what it meant when humanity went wrong.

Whatever happened from here, Doke End was about to become a circus of activity, and a ghoulish hotspot for years to come. While he watched through the screen, relying on the disassociation afforded technology, he noticed something. Each of the corpses were exhibiting different levels of decay. The body furthest from the entrance was, for want of a better word, more chewed and decayed than the others, while the other one, roughly on top of the trio, looked more recent. As if they'd been added to the cave in succession, one after the other, over a relatively short period of time.

Cam remembered fishing a body out of a river system far north of the Broads. A drowning. It had taken two weeks for the body to turn up. That had been an inland river, with ecological characteristics fairly similar to the Broads. That body had been in a similar state to the furthest one here.

Jessup, Drummond, Forrester. Was this them?

He didn't want to forget the five-day rule. If Jessup was here, with his DNA on the knife, then he'd be the most recent one.

But as he moved closer now to take pictures of each face, he felt more and more sure that Jessup wasn't here. Jessup was a thin and wiry man with haunted-looking cheek bones, whereas these men, or what was left of them, were still more substantial in frame than him. Plus… none of them looked recent enough. Which would mean Jessup's body was still out there… somewhere.

So… if not Jessup, who was the third guy?

It was another person who hadn't made it home, and it made Cam feel sick with the dread of it all.

He shuddered, remembered he was looking at decaying human beings, who were clearly the victims of the most heinous of crimes. His horror multiplied.

Easy Cam, he told himself. *It means you're human.*

But now he was beginning to feel like he was being watched. He knew it was only his anxiety, but he was starting to feel as if someone was behind him.

It felt like the woods near Middlewater.

It made Cam's hackles rise and his stomach drop. His pulse began to quicken, even more than before, and he could feel the familiar heat in his forearms.

Anxiety, growing to the point of attack.

He knew the signs well enough.

He had to get out. He had to get out now. He turned and tugged twice on the rope, which was the signal for

Thelonius to gradually wind the rope back in. He took it steady – and as Cam swam back up, he fought horrible thoughts of getting tangled and caught down here, ending up the fourth resident of this awful cave on Doke End.

Forcing himself to take one last look, Cam backed out of the chamber and silently prayed that he'd never, *ever*, have to go back in there.

34

'You look like you're going to be sick.'

Thelonius was stood over Cam, who had just heaved himself into the boat, and was now lying on his back on the bare deck boards. He was breathing steadily – in for three, hold for five, out for eight – while staring at the brilliant black sky overhead.

'I think I found our missing people,' he said quietly, stroking Nala's fur while she clambered onto his chest as it rose and fell. He couldn't – wouldn't – take his eyes off the cosmos.

'My god,' said Thelonius. 'There are bodies down there?'

Cam handed Thelonius his phone. 'Check the camera roll,' he said. 'Go to the most recent stuff.'

He listened as Thelonius took the phone, still in its protective case, and started scrolling.

'Oh my god,' said Thelonius. Cam could see him go pale, even in the dim glow from the phone screen. 'It's an underwater tomb.'

'That sounds about right.'

'You have someone to call?' He held the phone out as if it was a block of dangerous plutonium, and swallowed hard before speaking again. Even for the man Cam thought he was, this was clearly proving tough. 'If it's all right, I'd rather leave this one to the professionals.'

Cam took the phone, laid his head back and stared at the stars again. 'I'm right with you,' he said – and made the call to Rogers.

Within an hour, Doke End was swamped with more human life than it had seen in years – maybe even ever. Because of the lack of easy land-based access, the forces had converged on Doke End via boat, and now the once-silent water was suddenly covered in blue lights. Police boats, local vessels that had been commandeered, and rafts of people in high-visibility clothing. Cam was sure it wouldn't take long before a helicopter started swirling as well.

A dive team arrived and Cam recognised a number of faces from the Brindley car recovery a few months back. Some of them treated him more warmly than last time, replete with knowing nods. Cam got the impression his reputation was preceding him. Their boat pulled alongside Cam's battered dinghy, which had a delighted Nala and a fairly bemused Ed Thelonius sat in the back.

'You again,' said the team leader, Saj Malhotra, shaking Cam's hand from one boat to the next. Cam liked the guy, found him devoid of both nonsense and police politics, but right now all he could muster by way of greeting was a meek shrug.

'I believe you've got a nasty video?' said Saj.

'It isn't pleasant,' replied Cam.

'I was bored of my dinner anyway. May I see it, please?'

Cam had sent the video to Rogers, who was on her way, and would surely appear on one of these boats any time now – but it obviously hadn't been disseminated as far as the guys who were actually going to go down there and deal with it.

Cam passed across his phone. The men crowded around and over Saj's shoulders to get a look at what they'd be going down to face. As was often the case at times like these, the defence mechanism of gallows humour set in.

A couple of whistles rang out as the camera passed across the decaying faces. 'Bloody Nora,' said one of the other divers, before turning away.

'Yep, definitely won't be needing that dinner,' said Saj.

His dive team finished suiting up, and stood primed for disembarking. Ordinarily Cam would have felt a pang of jealousy that he wasn't part of the official team – on this occasion, however, he was happy to leave them to it. Instead, something surprised him. Something he hadn't felt for quite some time. A quiet sense of kinship with the other neoprened men, who were quietly steeling themselves, ready to visit Doke End's very own house of horrors. He sympathised with them in advance.

Cam directed them to the bank with a pointing finger. 'It's over there. Hit the bank wall and you should only be a matter of yards from the opening. It's behind a curtain of weed. Kept it hidden.'

Cam watched them slide into the water, passing various pieces of equipment between them, as well as a huge dark sack that contained what he knew to be body bags. One of the divers was equipped with an underwater camera rig, ready to document the entire thing.

'Be safe lads,' he said. 'It's grim and tight down there.'

Their heads slipped under the black surface, and they were soon out of sight except for the dancing beams of torch glare under the water.

'Bloody mad,' whispered Thelonius, as they watched the softly glowing cones advance towards the reed bed – and one by one, each of the torches went out as they went down the tunnel.

Within minutes, another boat arrived and this one did indeed carry, amongst a couple of other police escorts, Rogers. She stood on the bow, obviously cold, and somewhat breeze-ruffled. Rogers' jaw was grimly set, her long blond plait waving behind her like a flag. Perhaps she too was thinking about that video.

The driver of their dinghy lashed the boat to the others in an ever-expanding flotilla.

Rogers dug her hands in her pockets as soon as the boat was still.

'Well, that can't have been very pleasant,' she said to Cam. She had thawed a smidge since their phone conversation. 'How are you holding up?'

This was about as close to sympathy as Cam ever got from her. Every now and then, she betrayed the fact that she must truly care for him in a kind of begrudging collegial way. This seemed to be one of those times.

'I'm all right,' Cam said.

'You really do have a knack for finding the most disgusting shit, don't you? Like that one dog that always comes back with a mouthful of fox piss.'

Cam simply shrugged. 'What's the play here?'

'Well, I have to interview you in full, with an independent, to show that we did everything above board. But first, I need to oversee this… scene here, and to make sure these bodies are properly recovered. Then we can crack on with identification.'

'I suppose you'll have to speak to me as well?' said Thelonius.

'You prat about on my case, sunshine,' Rogers said, 'you earn yourself a poorly timed appointment and the shittest cup of tea this side of Nelson's Monument.'

Cam lowered his voice. 'Look, I know we're looking for him as a matter of urgency, but I'm pretty sure none of that lot down there are Tommy Jessup.'

Rogers paused, taking it in, before: 'You think he's still unaccounted for?'

'It seems so.'

'So… if you're right, who's the third body?'

'No idea.'

Rogers sighed, and momentarily squeezed her eyes shut, as if to block out the escalating madness. 'Well, isn't that just fucking peachy.'

35

When Cam was allowed to leave the scene, it was with the express instruction he go straight to the incident room – which had quickly been set up at the local sailing club.

Cockshot Sailing Club was open for the night, or at least some of it was, and in the meeting of the unstoppable force of the law and the immoveable object of long-established village world order, the force had proved stoppable after all: bingo night somehow hadn't been cancelled. It left one room of the club full of uniforms talking tactics and strategy, and the other full of a septuagenarian crowd that was part-intrigued, part-upset at the distraction from winning a set of steak knives and a couple of hundred quid.

After changing, loading his own boat up onto the trailer, and treating Nala to a cheesy-twirl thing in lieu of the promised sausage, Cam entered the sailing club just as 'Legs eleven' was called. He managed to sneak down past the bar to where the secondary function room was situated. The entire bottom floor was wrapped in glass and overlooked the blackened river and the breezed yacht masts, their cords pinging in the wind.

Cam, abruptly starving, grabbed a packet of cheese and onion crisps as he passed the bar. Suddenly desperately thirsty too, he ordered a pint of orange cordial to go with it.

The incident room, bedecked in sailing club paraphernalia and memorabilia, was now full of official bustle. The dark beyond watched them with expectancy from outside the windows here too, giving the room a goldfish-bowl impression.

Rogers had beat him there and was now at the head of the large central table, as he made his way over to join her. A laptop was open and angled upwards, her eyes fixed on it, while a host of other PCs, plain clothes officers and who-knew-whats hunkered around the table, all poring over their own electronic devices. As he walked, Cam caught sight of enough of the glowing screens to know what they were fussing over. It seemed that the photographs from the official dive had come in, and everyone was having a turn at rubbernecking.

Cam grimaced and looked away – he'd seen more than enough – so he sipped his cordial and thought of the oblivious bingo players next door.

As he took in the chatter of horrified excitement, he knew the story would explode any time now, well before an official statement was released, and would travel with wildfire intent. Speculation would follow and before anyone knew it, this whole area would become a hot spot for ambulance chasers, true crime enthusiasts, and plain old nosy weirdos.

And then there'd be the serial killer fans and aficionados, though how someone like this could be admired, even idolised, made Cam shudder.

Rogers finally noticed him. 'We were lucky to find somewhere with enough room for this cattle,' she said, joining him, and pointing at the assorted people in the room. 'At least one that had power.' She then lifted her tablet up, screen alive and ready. 'I think we can safely say that this one is Leonard Drummond.'

The screen in front of him was split. The left-hand side bore the close-up of what he guessed was Leonard Drummond's remains, versus on the right, a cheery picture of him in happier, and decidedly more alive, times. In the second photograph he was sat at an outdoor table, the parasol of which blocked out near-obscene sunlight. Just the sight of it threatened to heat the chill that was now deeply rooted in Cam's bones.

The man had short, cropped hair styled with an overt reliance on some product or other, and he had a drinker's paunch. A tribal tattoo sat on his shoulder and Cam wondered whether the man had any idea what it represented.

Rogers groaned theatrically: 'I'd say that's him. It's hard to make a hundred per cent ID when you've not got eyeballs or cheeks, but probably worth having it in our minds. Facial structure and hair are about right.'

'You check the ink?' he asked.

'The bodies are on their way here from Doke End now – we'll get a good look at them then. I'm guessing that will confirm it.'

'Why here?' Cam asked, thinking of the bingo players next door.

'Oh, I've worked in way worse. And this place had the best access for the ambulance.'

'What about the others?' asked Cam. 'Any ideas?'

'We've actually already confirmed one, near as dammit. Ryan Forrester. He has a distinctive sovereign ring. One of the bodies was wearing it. Even though he is fairly chewed up, it has to be him.'

Cam felt immediately grateful that Rogers wasn't swiping up pictures for him to look at. He spoke again before she got any ideas. 'So that makes two. And if the third one isn't Jessup, then… any ideas on our third man?'

'Nothing yet. But he'll be connected to the other two in some way.'

Cam thought. 'Yes, I agree. The whole thing – just doesn't feel right.'

'If you went down there and found any of that felt right, I would have you sectioned immediately, Cam Killick,' said Rogers.

'No, I mean… we're missing something. The motivations are weird, can't pinpoint them,' he said.

'If we knew why, sunshine, it would make everything an awful lot easier.'

'I suppose so,' Cam said unhappily. 'When do you want to interview me?'

Rogers took a look around at the people working frantically, then glanced out of the darkened windows at the river. A convoy of blue lights hovered above the water in the distance.

'The bodies are coming here when they're up and out. There's a fridge truck on the way to get them to the morgue. But when those boats arrive, I'll need to check in with the forensic pathologist. We asked him to come out and have a look at the scene, considering the hours he's going to end up putting into this. Maybe he'll let me have a look here so we can get a march on IDs, because time on this one really is of the essence. Are you all right to stick around, maybe do it after?'

Cam looked at his watch. He was due his concoction of meds, and boy did he need them, the sights, sounds, smells of the last few hours having cornered him into mental exhaustion.

It was as if Rogers could feel his indecision. 'If you are going to keep blowing these kinds of things up, then you really should be prepared to answer a few questions about them.'

Cam looked at her and could see that barely perceptible smile that let him know that somewhere, deep down, she held a small candle of admiration for what he'd done.

'As long as you don't make me go and look at all those bodies again?' he said.

'I think you've probably done enough where those are concerned. Now, I've got a couple of calls to make, so sit tight.'

Rogers walked to the sliding doors to go outside, but coming the other way were a couple of very interested chaps in sailing club blazers. The gold buttons strained so desperately that Cam thought they must surely buy those things a handful of sizes too small on purpose.

'What's going on in there?' said one of them in a haughty tone. He held a pink bingo dabber in one hand and waved it about like a bayonet.

'I'm sorry for the disturbance sir—' began Rogers.

'I'm the Commodore of this club, and I demand answers.'

Cam could see Rogers' expression change. She went from placating a member of the public to something entirely more scornful, and began imitating his accent. 'Ah well you see, the geese have gone to war. There's a feathered army approaching, beaks at the ready. I'd prepare myself if I were you, because it will be on the water where the battle will be won, and we'll probably need a bunch of posh toadies in daft clobber to stave off the winged hordes. Now, if you'll excuse me.'

And with that Rogers left.

'I don't think she took me very seriously,' said the Commodore to his friend.

Cam thought he might be right.

36

Some time later, Rogers stood outside the sailing club in a night that had dipped so fiercely in temperature, a freeze had to be imminent. She felt her very breath harden as it left her lungs, cold even before it had left her mouth, as she stood at the quay-heading waiting for the police transport to arrive. A set of twinkling navigation lights slid ever closer to her, bringing the horrors of that underwater tunnel with them.

This was going to be tough. She'd seen a lot of PCs rethink their careers in the aftermath of what she was about to see. She was about to undergo an ultimate test of mettle. And it wasn't just here in the present. The sight would last long after the seeing. Sometimes it was the smell that stayed longest, deep and psychological, the odorous spectre of cellular necrosis lingering long after the sight had disappeared.

At least Rogers knew what to expect, and could steel herself for it. That odour... no amount of showers or booze could get rid of. As the boat got closer, and took shape out of the darkness, she opened a packet a Fisherman's Friends bought from an all-night petrol station – because at least they held the worst of it at bay.

The mood was understandably sombre and weary when the vessel pulled up. First off was the forensic pathologist, a man who often, given the smaller size of the force, performed coroner's duties too. He got regular call-outs by the police, though mainly to declare someone dead when they hadn't answered their door in a few days, so this was a big career moment for him too.

His name was Thomas Black, never Tom, and Rogers extended her hand. 'Proper fun and games this one,' she said, noting to herself that it sounded like she was talking about a sick-ass Netflix show, and not a murderer's hidey hole.

'Yes, quite,' he said. Black had never been known for his glittering personality. Gallows humour had bypassed him in its entirety, and waved at him as it went. 'It's not the norm. We'll have to do what we can with it.'

Rogers knew he was understating it. Ordinarily, they would have spent hours photographing and meticulously recording the scene – but in this instance, darkness, time and the sheer awkwardness of the location meant that while all hands were on deck, they would be used appropriately. The crime scene would be pieced together back at the police labs, reconstructed using the photographs and itemised evidence inventory the dive team had taken at the scene. A clatter behind Black prompted him to dart sideways, to allow another officer to leap off the vessel and throw up wildly onto the deck.

'Good lad,' said Black.

Rogers watched steam lift from the hot spatter. 'Better out than in.'

'We're going to need extra help here,' said Black, his eyes still on the retching officer.

'What are you thinking?'

'This isn't run of the mill in any way, shape or form. I'm not sure we have the resources to cope.'

'Is this *we* as in all of us collectively, or just you and your staff?'

He finally looked directly at her. 'Both. This is something far more involved, far sicker. Far more complicated.'

Rogers didn't like that one bit. She'd never known Black to be spooked by anything – but then again, Black had clearly betrayed that he'd never faced anything like this before.

'Do you have a preliminary idea of cause of death?' Rogers asked.

'I should imagine the cause of death will be the easiest part to explain,' said the coroner. 'Answering as to why they were stashed at the bottom of the Norfolk Broads in some mad loon's murder grotto is anyone's guess. They'll want to write academic papers on this one, that's for sure.'

His eyes took on a distant quality, and Rogers waved her hand across them, back and forth. 'Hello, Black? You're here to establish how they died. *I'll* worry about all the Mindhunter crap. Anything obvious linking them?'

The pathologist looked at her, and, his professional intuition provoked, cocked an eyebrow. 'You seem to have something in mind.'

'We've had a murder weapon, but no murderer for a few days now. Nor a body. Until now – even though we don't think the victim we're looking for is one of this lot. Best guess we've got on method is a knife in the heart.'

Rogers was sure deep down that whoever had done this had a clear design, a crystal idea of what they wanted to achieve. And a clear design meant a regular way of going about things. He would follow some element of a pattern.

She was convinced, now she'd seen multiple bodies, that if one had died from a heart strike, there was a high chance the others might as well. Someone weird enough to go to the lengths they obviously had would be weird enough to follow a very set way of dispatching people.

'Yes,' said Black. 'The three victims here died via a penetrating injury of the heart, consistent with a stab wound. Blood loss and cardiac tamponade likely combined to do the job.'

'What is that?'

'When the pericardium is punctured, which is the sack around the heart itself, it fills with blood and this extra fluid makes it harder for the heart to pump. Not only is the heart punctured, but it is being choked by itself.'

Jesus, thought Rogers. 'I know your investigation is only preliminary,' she said, 'and these conclusions will go no further – but between us, any early assessments to give us a head start?'

'Well, all three were killed in a matter of weeks, possibly a fortnight, all indeed with puncture wounds to the heart. It was a very direct and precise job. Almost identical wounds on all three.'

'Go on.'

'They appeared to have died in what they were wearing, with clean incisions on the front of each chest, just above the sternum. The knife, and it was a knife all right, with a blade an inch wide and perhaps four to six inches long, went right through their outerwear.'

Rogers saw that ugly knife in her mind's eye – the one that Killick found to start this whole thing. 'Any other wounds that you picked up on?'

'None. No defensive wounds, either. These men, therefore, could have been incapacitated, but again considering the lack of ligature marks, I find this extremely unlikely. Our killer used surprise as a key tactic.'

'And you're confident it's the same killer?'

'That's up to you and your criminal profilers,' said Black. 'I would say there won't be many minds as sick as this.' That last statement hung uneasily between them in the quiet.

Rogers eventually broke the silence. 'Would it be OK for you and I to attempt some preliminary identification?' she asked.

'You want to do that here?' The coroner glanced beyond her shoulder, and nodded at the windows of the sailing club. Rogers turned to find several elderly faces pressed against the glass, her friend the Commodore at the front, watching the scene unfold with avid stares.

'Hell,' she said, exasperated.

And then she had a thought. She stepped on to the nearest sail boat and undid a clove hitch – which unleashed the mast of the overhead sail. It unfurled down from the tip, out to the pole that stuck out, whatever that was called, and acted as a huge privacy screen. 'That's a little better.'

The coroner shrugged and got back on board the transport vessel. Rogers joined him on board this time too, and the two were alone on the boat while the rest of the recovery team had gone inside for a winter warmer and presumably a discreet vomit.

Black unzipped the first cadaver and there was the first whisper of that familiar scalding stink that she knew would be there for a long time to come. It wasn't as bad as she thought, but then she remembered that putrefaction would have been slowed by the chilly underwater conditions.

Rogers stood at the head of the three bags, and looked carefully at the screen in her hand – although she couldn't stop herself from taking small glances at the death in front of her. 'OK,' she said. 'Tribal tattoo, left arm.'

A rustle. Rogers watched Black pull at limp arms, and she looked at the sky. Christ.

'I won't be able to see that until he's fully undressed,' said Black. 'Could you give me something else in the meantime?'

'Ear piercing,' said Rogers. 'Left ear.'

After a quiet moment, the pathologist sniffed. 'I'm afraid this one's left ear has been chewed off. The other one is clear. Anything else?'

'Hang on.' Rogers pinched and rotated the image.

'Back of the right calf, a small freckle an inch above the ankle on the back, dead centre.'

'You got that from Facebook?' asked Black.

'Yup.'

The pathologist sniffed again. 'This generation,' he murmured to himself. 'Oh yes, hey, we've got it.'

'That makes him Leonard Drummond. You'll eventually find a large tribal tattoo on his shoulder.' She instructed the pathologist to look for a signet ring on the other two, and sure enough, they could identify Ryan Forrester. Which meant that the third cadaver was still a mystery.

'Do you have a rough time of death on the last one before we go further?'

'Water always makes it hard,' said Black. 'Two weeks tops. If that broad was full of shellfish and they found this, which I'm guessing they did, this might have been as early as this week.'

'Damn.' Rogers knew that time frame wouldn't work for the blood on the knife in any event – even if it didn't have Tommy Jessup's DNA on it. They still had Jessup unaccounted for, not to mention his body. 'Damn,' she said again, to nobody.

That body didn't belong to Tommy Jessup. So if it wasn't him… then who the hell was it?

'If you find your killer's pattern,' Black said. 'You'll find your missing body. The people that do this sort of thing… they don't tend to stop until they've finished their supposed mission – or they get caught.'

Rogers looked off downriver, to a horizon she couldn't see. The architect of this madness was still out there. Without looking, she pointed at the last body. 'I'm going to need everything on our mystery guest please, and he's your priority.'

The coroner nodded grimly. Rogers felt a pang of sympathy for him. Death was his job all right, but, nevertheless, he had a long unenviable night in its company ahead.

37

After walking Rogers through every last detail about his discovery of what they were now calling 'the Grotto', Cam left the sailing club and hit the road. The exhaustion was finally catching up with him and he was convinced sleep would soon follow.

Actual sleep, he hoped. Not the kind that was constantly broken, nor rooted to the bottom of a bathtub with a straw in his mouth. He estimated it was possibly forty-eight hours since he had last had any semblance of restorative shut-eye. No wonder he was feeling too tired for his symptoms to really fire on all cylinders – even they were exhausted. Fed up, and desperate for comfort, a bright idea filtered through the grim fog – figurative and literal.

He checked the time, gambled and dictated a text through the hands-free kit.

It was late, gone midnight, but he was pretty sure that the recipient would be awake. She slept as badly as he did. His words were, for him at least, direct.

Are you still up?? Hell of a day! Would love an ear if you've got a spare one.

It was to the one person he felt he could actually talk to with more than a forced sense of transparency. He instructed Siri to send the message, and he held his breath.

The reply came back mercifully quickly, and his chest flooded with warmth when he read it.

Would love to. Front door's open, kettle's on.

Feeling steadier already with a firm destination, he made his way to Jess Tabernacle's residence, and the drive flew by in a frenetic battle between hope and darkness, as Cam's frazzled mind alternated between the two with the conviction and energy of a firmly struck ping-pong ball.

He knew exactly where he was going, no need for satnav, and the roads were deathly quiet, just the way he liked them. Through Ludham, over Potter Heigham Bridge and onwards to Thrigby, and Feather House, Jess's home, which was a white, two-storey pile in a mock-colonial style.

He turned down the drive and wound between the clinging rhododendrons on either side, along the fresh gravel that was a new addition since he'd last been here. The house in front of him now was resplendent. A full white coat of paint had restored the building to former glories, alongside a half-decent landscaping job, even if he did say so himself. It had taken them weeks, and a lot of thorn cuts. On the right of the property lay Feather Pond, formerly known as Brindley Lake. It sat merry, full and expectant, with moonlight shimmering on its surface like an Enid Blyton dream. The lights were on behind the bay windows at the front, under the pillars of the porch entrance, which gave the building a true sense of place and authority.

Cam parked up and Nala recognised it immediately, her tail frantically hammering against the leather of the front seat.

As they stepped up the front steps, where Jess's wellies stood proudly splashed with mud, waiting for the next dog walk, the very dog in question appeared behind the glass door pane. Wicket's tail wagged dementedly as he caught sight of Nala – while a shadow in the soft hall light preceded Jess herself.

She was wearing a grey, fluffy dressing gown with her blue hair held up over black reading glasses, and Cam didn't think a person could look more lovely if they tried. She opened the door, and the heat immediately came for him.

The building was now warm and homely, despite its cavernous personality; a far cry from the first time Cam had set foot over its threshold.

'In,' she said to the dogs. 'You too,' she said to Cam.

He smiled and entered, and they both looked down as the dogs reintroduced themselves to each other, in a mad flurry of fur and the sniffing of rear ends.

'Forgive me if I don't do the same,' said Jess, and Cam was so taken aback that he couldn't help laughing.

He felt the tension ease from his back, the pins and needles in his forearms evaporate, and the stabbing pains at the base of his skull withdraw. He gave her a light hug.

'Wow,' she said, recoiling slightly.

'Ugh, yeah,' he replied.

Jess pointed upstairs. 'The towels are up there and I'll boil the kettle again. I'm not having you coming further inside smelling like that.'

Cam nodded. The idea of hot water was a bloody good one.

★　★　★

He came back to the kitchen ten minutes later to find Nala and Wicket asleep at the base of the Aga, curled up into each other like a furry yin-yang on a scuffed old mat.

The rest of the kitchen had been transformed, restored to its original shape. A happy, worn breakfast table held court in the middle of the kitchen – where Jess herself sat with a cup of tea, reading an iPad.

'Tea's in the pot,' she said. 'And you can pour me another while you're at it.'

Cam grinned. This was just what he needed. 'Yes ma'am.'

'And if you're hungry, I can get a couple of bits out.'

'Bits?' he asked. It had been hours since he last ate anything substantial, and he was suddenly very aware of it.

'Well, mainly cheese and ham and some bread and stuff?'

To Cam, right there and then, a ham and cheese sandwich had never sounded so good.

They had a moment of what felt like easy domesticity as they prepared the various bits and pieces, and Cam found he didn't even need to talk about any of the terrible things that had happened that day – essentially the very reason he'd asked to see her. Instead, he simply asked how her day was. It was clear to him that being here, in her company, was more restorative and balancing than any therapy or medication.

After a few moments, hearing about the pensioner who'd got stuck in the lift at the department store while trying to take a five-finger discount on a packet of skimpy undies, Jess added the final piece to the table.

A half-consumed bottle of that blessed breakfast relish.

Cam couldn't help but laugh.

This – Jess – felt like home. And he loved it.

Now

I don't think he's coming back. Not tonight.

It's hard to admit that my fascination is most likely now an obsession.

But harder still would be to deny it.

I've just got to let it happen. This, after all, is an eye for an eye.

Now, as I stand outside his home, I feel that familiar euphoria sat on the horizon like a tsunami waiting to crest.

In the darkness, it is a nice home, a good home, but it is not one befitting *that* man.

This man needs a cave. Somewhere fortified. He's a creation forged from hailstone, burning metal and spilt blood. He shouldn't live in a place like this. Homely.

This paradox, and its unanswered questions, will only cement the fixation further.

I approach the stone cottage, and the security light blinks on.

It should unnerve me. It doesn't.

I wait a few moments, watching from the corn stalks behind his house. I know he's not here.

I've been here for hours, ever since the police arrived at Doke End, watching the house, imagining the things that I would find in there.

The artefacts and atmosphere of that man.

I walk to the rear of the house slowly, savouring every second.

What will I learn inside?

I don't wait. I take the stone frog by the back door.

There's a key underneath it, sat looking at me like a shiny insect suddenly exposed.

I leave it, and throw the chunk of stone through the rear window.

Creating such a sound, knowing nobody will hear it, brings the rushing euphoria immediately.

It is almost too big for me to control.

It's completely monstrous, this feeling.

How could it ever be beaten? Or bettered?

There are clothes in a basket in the back room. I smell the detergent on them.

There's a sink, with a bottle of cucumber and kelp hand soap next to it. It's so normal. I want to bathe in the details. I move into the kitchen.

It's so utilitarian and male. So devoid of characteristic touches, or so it seems.

The clock is blinking all four zeros. It tells me so much with so little.

The kitchen is spotless. No food remnants or scraps.

The two details confirm my suspicion. So much order, but he can't simply set his clock.

He's ingrained in the military – and there's something loose about him. Something unpredictable.

The living room now. The TV is caked in dust. I can tell he barely uses it.

There's a beanbag on the floor, facing the window. There's something almost meditative about it.

No art on the walls. No DVDs littering the TV console. Nothing to suggest taste, or enjoyment.

He lives like a tortured monk.

Bare floorboards like an ancient monastery.

What is he punishing himself for?

Why is he this way?

Up the stairs now. I find the master bedroom.

A double bed, navy bedspread, immaculate. Large picture window. No curtains. More punishment.

I get in the bed. Still in my boots, my work clothes. I roll over, put my face in the pillow, and breathe it all in. Try to get a feel for him. Use it to get a read. But nothing is coming back. I can usually smell fear. But I can't here. He's an enigma.

I get out.

I feel like if I can't know him, I have to remind him he's beneath. Show him my control. Show him I was here, and I own him.

He's been getting close, but at the end of the day, he's just another pet I occasionally offer time and favour.

I take the thing out from my pants, and focus. Concentrate.

The urine begins to flow.

Territory.

I'm in your den, diver, right now, changing its scent.

Re-marking it as mine. Now for the bathroom. The bath is there. A snorkel lies on a small shelf at the bottom of it. He uses it a lot. I can tell.

Mother always told me I can pass two millilitres, at any time. She always made me pass urine, even when I didn't need to. And she was right. I always found just a little. And she's right this time too, as I leave a dribble in the bath.

The bathroom bin is packed with little foil wrappers. Medication blister packs. I read the labels. Shocking.

This isn't the way I wanted it. This isn't good enough. He's not supposed to be damaged too. He's not supposed to feel like a brother.

No... He's not. He's been getting close, involving himself. Because he's broken and he doesn't know any better. We are not the same. He's not like me. He wants to be like me, that's what this is. He's been coming for me. He'll never be me.

What happens when a lion takes over the pride, when it feels threatened? It kills everyone and everything, and starts afresh. That's the only way. But he's not here. So, what is there?

His territory. You don't just mark it. You destroy it, and in doing so, you destroy him.

I go downstairs. Switch on the hob. Fill this disgusting place with gas. Take a kitchen roll. Tie one end around the oven handle, then unravel it carefully, all the way through the utility room and out the back door. Yes, that's it. All the way across the grass, out to the cornfield.

I spark the end with the lighter, and let the thin paper gradually take light.

As long as there's still the slightest ember when it reaches that kitchen, it will do.

But I look around. I still want him to know it's me. That I was here. That he's nothing, yet still belongs to me.

If I still had my knife, I'd probably leave it here.

As a signature.

But it's gone and somehow I still mourn it.

I suppose blowing the entire place into the sky will have to do.

38

Cam woke to the sound of a phone ringing, and a dog barking. His senses gradually came round, and made order of the sights around him.

He was in the en suite of the master bedroom at Feather House. Sometime during the night, old habits had conspired to die hard, as he found himself alone in the bathtub with a drinking straw in his mouth. Nala was stood next to the tub, paws up on the rim of the bath, as he pulled his head out of the water.

'I'm here, love,' he said.

He grabbed the nearest towel, dried his hands, and picked the phone up from the bath-mat where he'd left it.

He didn't recognise the number.

'Mr Cameron Killick?' said the voice on the other end. Like the number, it was a voice he couldn't place.

'Yes, that's me.'

'I'm PC Anderson with Norfolk Constabulary.'

Cam found it strange that it was a random police officer getting in touch to update him on the Doke End case, not anyone he knew. His point of contact with the police had always been DS Rogers and he wondered, with a sudden clench of dread, whether she was all right.

'What's happened?' he said.

'What are your present whereabouts, Mr Killick?'

This was all sounding very portentous.

'I'm over in Thrigby. I got here last night about midnight-ish.'

'I'm afraid there's been an incident at your home Mr Killick. A fire.'

Cam's mind flashed to Haven Cottage, the home he had bought with his military pension. A symbol of his rebuild and a promise to himself of a new life here in Nelson's county.

'Is anyone hurt?' he asked, looking down at Nala, who glanced up at him expectedly.

'No injuries as far as we can tell, but the damage is extensive, I'm afraid. Can you get down here as a matter of urgency?'

'Of course.'

'Thank you. I'll let the attending officers and the fire service know that you're en route.'

'Thank you. I'll see you soon.' He said it on autopilot.

Cam was stunned.

What could have happened? It wasn't in an area of regular footfall. What had been in the house that could cause any damage if it ignited?

He had stepped out of the bath and was towelling himself properly dry, when there was a knock at the door. He covered himself with the towel and shouted through the thick wooden door.

'Yes?'

'Is everything all right?' It was Jess. They had gone to bed in separate rooms after their late-night buffet.

'Yes, I'm fine,' he said. 'Just give me a sec.' He pulled on his clothes from the floor by the bath and stepped out.

Jess was in the master bedroom, wearing a black, pin-striped nightshirt. The black reading glasses were back up in her tousled hair.

'That was the police,' Cam said, in a daze. 'It seems my house has burnt down.'

'What? How?' asked Jess with eyes blitzed wide with incredulity.

'I suppose that's the big question.'

Jess suddenly jumped up, started for the door. 'I'll take the day off. I want to come with you.'

She was a good 'un, thought Cam. 'Thank you.'

39

Amazingly, it was the first time that Jess had been in Cam's van, and she took a couple of minutes to make herself at home. 'Big enough for all your tat, I see,' she said, as she turned to glance at the cramped shelves and changing area in the back.

As Cam approached the familiar S-bend in the middle of Neatishead village, he could see things were immediately different. There were more people flitting about than usual, and it seemed a bit darker. Hazier. He looked up over the rooftops to see a column of grey smudge, almost like a dark watercolour smear across everything.

That sense of scale and damage only increased as Cam got closer to the farm track that Haven Cottage lay on. Greeting him at the track entrance was a police cordon, and he gave his name to the attending officer, who opened the fluttering tape barrier to allow him through.

Once on the bouncing, potholed mess of the drive, he could see the track itself was clogged by additional vehicles. Police squad cars and two large fire engines blocked off the entirety of the thoroughfare.

But Cam couldn't see his home. He couldn't see Haven Cottage.

He thought they'd parked in the wrong spot, but as he got closer, he saw a collection of small landmarks and characteristics that told him that, no, they were parked just where his home should be.

The hedge that stood tight to Haven Cottage didn't have anything looking over its shoulder.

There was no second floor to the property.

The roof was gone.

Haven Cottage was, for all intents and purposes, no more.

Cam felt Jess's hand rest upon his knuckles on the gear stick. Nala and Wicket now had their paws up on the dashboard too, looking out. Wicket was still excited, but Nala was quiet. Cam was sure she knew how wrong things were.

He pulled up behind the police cruisers, and immediately saw Mr Edwards, the owner of the farm at the far end. He broke away from the officers he was huddled with, and came over to the van, a couple of German Shepherds in tow. He held a hand out to Cam, who took it.

'I'm bloody glad you weren't there, mate,' he said, before looking down at Nala. 'You too, poppet.'

'Thanks, Jack,' said Cam, as the dogs acquainted themselves in the ashen haze. 'Any idea what happened?'

'Not mine to tell,' he said, 'but anyone with a thimbleful between the ears can see this is arson. They've told me nothing, but there's half a brain in here, don't you worry.'

Cam looked at the wreckage of his home.

Arson. Deliberate.

Jack patted a heavy hand on his shoulder. 'Of course, if you need anything, Killick, we're only down there. Me and Dolly, we'll look after you.' He cocked his flat cap at Jess, with a 'Miss', and walked back up the track.

Cam felt detachment as he walked dazily over to the open gate of his property. Haven Cottage was now nothing more than four brick corners standing guard over a blackened heap of rubble and charred wood.

'I don't know what to say,' said Jess, tracing his knuckle with her own thumb.

'Neither do I,' said Cam.

He was sorely shaken, and concerned – not least because the entirety of his meds were in that house, and he'd have to go and get more as soon as possible. He was doing well, but the knowledge of their presence was sometimes a source of strength.

But they were replaceable with a trip to the pharmacy.

He was here and he was safe – and so was Nala and so was Jess. Even Wicket, too.

He hadn't kept any medals.

He didn't want them.

His dress uniform, he'd given away long ago.

Everything Cam Killick was, was in the here and now – and everything he hoped his future could be – was by his side and at his feet. And that meant that everything was, in some way, OK.

The next hour went by in a whirl of questions ranging from Cam's whereabouts to anyone who might be upset with him, in answer to the latter of which he could say very little thanks to the Official Secrets Act and common sense. There were also such banalities as insurance details.

It gave Cam a curious sense of refreshment and of hope – if, of course, you could discount the obvious attack on his life. The investigating officer took him to the back door – or what was left of it. The stone frog was still there, soot blackened, but intact – save for one of its bug eyes now carrying a large chip.

Cam picked it up, blew on it and wiped it with his hands. It would be his only memento from the place. He left the exposed back key where it was. No one was going to need that any more.

'Fire started in here,' said the officer, guiding him via safe footsteps to the remains of the kitchen. 'A massive gas leak. When did you last use the cooker?'

'Not a clue,' answered Cam. 'I'm more of a microwave meal guy.'

'Well, cooker was all switched on and blew out. There's just something else. A bit of an… aberration.'

He walked Cam to the back of the garden, just before where the corn stalks stood tall, and pointed at an object on the ground. The man cleared his throat. 'That's not one of your dog's, is it?'

Cam looked at the shape. Made a quick assessment, and even though he was no biologist, he knew it wasn't canine. 'No, it's not.'

'So that's… well, that. And this coincides with an opening here in the corn.'

As he looked up, Cam saw it before the man could even point to it. It was a parting of the stalks. Like a game trail.

A track.

'What are you telling me, officer?'

'Have you ever noticed anyone watching your property?'

'No.'

'Follow me, sir.' The officer led Cam into the field, following a clear track.

It had been carefully made, and the stalks hadn't been snapped – not a single one. But they had been moved to the side. Cam thought about bloody ET again, and brushed it aside.

However, it was clear.

Something, or someone, had weaved its way through the corn to Cam's property.

They came upon a small clearing on a very slight rise, and the officer invited Cam to enter it – before pointing back towards the direction they'd come from. Cam did as he was told, and turned to look back.

It showed a perfect, unobscured view of the back of Cam's house.

'Someone's been keeping an eye on you,' said the officer. 'And judging by what he left in your garden, and what he did to your house, I'd say he was a very dangerous, unpredictable character.'

'I tend to agree,' said Cam – as a full wave of shivers ran up his spine and jangled his nerves like a broken xylophone.

The other night.

He'd sat on that very step, and felt unnerved. Like he was being observed.

He didn't want to think that whoever had done this might be the same person who had created the Grotto on Doke End – but coincidences would only stretch so far.

He shuddered again, so fiercely, his teeth chattered.

40

Cam stashed the stone frog on one of the shelves in the back of the van, scooting some regulators over to give it pride of place, before climbing back up front to the driver's seat. Jess and the dogs were already in place, looking at him expectantly. The human passenger offered a tight sympathetic smile, and Cam smiled back. He was sad, but he was alive. Those two facts could coexist, and would have to do.

He saw he had a missed call from Rogers, and rang her back. The Detective Sergeant picked up quickly, speaking against a backdrop of chatter.

'Have you heard the news?' Cam asked.

'I'm afraid so,' she replied. 'I'm so sorry, Killick. By the time it had got to me, you were already there.'

Cam filled her in on the scene, and the oddities.

'It's our man isn't it?' said Rogers.

'Yes,' Cam replied. 'He's been watching me.'

'I think you'd better come in. No arguments.'

Before Cam had even opened his mouth, Rogers hung up.

He looked at Jess, who nodded. She was along for the ride.

Cam took one last look at the pile of rubble, chalked it up as another fresh start incoming, and left. Jess held his hand all the way into Norwich, tracing circles on his knuckles, and they stopped only to get a drive-through McDonald's – coffees, muffins and a couple of sausage patties for the dogs, who promptly inhaled them without pausing for breath.

Then it was onwards to the police station. Cam hoped – pleaded – that there'd been some breakthroughs regarding the Doke End Grotto. It would spin his mind away from the uncertainty regarding his living situation – but he was now forming plans of his own. This adversary wasn't playing by the normal rules, not by a long shot, so to have any chance of catching him, Cam had to adopt a similar unconventionality.

He churned as he drove.

On arrival, they were quickly ushered through by the desk sergeant who had been briefed that they were coming. Before they knew it, they were taken directly back up to the actual incident room, as opposed to the creaking side room at Cockshot Sailing Club.

Rogers was at a central table again, alongside a few other plain clothes officers, who Cam guessed were Norfolk CID.

'There's a coffee machine down the hall,' said Rogers, looking up from a jumble of printouts.

Cam and Jess simply raised their own fresh take-out cups.

'Well, la-de-fucking-da,' said Rogers.

'You know Jess don't you?' said Cam, stepping aside so that Jess and Rogers could shake hands.

'Of course,' said Rogers, 'it's good to see you again, Jess.' The two smiled at each other in that way people do at funerals. Nice to see each other, but the circumstances were regrettable. 'You still hanging about with this idiot?'

'Yes,' said Jess, 'And he's a proper good times-magnet isn't he?'

'If by good times you mean shit, I tend to agree.'

Cam ignored her and the jibe and tried to take in all the new information. Crime scene photographs had been printed out and put on screen dividers around the central table. There were many grim pictures of the cadavers, both in place and in the sterile setting of a mortuary slab.

He looked at Jess, who was now studiously looking at the floor.

There were coats thrown in corners, ties pulled off. Cam could tell that everyone in this room, and a lot of other people besides, had been very busy overnight – and that consideration for those not in their present train of thought was notably absent.

'So go on then,' said Rogers. 'What happened at your place?'

Cam shrugged. 'Best they can tell me is that it was arson… and someone has been watching my house. Whoever it was decided to act last night, but we don't know whether they were hoping to catch me in there or not. But the place… there's only a few bits of the ground floor still standing.'

Rogers paused to take that in, before glancing up at him earnestly. 'I am sorry, Cam.'

'Don't be. It'll be OK. I'm alive. Jess is all right too. All that really matters isn't it?'

Rogers actually rolled her eyes. 'Oh, what a surprise the two tormented souls are getting romantic.'

Cam couldn't help but smile. She was back. But his smile was punctured when Rogers continued.

'You've got plenty of time together, if she chooses to go with you.'

'Where to?'

'Protective custody. I would have thought that would be obvious.'

'You're kidding, aren't you?'

'That arson attempt last night was an attack on your life, Killick.'

'He knew I wasn't there.'

'Who?' Rogers put a hand on her hip. 'Who, Cam? Who is this person? That's right, we've got no bloody idea. And that was a warning, to you, to back off. You got too close to him, and when he finds out he didn't get you, then he'll most likely come back. And next time you might not be out.'

'But that's exactly what I want him to do,' said Cam, his own voice rising in pitch, and he realised with acute queasiness that other people in the room had started to watch the brewing argument. The plans he'd concocted had taken shape in the van, but he had to finish them off on the fly. 'I want to hunker down somewhere and lure him in.'

'That might work in Jean-Claude Van Damme movies – who knows, maybe you can even do the splits – but we are not doing that as a sensible and thorough police force. You need protecting. It's not that hard to get your head around.'

Cam was simmering with anger, and the sudden impotence of the situation. They wanted to bench him. 'I'm not just going to sit at home and do nothing.'

'Jolly right, you're not sitting at home,' said Rogers. 'Your bloody home got burned down by this lunatic. We need to set you up somewhere, sensible, and proper – and keep you there until this is solved.'

'I can catch him,' said Cam, and as the words left his lips, he realised he truly believed them. 'He's a psychopath, and he's loose. We don't have Jessup, we don't know his plan. We've got no idea what he's gonna do next. I can't leave this lunatic on the streets.'

'You're right,' said Rogers firmly. 'He's one of the sickest minds we've come across, and this is one of the most troublesome crimes I can think of. This man is dangerous and looking for you – and as much as you don't care about your safety, Cam, those around you do.'

Cam felt Jess's hand on his arm. 'Maybe she's right,' she said, looking up at him.

He softened, in an instant.

'Bloody hell,' said Rogers. 'At last, someone that can control him.'

Cam ignored her, and instead stared into Jess's eyes. 'I'll go with you,' she said.

He sighed exasperatedly.

'We've got a place we can put you,' said Rogers. 'A safe location on the edge of Norwich. We can sit you both there, that dog of yours as well, until we catch him.'

'Two,' he said.

'What?'

'Two dogs.'

Rogers huffed. 'Fine, two dogs.'

Cam softly shook his head. He hated this. Just hated it. 'When do we go?'

She pulled out a chair at the table. 'Right after you sit down and tell these fine people absolutely everything that you know about this person, and that horrible hole in Doke End. OK?'

Cam looked at the table and the faces around it. They were tired, but eager, and Cam could practically smell the air of commitment on them. It was a stay of execution of some kind, and at least it would satisfy the urge to help in the short term.

Behind him, there was a knock on the door.

'Come in,' shouted Rogers.

Into the room came a woman with long chestnut hair tied in a bun, wearing jeans and a navy down jacket. 'Chilly down this corner of the country, isn't it?' she said. The woman looked at Rogers and clearly made a guess. 'DS Rogers?'

'Yes – you're our specialist?' Rogers said, stepping forward to shake hands.

The woman had sharp eyes, and a nose that had been broken and reset more than once. She carried herself with animal grace, coiled and ready.

'Indy Macaluso,' she said. 'I'm the BIA from the NCA.'

'That's one too many acronyms for me to handle,' said Rogers.

'Sorry,' said Macaluso. 'The Behavioural Investigative Adviser from the National Crime Agency. Sorry, been travelling through the night to get here. Bit frazzled.'

'I hope the A-roads behaved themselves. Your areas of expertise?'

'Predictive profiling, prioritisation matrices, unknown offender assessment, all the good stuff.'

'Then we're very lucky to have you. Indy, this is Cam Killick – he's our diver who found Doke Grotto.'

Macaluso shook Cam's hand. 'Then I suppose I've got a lot of questions for you,' she said.

Rogers motioned to the table, and they all sat. Cam, for now, was going to play ball as best he could – putting aside his disquiet at being isolated and placed into protective custody, in favour of the greater good.

Because for now, the greater good was getting this maniac off the streets.

And the best way to do that was to help this team in this room.

41

Cam sat directly opposite Macaluso, and listened while the CID team took it in turns to bring her up to speed on everything that had happened the last few days. She took copious notes, and also placed her phone on the desk to record the conversation. She listened in silence, for the most part, but radiated an air of astuteness and focus that by themselves gave the investigation a much-needed shot in the arm.

Cam listened and felt in a lot of ways out of his depth with a lot of the terms used, but he did recognise some of the phrases from Ferris and Gupta's conversations on their *Norfolk Unexplained* podcast – particularly when the topic moved to the real outliers of human behaviour. Macaluso finally spoke, clearly and concisely.

'What we are talking about is the kind of psychopath who has gone past a certain point of control in their behaviour. There are approximately a million of them on Planet Earth at any given time, but these people are, for want of a better word, unicorns.'

She chopped her gaze between every person in the room, switching burning eye contact with each, as they listened to her spell out their quarry in no uncertain terms.

'The mind responsible here has his — and it is almost always a *his* — own concept of right and wrong. His own conscience and morals, with no real sense of consequences. No real sense of time, even. This person is not motivated by money, nor greed, nor jealousy. He is most likely motivated by the most animal and base of instincts. Sex might play a part here, but it is not his sole motivator. If he does find himself aroused, he won't want to be. He'll live a life of binaries. Things will be either positive or negative in relation to his own specific set of goals. But the fact he has lashed out at Mr Killick suggests a real anger, and a sense of retribution. He's been provoked, offended even, and this… arson of Mr Killick's home is his retaliation.'

She stood and moved around to the grotesque gallery at the end of the table.

'There is nothing random or haphazard or coincidental about any of this. If there is a pattern to his killing — which there clearly is — he would ordinarily continue along a similar vein. But he can't. You,' she pointed at Cam, 'discovered his grotto. His grand plan has either been ruined or it will have to change. He might even be finished, his game complete, but we won't know that until we've found Jessup or established the pattern behind his plan. If he's not done, the specificity of his behaviour — the mode of killing and keeping them in his underwater pantry to name just two — makes me think he'll keep on with his mission until it is complete.

'The three men in that grotto are connected, although, aside from Drummond and Forrester being friends, we don't know how — this is not random opportunism. Keeping their bodies suggested he wanted to savour their deaths. They are sacred to him, in some way. We need to find out who the third body is, and found out just how

269

many are in this group – which in essence is his kill list. This group most likely includes Jessup. When the group is eliminated, this man, this perpetrator, will most likely disappear. Mission complete. And now, to complicate matters, Mr Killick has clearly been added to the agenda. Although whether he's made himself part of the group to be killed is unknown.'

Rogers looked at Cam and Cam nodded grimly. Catching this guy was a huge priority and Cam was desperate, simply desperate, to set himself up as bait.

'But what about the fire,' said Rogers. 'Burning is a new one for him, and doesn't fit his pattern.'

'No, but I think that could fit with another part of the pattern and characteristics. I can only imagine that him acting out in this way is a direct response to this new variable in Mr Killick. Whatever Cam Killick did, he changed the game. And in changing the game, he changed the rules. In doing so he bought a haphazardness from our mystery man. And of course, he left his DNA at the scene.'

No one in the room needed to ask or confirm that Macaluso was referring to the shit they'd found by the cornfield at the back of Cam's house.

Macaluso moved on. 'You prompted something animal in him. Animals mark their territory with scat. I get the impression that you destroyed his territory, by discovering it and alerting the police. He then, in turn, destroys your territory, and then goes one further by claiming its wreckage. And burning is a very efficient way of destroying territory. In that sense, while it's a new tool for him, it fits his overall profile.'

'Taking a shit fits his overall profile,' said Rogers. 'I'll make sure to get that down.'

'Scat,' clarified Macaluso. 'This man... he's one complicated individual.'

Cam cleared his throat and tried to be as direct and confident as he could. 'Why don't we use his anger towards me to turn him away from the public. Put him on to me, let him come to me, and let's catch him.'

Rogers looked at him and rolled her eyes. 'We've had this discussion, Killick.'

'And it's the best option to keep people safe,' Cam countered.

'Good effort, but no. You're still going to the safe house.'

Cam looked at Jess, who nodded at him. Her orders, he would listen to.

He nodded back to her, but there was no heart in the gesture. He now felt properly useless. He was another pair of hands that could be out there hunting for this guy, but instead he was being rendered impotent.

'What do all your acronyms suggest we do now?' asked Rogers. 'No offence.'

Macaluso addressed the whole room. 'The answers will come from this room. The answers will be in the detail. The men in that grotto had a connection to our killer. You whittle down that connection and he'll be there at the end of it.'

The room went quiet for a moment, with only the thrum of the traffic outside – but the crackle was there. There was direction and charge to proceedings – but Cam was on the outside. Unless...

'Can I at least stay in here and help throughout the day?' asked Cam. 'Send me off at bedtime, something like that?'

Macaluso turned to Rogers, and said: 'This is your show.'

Rogers leaned forward. 'For the last time, no. I will not have injury to you on my conscience or anybody else's. And if you ask me one more time, I'll keep you so far out of this investigation that you'll find out what happened via the twentieth anniversary Channel 5 docudrama. Got it?'

Cam, at last, got it.

42

An unmarked convoy was waiting for Cam and Jess in the police station car park, after they had been escorted out by two burly officers. Cam was agitated just walking between them. He felt handcuffed and devalued, all at once. Wicket and Nala were delighted to see their owners as they arrived, and even more delighted when it seemed that they were going on yet another merry road trip together. Cam and Jess joined the ecstatic canines in the van, and followed the unmarked silver Mondeo out to the ring road and then off out of Norwich city centre.

'Well, this is novel,' said Jess.

Cam said nothing. He thought all this a waste of time and, when he was perfectly able to defend himself, more than a bit stupid.

They were barely out of the city when the bustle thinned out and they were suddenly pulling up at the Town House Hotel, on such a sleepy bend of the river that even the geese announced their presence in an altogether quieter fashion.

They followed the police escort into the car park, out of sight from the main road, and parked up by the water. It was a long, brick affair that seemed like three different buildings had been conjoined at some intersection in history.

Jess suddenly sat straight. 'Wait a minute, I know this place.' She span in her seat, looking at the well-appointed rear aspect of the pub and hotel. 'Yes, one of the Krays died here. Reggie, I think. He was allowed out on compassionate grounds with days to live, and he died here with his wife by his side.'

Cam knew the story, but didn't know the building. 'He was with Brown Bread Fred too, wasn't he?' *Norfolk Unexplained*, coming up trumps again.

The atmosphere was still and loaded, as they got out of the car. The police officer driving the Mondeo joined them.

'We'll be out here,' he said, already assessing the perimeter with cautious eyes.

Cam nodded, knowing he himself would be assessing the perimeter before too long – that is, if Jess would let him out of her sight.

Not that it was a bad thing, he had to concede. She was attentive and caring. She was looking after him, and her company was a balm on his fried, exhausted state. Plus, a night in a hotel with Jess Tabernacle could only be a good thing, right?

But the fact that he was inhibited in his movements, especially when he was under so much scrutiny, scared him. He was used to being able to move, drop everything, just go, in half a heartbeat. His head started to ache with the instructions he'd been given, and the fact that while this hotel was clearly lovely, and company even lovelier, he was essentially trapped. He hated the thought, and it started to prompt more agitation. He had spare meds in the car, and would have to take some, if he was going to get through the night without going bananas.

They didn't waste any time waiting outside and entered the lobby area, where a manager was waiting for them in a pencil skirt and a blouse that said, 'Don't spill curry on me.'

'Killick?' she said.

'I hope you've got something dog-friendly.'

'On this occasion, I think that's fine.'

The hotel was quiet, with very little footfall or obvious signs of activity. The only residents were likely the anglers who sat out the front, enjoying the stretch of river doused in sunshine that promised a hot spring – even if it couldn't manage extending it into the summer.

They were shown into a functional and well-appointed room.

'Think he died in this one?' said Cam.

The dogs immediately sprinted and threw themselves on the bed itself, unable to contain their joy at the new setting, the new adventure, and just being together.

Then Wicket promptly squatted, curled his back and—

'No!' shouted Jess, shooing the hound off the bedspread. 'I'd best take them out for a quick break I think.'

'We've been in the room about eight seconds,' said Cam. 'I'm sure that would have set a new record for hotel room desecration.'

His humour was a front, however – and a bad one at that. He looked around, and it felt like nothing more than a prison cell, albeit in shades of coral and magnolia.

Yep, I'm gonna go mad in here, he thought. He decided to attack it.

'Jess, listen… I… I can't stay here. I'm not asking you to get in trouble or anything, but I cannot stay and stare at these four walls. Not while there's a killer out there and I can help.'

Jess stood firm, and cocked her hip out. 'Do I have to full name you?'

'What do you mean?'

'Cameron Killick, do I have to full name you?' She said again, but there was a twinkle in her eye.

Cam sighed and sat on the edge of the bed. 'Yes, ma'am.'

'At ease, soldier,' she said, as she took the dogs to the door with a smile.

43

When the breakthrough came, it came with the imme-
diacy and polite intrusion of a very large bomb.

Rogers and Indy Macaluso were at one end of the table
going through a series of behavioural charts which left
Rogers' head both in tatters and swamped with fear. Time
was ticking by, and they seemed further than ever from
connecting the victims to a viable suspect. Worse still was
the notion that their spectre-like killer had been provoked
into changing his usual habits, making him doubly unpredictable and doubly dangerous.

Then, she saw it.

'Look!' she shouted, and she jumped up as if she'd just
discovered the theory of relativity. She marched to the
wall and the array of morgue photos upon it, and pointed
at one particular picture. 'It's there!'

'What's there?' said Macaluso, as she walked up to look
for herself at the photo of an empty eye socket. 'Who is
that?'

'Our John Doe. The unidentified third victim in the
Grotto,' Rogers said. She went back to the table, and
grabbed the trusty tablet which had become a third
hand in the last forty-eight hours. She shuffled through

documents and soon found the one she was looking for. 'The pathologist's report – here, in any historical scars or injuries, Black noted a grazing of the orbital bone.' She thrust the tablet under Macaluso's nose.

'So?'

'This victim has an old eye wound. A string of abrasions and scarring behind the right cornea. Essentially, the back wall of the eye was peppered with a very particular pattern of indentations. Left this guy's cornea unique like a fingerprint.'

'Where had they come from?'

'The coroner had no idea, but he photographed it. It reminded me of the pigeons my old man used to shoot.'

'You're losing me here.'

'Dad's an old country guy, used to take me on bird shoots. I'd have to pick up the birds, pop them in a basket.'

'Don't dogs usually do that?'

'He was allergic, and his doting daughter was the best alternative. They used to have a similar set of entry wounds from the bird shot he used. So, I had a look online. Found an archived article. *Eastern Daily Gazette*. Twenty years ago. Boy survives being shot in the head.' Rogers whizzed her fingers on the screen and held up another image, this time of an old front page. 'Group of scouts on a pigeon shoot. One of the boys at the back got excited, turned and pulled the trigger – right in another lad's face.'

'Bloody hell,' said Macaluso.

'The shotgun went off, and sent a load of pellet up behind his eyeball, scarring his orbital bone and cornea.'

'And he survived this?'

'Yes – and according to the article, he was awake through the surgery to get the shot out, could remember getting a good look down his front with one eye while the other eye was looking forward. They saved his sight and the eye.'

'Miracle of medicine,' said Macaluso.

'Which means we might have an identification. If it's the same guy, our third victim in the Grotto is Gareth Binns.'

Within a couple of seconds, keys were tapping all over the room, nobody needing telling twice that the identity of Gareth Binns needed pulling apart immediately.

'That's Binns with two 'n's, people,' Rogers said, as she tapped a couple more buttons and her tablet screen was suddenly mirrored up on the flatscreen TV.

The screen was a whirl of headlines, articles and front pages alike.

Local boy shot in head – survives!
Norwich boy survives hunting accident.

Then suddenly on the screen in technicolour was Gareth Binns, a young lad, but very alive.

'Let's find something more recent,' she said. She opened Facebook, to the feed page for the dummy account she had set up to crawl for information. She seemed to know exactly what she was looking for.

She typed the name in the search bar, set the filters to local, and picked the top profile.

The room was quiet for a couple of moments while a handful of photographs came up on the screen, each of Gareth Binns in various profile pictures. It was him. Even the rough facial structure was the same. They mowed through a quick cavalcade and a potted history of his various life events in the last couple of years until they hit something that made Rogers pause.

'*That,*' she said.

It was a swimming pool.

She had seen it before.

'We are getting somewhere,' said Macaluso.

'Let me just find the album,' said Rogers, flicking through the Facebook thumbnails.

And then suddenly there it was. The room stilled in an instant, all eyes on the screen.

Incontrovertible evidence.

Forrester, Binns, Drummond. The three dead friends together – with two others. By that pool on some holiday abroad. Sun hats and bad tans.

One of the two others was Tommy Jessup.

A group of five.

The caption underneath said, 'Mates for life.'

Another said, 'Thirty years strong.'

And just below that were the names of the people tagged in the picture.

Ryan Forrester, Tommy Jessup, Gareth Binns, Leonard Drummond and Ken Conroy.

'Now that,' Rogers said, 'is a breakthrough.'

44

Cam was upside down when Rogers called.

Jess had taken the dogs for a longer walk, and to get a few things from a local supermarket megastore, the kind of place Cam went out of his way to avoid – so he'd been left to his own increasingly frantic devices.

He'd paced, tried the TV, turned it off again, paced some more. He tried breathing exercises, did a two-minute plank, and was halfway through standing on his head for real.

He simply couldn't forget that there was a killer.

Twisted and warped.

Out there.

And he was prohibited from doing anything about it.

Cam righted himself, answered the phone and tried his best to keep all traces of sulk out of his voice. It was fooling no one.

'I know you don't like being on the outside, Cam,' said Rogers. 'And I can only imagine what you are doing to keep from going fully postal in that room. Call it courtesy, call it pity, but I thought I'd give you an update to keep your mind occupied.' Cam could feel in her voice that there was news coming – and he was quickly proven right. 'We found them. We've identified the group.'

Cam was suddenly ramrod straight, tasered by excitement. 'Who have you got?'

'We've got IDs on the three from the Grotto and they're part of a group of five.'

'So, there's two more?'

'That's right.'

'And Tommy Jessup is one of them, right?'

'Correct – and according to Macaluso, with Jessup already dead somewhere, that makes four out of five gone. Which makes one more to complete the puzzle.'

'Who's number five?'

'A guy called Ken Conroy.'

'We have to find him.'

'Ahem,' Rogers coughed theatrically.

'You…' Cam clarified. 'You have to find him.'

'Correct again. We've started. His house is empty. And he's not at work.'

'He's gone to ground. Your four best mates go missing, you get out of there.'

'That's what I'm thinking,' said Rogers. 'We've set up a stake-out on Doke End too, see if he comes back. Team on the water, out of sight. If he comes back, we'll have him.'

Cam was quiet.

'What?' said Rogers.

'I don't think he will.'

Now Rogers went quiet. 'Neither do I.'

'Come on Sergeant—'

Rogers interrupted. 'Don't even say it.'

'God damn it.'

Cam almost couldn't handle it any more. The frustration was kicking his anxiety into its higher gears. Being rendered useless was like having a gradually tightening noose around his neck.

'The police with you at the hotel aren't just there to keep you safe – they've also got a remit to keep you in,' Rogers said. Cam fell silent. 'Just stay put, get drunk or something and watch TV.'

'Message begrudgingly received and understood,' Cam said. 'And Rogers... I am grateful for the update.'

'Stay put.'

Rogers hung up.

Cam tossed the phone aside and threw his head back on the bed. He lay there and stared at the ceiling.

His innards were volcanic. He'd had his meds, but all they were doing was giving a different flavour and dimension to his agitation. Like trying to take apart a flaming bike while your hands are encased in oven mitts – the novelty was a distraction, and technically you weren't getting burned, but you weren't getting anywhere with the bike either.

He started his breathing exercises again. Tried to bring stillness and relaxation to his extremities, tried to fuse his blood with oxygenated warmth and calm.

All Cam could think of was a maniac killer, in the shadows, with a list of five names with four ticked off. It was only a matter of time before he surfaced to close the circle, before disappearing forever, his job done. He grabbed the remote, switched on the TV, but the abrupt beeps and lights from the aimless game show that appeared offered no solace or company – only ear-bleeding annoyance.

He thought about what else he could do to try to bring calm back, running through his repertoire of tricks – but everything he brought to mind was either useless or annoyed him before he had even got the chance to try it. He began to feel a bit like he was swirling in a bowl, getting deeper, as if he was on a downhill course in a vast drain of anxiety.

If Jess didn't get here soon, he'd go spare, he just knew it.

Jess. This was his chance with her. To show her the real him.

He got up and looked in the mirror, at his hair and stubble. He hadn't shaved in a few days now.

Why was it so long? Why did he look this way? Could he not have made an effort?

And then he realised that this was his own brain finding tricks to play on him yet again. He reached for a toothbrush – he could at least brush his teeth – but realised quickly that it was part of the emergency shopping trip that Jess had gone on – it wasn't even here yet.

The hotel room was getting smaller, he was sure of it.

He went to the window and looked out. The sun was dipping now, the day drawing to a close, and he wondered how on earth he would survive the night just sitting here.

Where on earth was Jess?

He started to pace again.

He started to make himself a coffee, but then realised that the extra caffeine would be no good.

He turned on the television again and cycled through the five channels over and over and over again, but every single thing on them made his teeth itch.

Nala wasn't even here to help him, her usual ability of sensing what he needed absent. Just looking at her usually calmed him down, gave him a sense of value and worth.

But even that was no longer present.

He was gasping, although he was only half aware of it. Everything inside the skin of his torso felt like bugs trying to escape. He listened out into the corridor, putting his ear against the door. He didn't know if the police guard was out there, but the silence outside was a crashing animal in its obnoxiousness.

Where are you, Jess?

Wherever Ken Conroy was, the killer was too. Lurking somewhere nearby, waiting to strike.

He had to get out. He walked over to the bedside table and took out the hotel notepad and paper.

He wrote a note and felt terrible about every word. He read it over three times until he felt it was the best of a bad situation.

It read:

Jess, I'm sorry I can't wait any more in this room. I have to get out there and do something. Please forgive me. Call me when you get back.

He knew this was a betrayal of trust, and a terrible way to progress any kind of relationship that he hoped to have with Jess. It was the worst possible start he could give them – if the start hadn't already been unimaginably bad. But Cam felt in all truth that a serial killer loose on the streets was bigger than any relationship between two people. He prayed that Jess could understand that.

Feeling like the worst human being on Planet Earth, he turned the television up, picked that mindless game show once more because it seemed the noisiest of the bunch, and listened at the door.

Nothing.

He sneaked back to the window, opened it and looked out.

The dew was already beginning to assemble on the lawn.

He climbed out, dropped to the soft, wet grass and slipped into the night.

45

As Cam marched, he muttered to himself angrily. He couldn't shake the feeling he was throwing away a chance at happiness with Jess Tabernacle by letting her down like this. He knew that by thinking this way, he was connecting an awful lot of dots that hadn't even been dreamt of yet but, such was his fried mental state, he couldn't help it. Nevertheless, it did feel better to be out and moving, even though he'd gone rogue.

As soon as he was within Norwich's ancient city walls, he grabbed the first taxi he saw, and instructed the driver to take him back to Neatishead. He wanted to look at the clearing behind his house. The spot in the cornfield where this beast had watched his movements.

From the backseat, he called Gupta, who answered on the very first ring, even though darkness had long since fallen. 'I was wondering when you'd call. I sent you a message, but you didn't reply.'

Of course, Cam thought. The Grotto would have hit the public news channels by now.

'I'm sorry,' he said. 'My house burned down.'

'If you're going to make a stupid excuse, at least make sure it's a good one.'

Cam didn't correct her, but caught her up on all the latest developments, then got straight to the point. 'I need to know everything you can get on Ken Conroy,' he said.

'You're going to be on the naughty step here, aren't you?' said Gupta.

Cam was trying not to think about it, his betrayal of both Rogers' and Jess's trust, and how he'd have to go solo for a while, without leaning on Rogers and her resources. Still, that was what Gupta was for. 'I know we're so close to ending this thing – there's one more name to go. I'm far more use out here than I am in there.'

'I do see your logic, but please don't tell Rogers I agreed with you.'

'So if you were Conroy and you were on the run, where would you go?'

'Let me have a look. See if there's anywhere he could lay low for a while. Maybe a second property, who knows.'

'Got it. In the meantime, I'm going to head back to my old place, and work through the tracks in the field. Maybe I'll see something someone else hasn't.'

They ended the call with Gupta promising she'd get back to him as soon as she had anything to report, and Cam half-heartedly promising he'd sort out his poor communication skills.

Within half an hour, Cam found himself standing in the charred husk of his old home.

Those four corners were still standing up to six or seven feet or so and it was like wandering around in the barest pieces of a huge, fossilised rib cage. His floor – or what was left of it – was strewn with rubble, and he stood in what used to be his living room, taking stock.

He was insured, that was no trouble, but the cost and effort of a rebuild was something he wasn't sure he wanted to embark on. If anything, being here tonight gave him something different, something he didn't expect.

That something was closure.

This had been a great home for him, the perfect base from which to build a new chapter of his life – but there was no necessity for it any more, simply by virtue of the fact it wasn't there any more.

It had gone.

And with it that chapter was gone too.

He was decided.

Whatever happened, in the coming hours, days and weeks, he was going to start afresh somewhere.

He left the building for what he imagined would be the final time and made his way to the field at the back. He knew that the trail would be tough to follow in the dark, but he wanted to see where it began, and in finding its start point, he wanted to glean what insight he could, by standing in the monster's footsteps.

Tracking carefully, he went through the field and soon found himself back at the clearing the killer had watched him from. He looked back to the remains of Haven Cottage, and shuddered at the thought of sitting on the back step, eating a sandwich, oblivious to who – what – was watching him like a predator monitoring its prey. The word *predator* made the hairs on his neck stand up so rigidly it felt as if they were trying to fold in on themselves. That was exactly the word for him. He was animal in nature and make up.

Another word that sprang to mind was *territory*.

Macaluso, the profiler, had used it.

The predator hadn't entered Cam's territory until it was time to strike. Instead, he had observed from neutral ground until he decided to come and make the claim.

It was trampled down, and the stalks crackled loudly as he stood on them. When he got to the centre, he span in place, looking at the circular wall of corn until he found it.

At the back of the small enclave was the faint glimmer of parting between the stalks.

He carefully looked through.

Another path. Leading away.

He pushed through, and started to follow it.

He was sure the police would have seen this – you couldn't really miss it, in daylight especially – but Cam's own curiosity needed satisfying at the very least.

He wanted to walk in this killer's shoes.

It wound away to the back of the field.

Cam knew what was there. No man with his record or training would ever live somewhere without having a full grasp of the perimeter. There was a tree line about ten metres deep, an apple orchard before it hit a gorse hedge behind it. Beyond that was another access track for the next farm along, representing their outer perimeter.

As he walked, his phone buzzed. A text, from Jess. He held his breath.

I'm disappointed and hurt, but I understand. I'll hold onto the dogs. Don't get killed.

The idea he'd hurt Jess was a knife through *his* heart, never mind anyone else's. He pocketed the phone, and carried on walking.

As expected, it didn't take long for him to hit the black-ened trees. The darkness within the tangled branches swallowed everything. He'd come prepared, and clicked on his dive torch. He started scanning the floor. The area was not often used by anything bigger than a muntjac deer – but now Cam saw that the overgrown grass had been parted by something much larger. Jack Edwards up at the farm had sworn that the talk of Norfolk big cats was true – so had Gupta and Ferris. This looked like a huge predator of a different kind. These fronds had been parted to allow access for something larger, something man-sized. Cam felt the buzz of his pulse quicken.

He followed the trail backwards through the trees which now traced along the side of the hedge. Whoever had been doing this had been quick, methodical and nimble, cat-like. Then… jackpot.

There, in the mud, was a boot print.

Cam froze.

It was large – larger than his own size ten.

This boot must be a size fourteen, meaning that statistically, whoever was after him had to be around six foot four, maybe even six-five.

You'd spot him in a crowd, that's for sure, thought Cam.

It would also mean, however, that he was quite the adversary.

The beast was taking shape.

Cam took a quick photo on his phone and kept following, eventually coming to the end of the hedgerow where a small fence stood. The man must have gone over it, and sure enough, there were flecks of mud on the iron bars.

There you go. Cam was getting a handle on their mystery killer. Walking his trail *was* giving him insight and feeling.

The phone rang, nearly blasting Cam out of his own boots with shock.

He worried he was in for an ear-bashing from Rogers, and didn't think he was ready for that yet.

He was therefore quite relieved to see it was Gupta.

'I've got somewhere you could check out,' she said.

Cam stood there in an errant shaft of blue moonlight, transfixed. 'Go for it.'

'All five of those men are the names on the lease of a snooker club in North Walsham.'

Cam's breath caught in his throat. That could be a perfect place to lay low. 'You're a bit of a genius, Gupta,' he said. 'Can you send me the address?'

'It'll be with you by the time I hang up. Oh, and it was Ferris who found this one.'

'Then please pass my thanks on, if she'll accept it.'

'She'll call you something unhelpful.'

Cam smiled. 'I imagine she might.'

46

Darting back through the corn stalks, now softly smoul-
dering blue in the moonlight, Cam checked his watch,
activating the glow-in-the-dark dial.

It was 9.30 p.m.

He retraced his steps, sprinting now. He didn't care
what he disturbed – he'd seen enough. Facts were at last
falling into place.

There was a monster of a man who wanted Ken
Conroy – and he just might be at the snooker hall.

Did this killer know about the group's business interest?
Who knew. But Cam simply had to get to Conroy first.

It didn't take him long, fuelled by adrenaline, and he
was soon running straight past the rubble of his home, on
up to the farm at the end of the track.

As soon as he entered the farmyard, gasping, German
Shepherds started barking from somewhere unseen.

Within a couple of moments, the back door of the
farmhouse opened, before Cam had even had the chance
to knock, and Jack Edwards stepped out. He was in a dressing gown and a flat cap, with a shotgun over his shoulder.
The dogs stood quietly by his knees, obediently waiting
for instruction.

'Bloody hell, Cam,' Edwards said, when he recognised his neighbour.

'I'm so sorry to wake you up,' said Cam. 'You said if there was anything I needed... well, I need something right now.'

'You pick your moments, don't you.'

'Is there anything I could use to get to North Walsham?'

Edwards looked off down the track and then back at Cam, his eyes narrowed by suspicion. 'Do I want to know what this is about?'

'Probably not.'

Edwards huffed, and retreated into the house for a couple of moments. He emerged with a small key on a battered leather key ring, and tossed it to Cam. 'Might not be ideal, but my old Norton is in the third barn at the back. If there's any chance it can come back in one piece, I'd be grateful.'

Cam held the keys up, and nodded. 'I'll do everything I can to get it back with you tomorrow – and thank you.'

'Go easy on the throttle, she's quite a bit older than you.'

Cam soon found the barn, counting as he ran past the hunkered blocks in the dark. He threw the huge doors open to find an array of abandoned machinery, most of it tired and rusted.

But there in between them all was an ATV – and a motorbike, black paint and chrome. A faded decal on the side of its fuel tank read 'Norton Commando'.

It was perfect. Cam felt a quick adrenal fizz, as he jumped aboard.

He burst into North Walsham in a combined barrage of a screaming 750cc engine and a screech of tyres that he suspected weren't exactly road-legal.

The address Gupta had sent him was on Main Street, the central spine of this quiet market town. What Cam knew about North Walsham could be put on the back of a postcard, mainly because there was no waterway running through it, therefore no work reason to visit.

Rack, the name of the snooker hole, was written in block letters which stood proudly across the top floor of a row of shops. Cam went past the front, and saw there was no front entrance, and it was dead, no lights glowing in the upstairs windows. But then again if you were the last person on a killer's wish list, you'd keep it dark as well.

Cam parked the bike at the end of the street in the neon wash of a bookie's garish shopfront. He retraced back up the street on foot, ducked down a side alley to approach from the rear. There was a tiny back lot below a metal stairway that led up to the establishment's door. He hopped up the steps on the balls of his feet, although the soft tings of his shoes still echoed across the soaked back alleyways.

A little porch stood at the top of the stairs, again fully darkened. Cam stood on the raised platform and tried to peer inside, but a black curtain was lowered across the PVC door, rendering all visibility zero.

Instead of giving up, he reached into his pocket for those trusty petrol flap pliers.

It didn't take him long before he was in.

He stepped into a small reception area cloaked in shadows, past a small desk with a till, and was suddenly in what looked like a converted office space with four snooker tables in it.

It stank of old ale spills and cigarettes, and at one end, a dim bar sat dormant while the drinks fridges glowed softly beyond.

There was no one here.

Cam headed towards the back and, as he moved, heard the whistle before he even saw what was happening.

The soft breath of something flying through the air.

Instinctively, he ducked and moved backwards in the same motion, away from the source of the sound, and at the same time, lifted his right arm up to shield his head.

A snooker cue swung out of nowhere and caught him on the underside of his right bicep, but he'd caught enough to dull the blow.

Cam pinched his arm down quickly and caught the cue mid-strike, trapping it in his elbow. He then span one-eighty, twisting his entire body weight, pulling the cue with all his might forward.

The makeshift weapon was ripped from its owner's hand.

And Cam stood up to face his assailant.

But confusion hit him with more force than any pool cue could – because standing in front of him, living and breathing, was a tired, scared Tommy Jessup.

47

Rogers laid into him as soon as she picked up the phone. 'You blistering idiot.'

'I know I'm in trouble, but I think you might forgive me.'

'Unless you're about to deliver me Richard Gere in his white suit on a silver platter, I don't think so.'

'I've got someone here you're going to want to talk to.'

'And who might that be?' said Rogers. 'You know we're working hard as we can here, all of us, and you're pissing about jeopardising your own health and the general public's. Not only that, you might just put the mockers on this entire investigation—'

Cam breathed in and interrupted. 'I'm stood here with Tommy Jessup.'

The line went quiet for a moment.

'Stood?' said Rogers, eventually. 'What, are we talking like *Weekend at Bernie's*?'

'No – it seems we've got things a bit wrong.'

'And he's living?'

'Yes, he is.'

Rogers was quiet for a moment before she remembered what Cam had done. 'You are in a lot of trouble. You understand that, don't you? Not just from me.'

Jess. Cam winced. 'Understood, but I'm afraid we're going to need picking up.'

'Yet again, Killick, you've found a way to make sure words fail me,' Rogers said, before the line went dead.

Cam pocketed the phone, and sighed, leaning back on the steps behind Rack. Jessup was staring at him, with wide eyes and a backpack over his shoulder. 'You thought I was dead?' he asked quietly.

Cam looked down. 'Yep. Best get your story straight because you're going to have to tell it.'

'Shit,' Jessup said, before looking towards the alley leading to the main road.

Cam saw it. 'If you're thinking about running, there's a sicko out there who's looking for nobody but you. Fancy your chances?'

Jessup looked back at Cam. 'Think I should come in for a chat after all,' he said, dropping his backside onto the steps next to him.

The police car that came to pick Cam and Tommy up arrived some fifteen minutes later. Rogers was waiting for him at the door of Norwich Police Station with an expression that suggested he keep a five-metre distance from her at all times.

'Never mind the trouble you're in from me, you deserve a smacked arse, and not in a kinky way. Rest assured; she is not happy with you.'

'I know.'

They took Jessup up to the squad room, which was still full, but the faces were now full of quiet disbelief at who had just joined them. Cam nodded sheepishly to its occupants, turning his attention back to Jessup – who was just starting to get the riot act from Rogers too.

'Sit down, you little twerp.'

Jessup did.

'Let's have a little getting to know you, shall we – since we've been looking for you all over the place for days now. How about we start with how in the hell we have a piece of your heart on a knife this good-for-nothing swine found in Doke End?' She pointed at Cam. 'Yet you're sitting there, oblivious as a fucking post.'

Jessup looked up with blank incomprehension. 'A piece of my heart?' he said.

Cam spoke from his place by the back wall. 'Cardioid tissue.'

'Cardioid… *tissue*,' said Rogers. Cam could see she was molten now. 'We've put so much effort into finding you, not to mention identifying you, I've got half a mind to turf you back out to the mercy of whatever lunatic has been killing people and stashing them in underwater murder pantries.'

That, at least, prompted Jessup to appear shaken.

'You've seen the news, haven't you?' Rogers continued. 'You've seen what's happened to your friends.'

Jessup looked whiter than usual, and his eyes sank even further into his head. 'So that was them?'

Cam knew the names hadn't been released yet, but Jessup had obviously connected his own dots.

'Yes, it bloody was, sunshine.'

'You knew something had gone wrong earlier?'

He was badly shaken now, but nodded. 'We were supposed to meet at the King's Arms in Ludham for the Norwich game. They've got Sky Sports. We never miss Norwich games on telly, not since we were kids.'

'Did anyone attack you in the meantime? Threaten you?'

'Nobody.'

'So, you just went to ground and got to hiding in that snooker hall of yours?'

'Well, it's been two weeks since we were last all together. One by one, it seemed they'd all disappeared. Ryan's wife got in touch, asked if I'd seen him. And Lenny's latest girlfriend. Gary's a loner, but he wasn't answering his texts. Then Ken wasn't either. Nobody was. With all four of my mates missing, I panicked. Thought I'd better disappear as well. I've been there three days now, but why they're dead I've got no idea.'

'What about when we released your name? Asked people to come forward with information?'

'I wasn't leaving that place. And then I thought that whoever was after us might leave me alone if he thought I was already dead. I thought I could hide until it all blew over.'

'So, sixty-four million dollar question – how did Diver Boy find a knife with your heart tissue on it?' Rogers pointed at Cam again, who was just grateful not to be the focus of her ire for once.

'It can't have my heart tissue on it,' said Jessup incredulously. 'I've not been stabbed!'

'Well, that's becoming apparent it, isn't it, sunshine! We've got DNA from your place which matched up. Your father's DNA to be precise.'

Jessup looked genuinely confused. Cam felt something drift suddenly, untethered, something very wrong. 'My dad… I've not seen my dad in years.'

'But what about Jessup and Son Landscaping?'

'I mow lawns under that name because it sounds better! Sounds more established! It's just me!'

'Just you?'

'Well, I might have a son out there somewhere,' he said, looking for someone who would appreciate the lascivious twinkle he was offering, but found no takers.

'We got it off a coffee cup outside that floating trailer of yours.' Rogers looked at Cam to make sure this was right, and he nodded.

'I hadn't used it. I mean sure I had, but not that day. It wasn't my dad either, that was… that was Jim Conroy. I gave him a coffee earlier this week when he came round asking where his son had gone. I gave him a brew while I told him that I didn't know.'

Rogers almost had to sit down. Her knees felt like they were crumbling, along with every assumption she'd made about this case.

The facts had to be realigned in her head, and placed in new slots. How could they have been so stupid?

The DNA match between knife and mug had been a familial hit – whoever had used that coffee cup was the father of whoever had been stabbed in the heart. That wasn't in doubt. They just had the wrong father and the wrong son. And the wrong murder victim.

All the logic they'd worked from was valid. And yet… She looked at Cam, to see that the penny wasn't quite dropping for him yet.

'It was Conroy,' she said. 'Conroy's DNA on the knife. Conroy is dead… We've been going down the wrong track all this time.'

The room fell silent, the scale of the error echoing.

Indy Macaluso spoke up. 'Is there any chance I could ask a few questions here,' she asked. 'I don't want to step on any toes.'

Rogers sat down at last.

What a fiasco, she thought. *And I… I was in charge of it.*

'Yes,' she said. 'Please go for it.'

Macaluso walked forward from the back of the room. 'I have to ask you, Mr Jessup, whether anyone would have reason to harm you and your four oldest friends?'

'No clue!' said Jessup, himself offering disbelief now. 'I've been scratching my head, and I still can't think of anybody who'd want to harm us or that could harm us like... like what happened to the lads.'

'We've spent a bit of time looking into you *lads* today. You're always into a bit of rum stuff, right? The odd dodgy dealing, the odd bits and pieces here and there, bit of recreational drug use. Do you ever think you might have rubbed somebody up the wrong way?'

'It's all just banter, isn't it?'

'Ah, yes, banter,' said Rogers sarcastically. 'The common excuse of the blithering idiot.'

'It's the truth though,' said Jessup. 'Yeah, we've been into scrapes as lads and as mates. But we've never harmed anybody, like *actually harmed* anybody!'

Macaluso stopped her walk around the room, and looked dead straight at Jessup. Got down to his level, bored into him. 'Are you sure?'

'No.'

'I ask you again. Is there anyone in the past who might have reason to build up such resentment for you? The reason I'm asking this, Mr Jessup, is because so much of what has happened to you and your friends looks like the work of someone who is totally committed to a particular brand of revenge. A particular shape of justice – which might have something to do with the past. Was there ever an occasion of injustice? Anything spring to mind?'

'No! Nothing!'

'Any time when the five of you got someone into trouble?'

Jessup started to shake his head, but something stopped him. Rogers could see the tell behind his eyes as a puzzle piece dropped into place. 'Yes. Now you mention it, there might be. But it was ancient history, years ago.'

'Tell me,' Macaluso implored.

Jessup smiled oddly, then brushed it away again, as if he was running through said old occasion in his mind and trying it out for size as a motivation for all this.

Then Rogers remembered something. Something jumped out of the landfill of her own memory. She stood and reached across the table through the stacks of old newspapers they'd been combing. She soon had it, and held up the old edition she was looking for.

Local boy shot in head – survives.

'On this hunting trip,' she said. 'One of you got shot.'

Jessup looked thoroughly rumbled. 'Yeah.'

'The article says this boy Gareth Binns was shot in the head, but miraculously survived. Bird shot in the eye, but you know all that. You, were there of course. There were six boys present, with one boy expelled over the incident. The others said he'd pulled the trigger.' Rogers glowered over the table. 'Who was that?' she said. 'Who did you lot blame?'

Jessup almost laughed, but it was a nervous reflex devoid of humour. 'But it can't be, we've not seen him in years!'

'The name,' said Rogers again, firmly.

Jessup looked down at his chewed fingertips, as if the weight of whatever it was they'd done was finally beginning to have an effect.

'Bix,' he said finally, looking up. 'His name was Bix Lindbeck.'

Then

I like the forest, and I like the trees. I like the animals, the big, the small, the tall. I like their fur, their little movements. I like the smell of everything here in the forest, particularly the dirt.

'Lindbeck, hurry up!'

I wish the teacher would shut up. I'm so fed up of listening to his constant yammering, constantly telling me what to do and where to go.

I hate that it always draws attention to me.

He might be the worst of the lot.

'Yeah, come on, you're slowing us down.' A nasty voice nearby.

God, they've caught on.

'Yeah, Bix,' someone else says before a heavy, pointed shoulder barges me in the back.

I fall forward and catch myself. It was Conroy who pushed me. He speaks again really quietly. 'Hurry up, you fat fuck.'

The rest of them laugh. It's so hard not to cry. Why do they do this to me every day?

I get barged on the other side, which bounces me back into Conroy. 'Hey, watch it fat fuck, you're messing my trainers up.'

I look down and see the white trainers that Conroy has decided to wear, a stupid idea for nature and this excursion, and I know it wasn't me.

He knows it wasn't my fault too, but that doesn't stop him. It never stops any of them.

'Look what you've done, you piece of shit,' he seethes.

'Boys, quieten down,' says Mr Forbes at the front.

Why can't the teachers see?

I want to shout. I want to scream. But I can't and I won't. It would do no good.

The teacher never listens, and even if he did, it would only get them into trouble and they would pick on me more.

'Yeah, watch what you're doing,' says another voice.

That's Jessup. I hate these boys. They're together all the time, a nasty little herd. They have a friendship that I would love to have. But that isn't for me.

'Yeah shut up, Bix.' His voice gets louder, and sing-song. 'Bix, Bix, he's got three dicks.' The other boys join in, chanting along.

I can't take much more of this.

I wish that it'd all go away, me included. I just don't know what I did to make them act so horribly to me.

I know I'm sensitive, and I know that showing them it upsets me makes it worse.

I ignore them and try to drop to the back of the group. Why did I have to be with this group of five and Mr Forbes? Any other group would have been better. And, if the truth be told, I was really looking forward to today. I was quite interested to see what would happen if we got one.

If a pigeon got shot, how would it react. How would it behave? Especially if it didn't die immediately? That last thought excites me quite a lot.

I don't talk about these things, but they're what I'm interested in.

And I wanted to have a go with the gun. I think it would be interesting to pull the trigger, to have that power in your hand.

Instead, they keep having it themselves for five minutes each and nobody lets me have a go, not even the teacher, who thought the five minutes idea was great.

One of the other boys starts talking now. That is Forrester. 'Bix ends with an X. Do you know what else ends with X? Sex.'

I'm going to go red. I can feel it.

'But I bet you've never had sex, have you, Bix?'

I feel dizzy.

'No one's ever going to have sex with you though, are they Bix?'

'You're strange and smelly, aren't you?' Leonard Drummond.

'He fucking stinks.' Ken Conroy.

'Three dicks and still no sex.' Tommy Jessup.

Gareth Binns creeps up behind me and sniffs loudly.

'Ugh, he smells like cow shit.'

That's probably right, considering I do muck out the animal sheds. But that's what father makes me do, and it's not my fault.

Father would sort these boys out. Father would never stand for this. He'd sit them down and have a huge serious conversation with them, just like he has to do with me, and they'd never misbehave again. I wish that would happen. It would fix everything.

There's a flapping behind us, sharp and sudden, and I can hear a bird taking off.

'There's one!'

Everyone looks to the sky to where wings beat in a hasty take-off, and sure enough, a pigeon crosses the grey cloud cover, all alone.

'There!' shouts Mr Forbes – when a loud, deafening crack rings out.

I cover my ears.

The gun has gone off.

Someone has taken a shot.

The gun is shoved into my hands. It still feels like it echoes with the shot that has just been fired.

The teacher turns around and I'm holding the gun, and Gareth Binns is holding his face.

He's screaming. 'My eye! My fucking eye!'

'Who did that?' shouts Mr Forbes as he runs over.

There's a little blood, but not much. That blood is very interesting. It looks to me like puzzle pieces, falling out of his eye. He doesn't look too bad considering, but I remember it's bird shot.

'Lindbeck, you careless prat,' shouts the teacher.

I'm still holding the gun. I didn't do this. I know I didn't do this. It was Conroy. I know it was. But he's looking up like it couldn't possibly be him.

'Yeah,' he says with mock hurt. 'How could you do this?'

I'm stunned into silence.

'Bloody hell,' says Mr Forbes. Gareth is now doubled up in pain and he looks up at the sky.

I get a good look at it. It's amazing. Really.

It looks like the bird shot has peppered his skin in a graze. But the eye weeps.

'It was Bix,' shouts Ken.

'Bix tried to kill him!' Ryan Forrester.

'Why did you do that, Bix?' Tommy Jessup.

The chorus is all around me and before I know it, Mr Forbes has got me by the collar and is dragging me away.

'You little psychopath,' he spits in my ear. 'Let's see what the head makes of this.'

Soon after

I can't believe I've had to wait all this time, a couple of days I've been at home worrying like mad. I didn't do it. They all know I didn't do it.

And now this meeting with the headmaster, it's almost too much for me.

It's like the teachers waited and waited, for me to feel as much dread as possible.

I've been sick so many times this weekend after what happened on Friday, I can't seem to be able to hold anything in or down.

Mother and Father think I've come down with something.

But I know it's not that.

All six of us sit outside the office, and I know that it's my word against theirs.

It's David and Goliath.

We go into the room at last and it almost feels like a relief.

I can't bear Gareth Binns staring at me any more with that one good eye. The other is behind a white patch, that he's already managed to get muck on.

I can't look anywhere though. They all look at me like they hate me.

I think what's happened is that they've told such a lie, such a committed lie that they must all believe it, like the line of truth has been so blurred they don't even know what the real story is any more.

It's tremendously upsetting to know that your word really doesn't mean anything.

Horribly, finally, we are taken in to the head's office.

We sit down, at chairs already laid out. Me and the five other boys. They still all look at me in horror and hatred. Mr Forbes is there, and so is the headmaster, Mr Gilman.

'Would anyone care to tell us,' says Mr Gilman. 'What happened on the pigeon shoot on Friday?'

There is quiet until Mr Forbes speaks. 'We finally saw a pigeon and it appears one of our team got too excited and pulled the trigger at one of his friends.'

He's staring at me.

The fact that he's supposedly talking about me is bad enough, but the thing that really hurts me more than anything is the fact that he's referring to us all as *friends*.

I am their victim, I am their prey.

They have never treated me as a friend.

How do I defend myself here?

I didn't do this, but no one will believe me.

'And it was you, Lindbeck, who was holding the weapon,' says the head.

I can't say anything. I don't feel able.

'Is this true, Lindbeck?' asks Gilman.

My voice is shaking. 'The gunshot went off, and then we all looked in the sky, and then there was screaming and the gun was put in my hands. Ken Conroy put the gun in my hands, sir.'

But the boys on my right erupt.

'Liar, sir!' Tommy Jessup.

'We saw it with our own eyes!' Leonard Drummond.

'He's having you on, sir.' Ryan Forrester.

The head looked at Mr Forbes, and Forbes simply nodded.

'This isn't the truth, sir,' I say. 'It was Ken Conroy who had the gun, sir. It was Ken Conroy who pulled the trigger.'

'He's lying, sir!' screams Ken Conroy. 'I swear on my family's life he's lying!' Ken Conroy is on his feet now.

'I've heard enough boys, out you go,' says Gilman.

It's over?

'Lindbeck, you stay there.'

They all shuffle out. I can hear sniggering. Mr Forbes has gone with them.

I'm shaking.

'This is unacceptable,' says Gilman.

'I didn't do it, sir,' I say again, but I know no one's listening.

It's like my pleas are falling on deaf ears. They always are.

'We'll discuss the future with your parents. I'm going to call them immediately.'

Expulsion. No…

But now he stands up and takes the birch from behind his desk.

I've heard about this.

Heard that he used to use this, but I refused to believe it.

He can't possibly be using that.

Those days are over, aren't they?

'Stand,' he says. 'Hands out.'

I step forward and raise shaking fingers and he smashes me across my knuckles.

Punishment.

Punishment.

Every time he hits me, my vision seems to go white with anger.

How could he be doing this?

'Stand straight, boy,' he says and then he comes behind me.

Why can I smell him?

Why is he this close?

He's undone my trousers.

I can feel his huge, calloused hands on my belt.

Why are my trousers falling to the floor?

I stand there as I feel his thumb creep inside my waistband and pull down my underwear.

I have never known such horror.

I am terrified.

'There we are,' he says and he thrashes my backside again and again with the birch.

I almost can't handle this any more.

I almost want it to be over.

Not this. I mean everything.

I want it all over.

I want to be dead.

48

'It was kid's stuff!' shouted Jessup, but his body language betrayed the fact that he knew just how seriously this might have hurt the innocent young man they'd framed, Bix Lindbeck. Cam felt a unique kind of disgust for the man in front of him. Jessup's excuses sounded like many he'd heard over the years.

We were only messing.

It was just a joke.

It was banter.

None of that, he thought, would make a jot of difference to Bix Lindbeck.

'What happened to the boy you blamed?' Cam asked, stepping forward from the wall.

Jessup looked around and held his arms out in appeal for some kind of understanding, but it wasn't coming. 'After he was expelled, we didn't see him again, not really. Every now and then you'd see him knocking about. Norfolk's not that big a place is it!'

Rogers interjected. 'Everyone, get what we can on Bix Lindbeck, now.'

But Cam wasn't done with Jessup. 'What happened to him after?' he repeated.

'I don't know, but he was just dead weird,' said Jessup. 'Think he went off the rails.'

'Define off the rails for me please, Mr Jessup?'

'Well, he didn't get back into any school, I don't think. Think he started working out of his parents' place, but we knew his parents were absolute nutters, they wouldn't have been happy with what he turned into.'

'What about his parents?'

'Well, they were foreign for a start—'

Rogers took two steps towards Jessup and towered over him. 'You use that word in that way, or say anything like that again, I'll take you to your old mate Lindbeck myself.'

Jessup went red and cowered, but he started speaking quickly, as if trying to save face. 'They were very strict. Think he was really scared of them. If his clothes were ever dirty, they'd give him a right telling off.'

'I bet you liked getting those clothes dirty for him, didn't you?' said Cam.

Jessup didn't answer.

'What else?' said Rogers.

'I think his parents died years ago and I have no idea what happened to him since then.'

One of the other officers around the table spoke, looking up from a laptop. 'Parents, Gun and Bo Lindbeck. Were Swedish immigrants back in the fifties. Became parents fairly late in life, had a son – Bix – born in 1987. Parents died around the year 2000. Address is a PO Box in Acle.'

'Check the DVLA?' said Rogers.

'Will do.'

'Do you have any idea where he might be, Mr Jessup?' asked Cam. 'Any idea where this farm is?'

'No idea.'

Cam was thinking about that footprint he found in the woods behind his property and about just how large Bix Lindbeck would have to be.

If, of course, it was Bix who was responsible.

'I don't know anything about him,' said Jessup. 'Haven't thought about him in years.'

'Well, it seems he's thought about you.'

That same officer spoke up from across the room. 'We've got teenage trouble. 2002, a Bix Lindbeck was arrested trespassing on a livestock farm over near Salhouse. Bothering the animals.'

Animals, Cam thought. *Livestock. The disappearances in the area, the ones Gupta, Ferris and Martin at the tackle shop were all talking about.*

Jessup snorted. 'That sounds about right.'

Everyone looked at him with pure derision.

Jessup put up his hands. 'He was always going on about becoming a vet, that's all.'

'So, he has not turned up anywhere else?' asked Rogers.

'Hang on... yes. Ugh... oh dear. Another altercation with police in 2003. A charge of animal cruelty was levelled against him, but he didn't answer it.'

The room was silent, until the officer continued.

'Turns out he appeared tearful at a vets in Wroxham, with a baby pig. He'd tried to do some sort of haphazard surgery on it. He'd butchered the thing.'

Macaluso stepped forward. 'It seems the expulsion, and whatever fallout happened after, sent him on a very different path. One where he carried on the life he was hoping for, but through a particularly broken prism. He's animalistic, yet nurturing. Extremely violent, drawn to blood and what it means. I dare say that all of these characteristics he went on to exhibit were there all along. It just needed a break point for them to really manifest.' She looked pointedly at Jessup.

Rogers leered at him. 'You and your little shitty mates were poking a card-carrying, once-a-generation psychopath murderer – and you didn't know it. You made him who he is. Well, it's bitten you all on the arse now, hasn't it?'

Macaluso spoke again. 'Don't forget – all his actions and retaliations exhibit a reverence for territory. Even the actions at Killick's place last night. Including the bowel movement outside—'

'Bix took a shit at his house?' said Jessup with wide, delighted eyes.

'Shut up,' said Rogers. 'We need to find him.'

'If he's gone out of his way to re-establish his territory and boundaries, he'll have gone back to his own, to restate the claim, refortify.'

Rogers shook her head. 'We've got a team on Doke End, remember? If he's gone back there, we'd know about it.'

Cam leaned forward. Every minute of the last twenty-four hours, he'd been building a plan in his head. It started as just pieces of an idea, triggered by something he'd seen. But the more he learned about the background of their killer, this Bix Lindbeck, the more he thought it would work. 'I've got an idea. Surely now is the time to try something different.'

'Don't Killick, just—'

'Please, Rogers. Listen to me. Listen to what you've just heard. This guy is so close to completing his circle – a circle I've somehow now entered. Which means that Bix Lindbeck is going to pay great attention to three things.' Cam turned and pointed at Jessup. 'Him.' He then swung his finger to the ID pictures tacked to the walls. 'Those bodies.' He jabbed a thumb at his own chest. 'And me.'

'He's right,' Macaluso said. 'Those are the pieces of his pattern.'

Rogers slowly shook her head.

'Please Rogers, just give me one chance,' Cam said. 'We've got what he wants, and if we frame it right, we can force him to show himself. But we've not got long. If he realises we've got Jessup, he might cut his losses – but while his objectives can still be met, we've still got a chance.'

Rogers looked away, and cast her eyes across the artefacts of the case, which were everywhere. All this degradation. All this desecration. The violence, and horror. The danger of this man, being left free to roam.

'If I said yes,' she said slowly, 'what are you thinking?'

'We go fishing,' replied Cam.

49

A frantic few hours passed. Killick's plan was absurd, surely couldn't work, but Macaluso admitted the reasoning was sound. Rogers was aware that they'd made a serious error in misidentifying the DNA on the mug from Middlewater, and was keen to bring a resolution. If that meant embracing Cam Killick and the unconventional, so be it.

'Are you sure about this?' she said to Killick, as he lay back and let the thick black polyethylene swaddle his shoulders.

'No,' he said, taking in his surroundings.

'Do you think you'll be warm enough?'

'Not sure,' he said again. He looked nervous, which, given what he was about to do, she could understand entirely.

'Don't make me regret this – and remind me to book you in for Sectioning when this is all over,' said Rogers. 'And I never gave you that taser, got it? I can't let you go out there with nothing.'

'Keep an eye on me,' he said. 'And remember what I said.'

'I remember,' Rogers replied.

Killick nodded firmly once – then she zipped the body bag up over his face, and slid the cadaver tray back into the belly of the mortuary van.

Rogers now sat in the back of a police Transit, alongside Indy Macaluso and a handful of uniforms. It was four in the morning. Most of the officers had been pulled in from the canteen, late in their overnight shift, and were happy enough to while away the final hours of their working day escorting a senior detective on an expedition.

Their operation, if you could generously call it that, was put together and executed with haste, and had the feeling it had been thrown together with packing tape and parcel string. Those podcast lunatics had done their job too, and put out a very compelling news piece on their newspaper's website. They had actually been good for something after all – or they would be, if this madcap idea worked.

'GROTTO BODIES IDENTIFIED,' said the headline. The sub-headline went on to read: 'Three victims recovered in Upton burial site identified. Moved to local funeral home.'

Apparently, the *Eastern Daily Gazette* editor had been furious at being woken, then being asked to blow such a story in the middle of the night when no one was paying attention – but when Rogers had told them it was part of a heroic plan to catch a serial killer, they were much happier to pull the trigger. The article went on to state that the bodies were being held overnight at Alcock and Sons Funeral Directors, and that this would be 'the last time they'd be together before being released to the families first thing in the morning'.

Cam hoped that line would be the kicker; the one that would trigger Bix Lindbeck into action.

'Oh my god,' said Rogers quietly.

'He took the bait?' asked Macaluso.

'I don't believe it, but... I think so.' Rogers watched the computer screen, and the map which sat open in an internet browser window. On it was the local road network – and a picture of a small blue dot picking up speed along one of the A-roads north of Norwich city centre. It represented the location of a phone GPS signal, which was beaming out from the back of an unmarked funeral transportation van.

It was racing off, back towards Upton.

Bix Lindbeck had taken the opportunity to reclaim his property.

'Dead bait don't move,' whispered Rogers. Killick, that daft bugger, had been right.

'What was that?' asked Macaluso.

'Nothing – driver, let's get moving. I'll direct from back here.'

Cam felt partially frozen solid. The van was refrigerated, and when he climbed into the body bag, he thought it would give him a modicum of warmth. Kind of like a sleeping bag. It did no such thing. But when he heard the back door of the van open with an echoing clunk that was very close to his feet, adrenaline warmed him up so quickly it could have burnt his innards.

The plan had been simple but tough enough to attempt to execute in under a couple of hours.

Find an amenable local funeral director.

Make sure they had a refrigerated van.

Leave the garage unlocked, and the keys in plain sight.

Load it with three 'bodies' on the racks which held space for four cadavers, two up, two down, the bag tags labelled Forrester, Drummond and Binns. The top two loaded with whatever they could find, just enough to resemble the human form – and the bottom one with Cam himself, phone in left hand, location sharing on and configured via a tracking app to Rogers' laptop. In his other hand, primed and ready, a Taser X2 model – fully charged.

Next, was leaving the place, then instructing the podcasters it was time to put out the bulletin that the bodies were there for a limited period.

And then, they had to wait.

It took a couple of hours, Cam fighting every demon he had, before the van door was eased open. He'd gone through his breathing routines, his relaxation techniques, reciting the alphabet but with fruits and vegetables (apples, bananas, celery...), doing everything he could to place himself in a Zen-like state, to try to get through it. Strangely, the weight of the bag on his face and extremities, and the pressing cold, felt a bit like being underwater. It helped him beat back the mental toils.

He heard a boot scuff. A jangle of keys. The weighted quiet of a night he couldn't see, and the presence of a monster he could only imagine.

Then the van door shut again. When the engine started up, Cam knew his plan had worked.

The idea was that Bix Lindbeck would come to the funeral home, unable to leave his prizes to be separated and buried on terms that weren't his. He'd break into the building, and look for them inside. He wouldn't find them, so he'd try the garage, and see this very van hooked up to the mains, with the refrigerator compartment running, and realise his quarry had already been loaded up, ready to go. He'd look for the keys, find them handily on a nearby workbench, see three body bags in the back and make a break for it.

And Rogers and the police unit would follow.

The van reversed with a series of beeps, before it rumbled onto the tarmac of what Cam knew was the back yard of the funeral home. With a lurch, he felt momentum swinging as the van reversed in a tight circle, before the accelerator was driven home with purpose, and they sped away.

Cam checked his phone, saw he still had reception. It was crucial to have mobile coverage for as long as he could now. As long as it did, it could ping its position to his chosen recipient. In this case, DS Rogers.

It was also a matter of pride, of protection, of decency.

He needed to go toe to toe with the predator, bring him down.

He listened, and waited. Squeezing the handle of the taser, he was beginning to realise that his fear in this situation wasn't merely of the unknown, it was based on what he knew his quarry was capable of.

He was in the maw of a man who killed with no compunction, and presumably no compassion. Someone who could bring bodies down underwater and leave them in a horrible make-believe of dehumanised disgrace.

On his travels with the SBS, he had encountered real evil on occasion. People on not just his opposing side, who revelled in the blood that they shed. But never a serial killer, which is exactly what he appeared to face. It was this nudge of the unknown that scared Cam. This was a darkness he couldn't prepare for.

They sped through the night, Bix Lindbeck and Cam Killick, two very different creatures, in a one-on-one battle for supremacy. Only, one didn't know the other was there.

The other benefit of having his phone meant that Cam could see where they were going.

He watched the blue dot on the map speed through Sprowston, and onto Rackheath and Salhouse, before heading to Upton. It seemed he was heading back to where this all started, before the bumps of the suspension heralded a turn-off after Salhouse Broad, and it seemed they were blasting through softer terrain, if the hushed sound of the towers was anything to go by. The blue dot on the phone was careering through pure green – and that's when the phone went dead.

The signal had gone – like it so often did in the Norfolk wilds.

Cam was alone with a serial killer.

'We've lost him!' shouted Rogers. 'He's lost reception.'

The driver eased off the accelerator as he awaited instruction, but the loss of momentum felt like heartbreak to Rogers. 'What should I do?'

'Keep going – head to where we lost him, and we'll pick up from there.'

'Where were they headed?' asked Macaluso, as all the passengers in the rear of the police transport van lurched forward as the accelerator was jammed down again.

'Salhouse. I've got a pin-drop, but it's in the middle of nowhere. We'll have to fly solo until we get there, and try to work out where they went.'

'There's nothing on the map where he disappeared?'

'Nothing,' said Rogers. 'It's just a big stupid block of green. No roads, no nothing.'

'This is dangerous,' said Macaluso.

'Don't try to cheer me up too much, please.'

'No, I mean, this is really dangerous. We're heading onto his turf now. His territory. And you know how he feels about that.'

Rogers knew exactly, and fell silent.

Damn you, Cam Killick, she thought. *I can't believe you talked me into this.*

And you just might have got yourself killed.

50

The road, if it was a road, was undulating, indirect and, because Cam was lying on a steel slab in a mortuary van, really uncomfortable. His vertebrae clanged with every bounce, which seemed to get worse the further the van travelled. He began to plead for the journey to end, even if it meant the end of the road for himself.

The van pulled to a stop, and Cam tensed. By making sure his body bag was on the bottom, beneath the other two bags, he was hoping he'd be the last body bag to be removed from the vehicle – and while Bix Lindbeck was occupied with hoisting the first bodies away, Cam would get out and ready himself with the advantage of surprise. On the other hand, if Lindbeck picked up his bag first, he'd have to play dead, take whatever bumps and impacts until Lindbeck put him down, and he went to get the others. He was relying on the notion that Lindbeck would want to keep all three bodies together.

The front van door opened. Footsteps, outside the van, over the hum of the refrigerator. Thumping, heavy, towards the rear. Cam held his breath – but the rear door wasn't opened. Instead, the whine of a metal hinge, alongside the footsteps.

Cam realised it was a gate being opened.

Footsteps, the driver's door again, and then the van lurching forward.

It soon stopped again, as the door, footsteps and hinges proceeded again – ending with a thick clunk.

Territory, thought Cam. He was in Bix Lindbeck's den now.

The van pressed on, but the idea of being in this killer's territory set off a mammoth wave of panic through Cam's whole body.

He shouldn't be here.

He'd made a massive mistake.

Rogers had been right.

He should never have used himself as bait, dead or otherwise.

No.

No.

Stay cool, Cam.

Hold it together.

You can't stop this killer if you crumble now.

He grit his teeth, tried to fill his lungs with as much oxygen as he could, even though the body bag, while breathable, didn't offer a chance to take big gulps. He pictured himself lying in his bath, his dog on his bathmat, listening to him snore. God, he missed Nala. How he needed her now.

He felt his pulse lower, and his composure gradually return.

The van trundled on before, mercifully, it seemed to hit gravel, then shortly after, it stopped.

The engine was killed.

Now was the time.

Cam tensed again. The door again. Heavy footsteps on gravel. The back door of the van opened. And the beast stepped in.

Cam stayed so still, it somehow hurt. Steps, up and into the van, so heavy they wobbled the entire vehicle. Cam lay totally floppy, in case his bag was selected.

Play dead. It was almost impossible, feeling this tense, to lay completely inert and relaxed. *Play dead, dammit.*

With a deep scrape, Cam heard one of the other bags being lifted.

He didn't want to breathe out just yet, in case it made a movement.

With a couple of deep grunts and the clank of footsteps, Cam pictured the surely huge form of Bix Lindbeck hoisting the body bag up over his shoulder. The van lifted on its suspension as the combined weight stepped out.

Footsteps on gravel receding into the distance.

Go.

Now.

Cam poked his finger through the gap he'd perfectly left in the zip, and pulled it down with a hissing metallic *thwip*.

Dawn light was crashing into the open rear doors of the van as, sure enough, he lay there next to the remaining body bag. All he could see outside was a gravel driveway leading up to a metal gate, that was wrapped heavily in barbed wire. The fencing around the gate was thick with razored wrapping too.

He climbed up and out, and hopped down, making sure to stay light on his feet, even though his body ached as it recovered from the battering of the ride over here.

He peered around the side of the van's open door, and it was clear he'd found it.

Lindbeck's Mill.

Mist hunkered around its foundations, giving the impression that the group of dilapidated buildings was floating on a cloud.

Everywhere was silent.

No birds. Not even now, at dawn.

The van was parked in a gravel turning-circle, some forty metres from the mill itself.

There was a central tall building in white stone, three stories high, while next to it sat a couple of outbuildings in a yard beyond. In front, tight to the main part of the structure, lay a large pool, which carried a thick layer of desiccate on top – bits and pieces of old wood that had been left there to rot. The building was clearly an old mill but it surely hadn't been used for its original purpose in years. All of this, it seemed, was surrounded by thick woods on all sides, an island away from the rest of the world.

It would have been impressive at one stage in its life, but now it was a sad testament to an industry that was no longer needed. The upstairs windows were cracked, no glass in any pane. The whitewashed stone of the building was tired, chipped and moss-covered, and the building itself looked derelict.

Cam couldn't see Bix Lindbeck. There was no peripheral movement anywhere. The buildings gave the impression of abandonment, even though they were obviously in use. As silently as he could, he ran for the outbuildings, looking for somewhere to hide, where he could try to find a way to get in contact with Rogers.

He ran to the corner of the outbuildings, two of which sat in an L-shape behind the old mill itself. He picked the gable end of the nearest one, and tucked in tight.

Cam sat and watched for a few moments. The homestead looked out over a long, rolling meadow, off to distant trees a couple of hundred metres away. He took out his phone once more. Still no reception. If he needed back-up, he'd have to hope they'd take the initiative and get inventive.

His nerves began to rise again.

This was like finding a bear's den, and wondering where the beast was hiding.

He took out his phone, sent Rogers a location pin.

He hoped, in the coming moments, he'd chance through a pocket of reception, and the message would send automatically.

Staying low to the ground, with the taser raised, he came around the corner and checked the back yard of the property. No sign of life. He needed to get a fix on Lindbeck. Where was he? The aged wooden back door of the mill was shut, and he hadn't heard it open or close.

Maybe Lindbeck was back around the front of the building somewhere?

He had to chance it. The back yard was completely open, and he'd have to move across it. He'd have to make a sprint for it, to try and get to the gable end of the mill wall. So he could look out towards the pool and meadow.

He stopped. Hunkered down. Listened.

Nothing. The air was still. Still no birds, like even they knew a predatory force was about.

If all their assumptions were correct, the evil he was looking for had been provoked and brought into being by a completely different kind of evil – the evil that children can so easily do to each other. It lent him an unwelcome sympathy for the monster he was hunting, and it left him feeling strangely off-kilter.

Head down in a crouch, he ran for the near corner of the mill. He tried to stay light on the balls of his feet, and pounded across the old dust and rocks of what used to be the driveway when he saw something on the ground.

It was a small triangular segment of tyre track, but this wedge-shaped imprint was surrounded by small neat lines, going crossways, this way and that.

They were the marks of a sweeping brush.

The tracks had been swept clear.

Cam felt the muscles between his shoulders tighten involuntarily. Lindbeck had swept these tyre tracks, to make it look like the mill was as empty and abandoned as possible.

Cam pulled out his phone to check for signal, praying for a bar, when he heard something. He thought he was mistaken, and the hand that held the phone drifted down to his side. He looked across the rear courtyard of the property, but couldn't see anything. He turned and looked the other way and couldn't see anything there either.

What was the sound he had heard? It had been something metallic, maybe metal on stone. It was muffled, but it was here. He listened so hard his ears hurt. He followed along the edge of the building to look along the gable end corner of the mill and looked out at the meadow.

And there, standing in the field, was a sight that froze the blood in his veins.

Staring out at the edge of the pool, his back to the mill, was a huge man in tattered overalls. His hair was long past his shoulders, and even from this distance Cam could see that it was knotted and filthy. He couldn't see the man's face, only the width of his torso.

The man was huge.

Silence was everywhere.

And on the surface of the pool, the black body bag he'd lifted from the van drifted for a quiet moment, before it slipped away in a quiet gurgle.

Cam couldn't move, rooted to the spot in shock and fear.

His plan had been to surprise Lindbeck with 1,400 volts, and call the cavalry when he was incapacitated.

Cam didn't know what to do. He didn't know whether his legs would move even if he told them to.

And then that metallic clank again, louder. More insistent. The huge man in the field turned to see where the sound had come from.

And the man saw Cam Killick standing there.

And, worse still, Cam recognised him.

51

The horror Cam felt when his eyes met with that man's was almost too much to bear.

When the man saw him, the eyes that looked back were bleak and black, open wide. And then he *screamed*.

It was so loud, so feral, from a place inside him where natural order and blood were the only things that mattered.

Cam tried speaking but the words wouldn't come out, and then the man started to run. Huge pumping strides. He was huge, six foot six at least. And so broad.

When Cam had seen him, the customer in the shadows at Martin's Bait & Tackle, he'd had no idea he was this large.

Nala had barked at him. She'd known all this time.

The ground beneath Cam's feet seemed to shake as he ran, and his speed was something to behold. If this was a battle Cam was going to win, he'd have to use his head – because in a battle of strength, surely Lindbeck would hold every advantage.

He ran back around the corner end of the building, turned and dropped low, to his haunches. Surprise was his weapon, and he had to put everything into making it count. The footsteps pounded closer, a ragged, gnashing breath accompanying them, and as soon as Cam felt the man round the corner and enter the courtyard, he rose and pointed the taser at the man's back.

Lindbeck froze, as Cam pulled the trigger. The two probes darted across the two-metre gap between the men – but Lindbeck span. Only one of the probes caught him in the substantial meat of his right shoulder. The buzz of charge ran out, but Lindbeck ripped out the probe, tossing it down angrily.

Cam was defenceless, as the huge man lunged for him, anger and pain and betrayal writ large on every twisted feature. He ducked, but the man's arms were so long, they quickly closed on Cam's own arms and shoulders, and he was thrown to the floor with such force he felt like he'd been charged by a buffalo.

He rolled in the dust of the courtyard, and tried to stand, but Lindbeck had him by the head, lifting him bodily. Cam kicked and thrashed, and caught Lindbeck's torso, causing him to lower. Cam reached up, and took the pressure point on one of the huge man's hands – the one between the thumb and forefinger of the left hand – and dug with all his might into the muscle and nerves. Lindbeck dropped him, and Cam rolled back.

He had to find safety and regroup.

Nothing would quite stop the force of darkest nature that was all over him.

He ran for the back door of the main building, but couldn't get in. It was locked.

He turned, needed to find an advantage from somewhere, an advantage in surprise.

At the back of the courtyard there looked to be some animal sheds.

There must be something in there he could use, if only just to hold him off a little longer.

Rogers please check your phone – let that location pin have got through.

He ran for the nearest one and ploughed through the door into an open shed, thinking now that his plan to use himself as dead bait was the stupidest idea he'd ever had. As he charged through the door, the smell of animal detritus was almost overwhelming – but it was mixed with something richer, something altogether darkly sweeter.

There were pigs everywhere. Too many of them, packed in too tight. There were goats too. Chickens. The odd sheep.

Could this be? The missing Upton livestock?

They parted as he entered, alarmed by the abrupt human presence. As they spread backwards, it revealed the filthy floor – and what was at the back of the shed.

Another sight that would live with him forever.

He stopped frozen, coldly stunned, revulsion grasping right up his throat.

There was an old, wrought-iron bed pushed up against the wall.

And there was a man lying in it.

A pig, blissfully unaware of Cam's arrival, was troughing away at the man's legs. The powerful motion of its jaws was causing the bed to rock back and forth, clanking against the wall – causing the noise which drew Cam into this hellish place.

The man was gazing at Cam with empty, lifeless eyes.

Cam recognised him.

He wasn't the same as the pictures, not by a long shot, but there was no doubt about it.

It was the missing man, Kenny Conroy.

The fifth piece of the puzzle.

Cam approached carefully, his jaw sagging. The feasting pig moved away, but Cam refused to look at the man's legs.

He was still in fishing greens, although the jacket was folded over the headboard, and the shirt had been ripped open to reveal his torso. On the floor was a bucket with unspeakable things in it. The bed clothes were sodden with filth. It seemed to Cam that he couldn't have been dead for all that long.

Cam got closer and found an unmistakable scar on his chest, stitched up with cat gut, inflamed and reddened. A knife wound, right there where it should be, over the heart. This was Conroy all right, but his experience at the hand of Bix Lindbeck had left him a husk of the man they'd seen in the Facebook pictures.

'He was alive for a while,' a voice said from behind. It was deep, and pleading.

Cam turned. At the entrance to the animal shed was the huge man, stepping down on to the dirty floor.

'Bix Lindbeck?' said Cam, carefully.

The man looked at him through that tattered hair, and nodded slowly.

'I saw you at the fishing tackle shop, didn't I?'

'You did.'

The eyes looked back at Cam so full of regret and hurt.

'What happened, Bix?'

'Life was going on,' Lindbeck said, 'until I saw them on Doke End, my Doke End, and it had to change. Never again, never again.'

'I know what they did to you, Bix. It was terrible. Nobody should have to go through that.'

'But they made sure anyway.' Lindbeck pointed at the bed.

'They were horrible to you.'

'And I showed them.'

Cam didn't know what to say to that. Academically, Bix Lindbeck really had shown the bullies why they should never have messed with him, but it was a few hundred miles away from any kind of justice Cam could morally agree with.

'Bix, whatever they did to you, you can undo.' Cam knew this wasn't true, but he said it anyway. He knew that nothing would undo what Bix Lindbeck had done. But Cam had to try, for his own sake at least. As mild as he seemed now, Lindbeck carried himself in a way that ignited awe and fear. It was far removed from the hunched, shuffling form he'd seen in the shop.

'I couldn't undo what happened to him,' said Bix. 'When they get like that they're broken forever.'

'You tried to fix him.'

'When he didn't die straight away, I felt bad. Didn't like the way he looked at me. Tried to fix it.'

'Like the animals you like to fix?'

Bix seemed to like that, softened, but then looked down. 'Couldn't fix that one.'

'What happened to him?'

'It was all going like normal,' Bix said. 'The knife slid in just fine. But then he didn't die, and then he started to cry, and then I started to feel bad because I used to cry. I used to cry all the time because of them.'

Cam looked down again at Conroy, who stared back, unseeing, unhearing. 'You lost the knife on Doke End.'

Bix nodded. 'Yeah. I patched him up. Felt bad about it. Thought I'd keep him alive as long as I could. See if I could fix it. Mother always said not to let anything suffer, unless you think you can make it better. Must have died last night.'

338

Cam couldn't imagine just how much Conroy had suffered here in the last few days.

'Had you ever killed anyone before, Bix?' Cam asked.

'Never. Not before I started seeing them appearing on my Doke End. Once I'd got one, I had to get them all. This is mine.'

'And make them part of your territory?'

Lindbeck's eyes seemed to grow intense, as if he'd encountered someone who finally understood. 'Yes. They trespassed.'

'Bix, I'm telling you, we can get you out of here,' Cam said. 'Somewhere, away from all the world's bullies, away from people who would do you harm. Get help.'

'Don't need help,' said Bix. 'Just want to live here, at home, with my animals.'

And then behind Cam was that rattle again, metal on stone.

The pig had shuffled closer, started gnawing again.

Then, from the courtyard outside, a female voice shouted: 'Hello?'

Cam recognised it.

It was Rogers, that brilliant, stubborn cop who thought he was an idiot. She'd made it.

Lindbeck looked at Cam, the betrayal writ large on his face, a pure animal rage beginning to swarm and convulse in his eyes, and then he turned and grabbed a pitchfork, stood by the wall.

He threw open the door, and ran out into the courtyard.

52

Rogers entered the courtyard of an old farm that could surely have a side hustle as a slasher movie film set, when she started to hear voices. There didn't appear to be any conflict, anger or rage, so she decided to speak. Join in, as it were.

What she wasn't prepared for was for Cam Killick to scream her name – and then for the biggest man she'd ever seen emerge from one of the outbuildings carrying a pitchfork.

Oh, so this is how I die, she thought.

She didn't even have time to say or do anything before the man was almost upon her.

The pain in his eyes was cavernous, a black hole with whirling constellations of grief, and hurt. She didn't think such depths of feeling could ever be reasoned with – so she thought on her feet and grasped for anything that might work.

She found it. With her hands out in front of her, she shouted: 'We've got the last one. We've got Tommy Jessup.'

Speaking about Lindbeck's last remaining puzzle piece, the one that eluded him, stopped him for a second. 'Where did you find him?'

Rogers spoke fast. Keeping him talking and occupied was her best chance for survival. 'He was hiding at a snooker hall. It was theirs. Those horrible boys. Did you know about it?'

'No,' he said.

Killick appeared behind him. The look on his face was grave, ashen.

'We can stop this,' she said.

'We can get you somewhere happy, mate,' said Killick.

And that seemed to soften Lindbeck. But it seemed suddenly to melt him too much. Tears began to fall.

He started to cry uncontrollably, and looked up at the house. 'She's going to be so angry with me,' he wailed.

'It'll be all right, Bix,' said Rogers. 'We'll explain everything. We'll tell her what they did to you.' Rogers was clutching at straws, but her appeal was genuine. But what this massive broken murderous man had done would be hard to explain to anyone. 'Is she your mother, Bix?' she said.

Bix looked at the house again.

Killick looked at her and shrugged. He didn't know either. They'd been dead years – but if the long dead corpses of Bix Lindbeck's parents were in there somewhere, she'd give it a miss, thanks. Preceded by a sudden growl, the police transport van suddenly burst through the main gate up behind them, and sped down to the courtyard. The sirens suddenly hit, which were deafening in the enclosed space.

In the confusion, Lindbeck ran for the back door of the house.

'Conroy's back there!' shouted Killick, as he ran to follow Lindbeck into the ancient mill. Officers began to spill out of the side of the vehicle.

'Don't you dare!' said Rogers.

'What else am I gonna do?' he said, barely breaking his sprint.

And then he was gone, inside.

She turned to the outbuildings and the door Killick and the giant had emerged from.

From the look in Cam Killick's eye, something told her whatever was in there would be far from pleasant.

53

The house smelled of must, and something dead. Not recent dead either, but that long clung-to notion of something passed. It was a memory of decay more than anything else. Cam shuddered at what the rooms of this desperate place might contain.

Cam didn't know where Lindbeck had gone, until he heard footsteps along one of the downstairs corridors. The floor was stone and those boots and heavy footsteps weren't masked, providing an echo chamber. Cam ran in the direction of the noise and saw, at the far end of the corridor, the huge man shambling down a short flight of steps.

Bix Lindbeck was now in flight mode – something about his conversation with Rogers had changed everything for him. As Cam reached the end of the corridor and threw himself down the short stairs, he thought that maybe calling for him would be the right idea. 'Bix!' he shouted.

When Cam reached the bottom of the short flight of stairs, he arrived into an open-floored chamber which contained a mill wheel and a dark pool, and he was just in time to see Lindbeck hurl himself into it. There was something in his hand. He dropped underwater, steam lifting from the rolling surface. At the far end of the room was a low opening in the stone wall to allow the water to pass in and out. Cam was sure he had found the mill itself.

Cam ran to the water's edge and looked down. The pool was just as murky, still with all that desiccant on the surface, twigs, branches, leaves, all pulled to the edges with a film of accumulated filth. It looked nothing short of freezing, but what choice was there but to dive in?

He took a deep breath, rotated his shoulders once to get blood flow running through, then threw himself at the pool. It was like being hit by a train made of ice, run through by an actual Polar Express. He was pretty sure that Lindbeck was trying to get out under the wall opening, and Cam swam for the gap in pursuit. He had to duck under the water to get through, and it felt as if his ears were going to drop clean off his head. The freezing pressure on his extremities was almost too great to bear.

He opened his eyes, as he forged out through the opening into a pool in the open air outside – and saw a couple of vehicles, sunk to the bottom of the deep pool. There was a fishing boat, and an entire 4 by 4. Cam didn't know who they belonged to, but he bet it was Lindbeck covering his tracks.

Shimmering sunlight overhead, he reached for the surface, and emerged from the water – only to be dragged back down again immediately. Something was pulling his leg with such force it made him immediately think of a shark attack. Hands were around his middle, pulling him down with obscene strength. Cam opened his eyes, and through his hazed, swirling underwater vision saw Lindbeck's hair thrashing as he tried to drown the smaller man.

The tightness around Cam's chest made his lungs pump hopelessly for air that wouldn't come. But somehow, he felt calmer.

The underwater world wasn't Bix Lindbeck's territory. It was Cam's. And he'd had a career fighting in it.

He lifted both hands, grasping a handful of Lindbeck's hair with one, and jammed the heel of his other palm into the base of the beast's nose – sending massive pain through the infra-orbital nerve – another pressure point. It was a classic restraint technique, and he pressed as hard as he could.

But Lindbeck wouldn't let go. Cam could hear him screaming, muffled, but he wouldn't release his grip.

Cam let go of Lindbeck's hair, and reached for his left ear, and gripped and twisted with everything he had.

The two pressure points combined at last to slow the monster down, and he let go.

Cam fought for the surface, and crashed through, finding himself in the pond outside Lindbeck's farm, gasping into the chilled morning air.

He swam for the bank, only to see Lindbeck's huge form reach down on the grass and pick up that item he'd gone back for. It was a small container, but Cam couldn't get a good look at it – only that it was shiny, and oval, as Lindbeck scrambled off into the trees at the edge of the meadow. Cam pulled himself out, and started to run after him, his clothes frozen bandages.

He felt his own legs start to seize up and his arms begin to judder, but the same problems didn't seem to bother Bix Lindbeck as he sprinted through the trees.

'Killick!' came a voice somewhere behind him, and Cam glanced back to see that Indy Macaluso was charging along after them, sprinting through the long grass, entirely weaponless, cruising on bravery alone.

That at least made two of them, when it came to trying to take Bix down. Cam was big and bold enough to admit that, after everything, he didn't think he could take Lindbeck by himself.

They ran, chasing and tumbling through the dense under-growth, Cam just ahead of Macaluso. Lindbeck was still ahead of them, the predator having yielded and become prey, and they were gaining – but in the distance, the trees opened out again. The forest was beginning to part. Water yawned at them, reeds swayed, and trees stood vast and ancient.

Cam recognised it immediately.

Of course.

Doke End.

Where it all started.

Where it all was to end.

Cam sprinted harder, shouting Lindbeck's name, plead-ing with him. He was running straight for the water. Cam was desperate to stop him, desperate to pull him back, desperate not to have to dive into the icy drink again, but all the while prepared to do so if it meant bringing Bix Lindbeck's murderous spree to an end.

As Lindbeck got to the water's edge, Cam bellowed one last time: 'Bix, stop!'

And the huge man did.

He lowered to his knees.

Cam approached cautiously, but he could see that Lindbeck was hell-bent on doing something, although Cam couldn't see what.

He got closer and could see a soft smoke drift up from the water's edge where Lindbeck was leaning, and suddenly realised.

'Wait,' Cam said as Macaluso reached him.

They watched as a small white cloud slowly drifted from Lindbeck's feet. When the cloud stopped, Lindbeck's shoulders stopped moving at last and Cam gradually approached him.

Lindbeck was on his knees, staring straight ahead, at the cloud of ash that was floating across the broad stretch of water, the remnants of which were dappling the surface.

Cam glanced down at the empty urn at Bix's feet. 'Mother?'

'And Father,' Bix Lindbeck said. 'I was scared of them, and they were too tough on me. But I promised them.'

'They're at rest now, mate. Nobody can do you harm any more.'

Bix just nodded.

The two men remained there in silence for a moment, one sat, one stood, staring across the dawn water – when Bix held his hand up to Cam like a child.

Cam looked at it, then looked at the man himself. He saw the young boy whose life had been forever altered by the actions of others, whose adolescence had been stolen by cruelty – a cruelty he then came to embody and replicate. Somewhere, despite what this monster had done, Cam, on a plane of understanding he didn't want to acknowledge, felt sympathy for him.

'Can you take me away now?' said Bix Lindbeck.

Cam looked at the man and took his hand.

54

Rogers hadn't been prepared for the contents of the animal feed shed.

She expected another macabre sight, for sure, like the one Killick had found at the bottom of Doke End, but instead she found something even more unsettling.

A human being, clearly damaged in the most irreparable of ways, recently dead while being feasted upon – the human state laid at its most bare. Rogers didn't know how to handle it, so she simply walked over to the man and sat on the edge of the filthy bed, so the pigs would keep away.

She only left when the paramedics arrived at the scene. When they eventually came in and found Rogers seated at the foot of a bed upon which was *that*, the shock was all too evident on their own faces.

She left the room, and as she got back out into the courtyard, she breathed in clean air for what felt like the first time in her whole life. The smells in that room, and the look in the man's eyes, would haunt her forever. She walked round the front of the property, just as more police arrived, and Lindbeck's Mill was suddenly awash with sirens, and the flickering of blue lights up stone walls, all under canopied treetops. When she emerged around the side of Lindbeck's Mill to look out at the field, she saw in the distance Indy Macaluso walking a short distance ahead of Cam Killick – who was holding hands with none other than Bix Lindbeck.

Rogers strained to look, but couldn't see anything by way of restraints. Killick had somehow subdued the man. The police behind started to run towards the men, but Rogers paused them. 'Give them a moment,' she instructed. 'And take the big guy gently.'

She waited and tried to put on her own kind expression, while the three people walked across the grass, round the front pool to meet her. Rogers held out her hand to Lindbeck. 'Hello Bix,' she said. 'My name is Claire.'

She turned to the assembled officers. 'Bix here could probably do with a warm drink and somewhere quiet. Can we sort that out for him, please?'

Bix looked from Cam Killick to Rogers. She found it so hard to square away the intense damage that those eyes held with the horrors that she had seen at the hands of the eyes' owner.

'I think that's a great idea,' said Indy Macaluso, ushering the officers along.

'Can you come with me?' asked Bix Lindbeck. He was looking down at Cam Killick.

Killick shrugged gently.

'Of course I can, mate,' he said. 'If that's what you'd like.'

Rogers simply looked at Cam Killick.

And nodded.

Epilogue

Jess crossed the River Bure in a small rowboat. She had with her a carrier bag containing, among other things, a five-pack of T-shirts, a couple of pairs of jeans, a five-pack of underwear and some socks. There was bread, milk, a bit of cheese.

'Ahoy,' shouted a voice behind her. She turned to look and saw Cam, Nala and Wicket on the veranda of a single-storey houseboat, moored to the riverbank, next to yet another of Norfolk's famed reed beds. It was a long tin box, not unlike a static caravan, but on water and wrapped by a deck.

He was smiling. She liked to see him smile.

Jess got to the steps, and tied up. Cam held out a hand to lift her up the short ladder onto the deck. 'You are aware this is the twenty-first century,' she said. 'You don't have to live like this.'

'It's working so far,' he said. He'd only been there a matter of days, but already she could see what this was doing for him. Living actually on the water was perfect for him. Cam Killick and H_2O, a match made in heaven.

Nala and Wicket marauded Jess to try to get at the bags, but Cam took them from her and passed them through the open window, into the kitchen.

A few months ago, he'd helped her set up her new home at Feather House, and now, she was returning the favour. They had spent the last two days ferrying things to and fro across the water from the village of Horning. When Cam had started looking for a new place, he'd been so inspired by a place called Middlewater and their 'floating caravans', as he put it, that a houseboat had been the only option. He'd found one up for rent in Horning, just down from the Heron's Reach pub, and the remains of the *Southern Comfort* paddle cruiser. Firmly choosing to forget the historical horrors of both those things, Cam decided this was about as perfect a new start as he could get.

Jess looked out, and saw another woman over on the deck of another houseboat, further up the water. She was enjoying a moment of that early spring sunshine. They waved to each other. Cam came out, and by God, he waved too. Jess thought this camaraderie would be good for him, this kind of neighbourly quality.

She wanted things to be good for him. He needed a steady period.

The last few weeks had been swamped with explanation and haunting revelations, drawn out with expert skill by Indy Macaluso. Cam had been there for all of it, and Jess, in turn, had talked it through with him, to help him process what he was hearing.

Through extremely strict, almost brutal parenting, Bix Lindbeck had developed an insular nature and an extreme love for all things animal, perhaps because animals could never say anything bad to him. He appreciated their values, the fact that if things needed to be done they simply did them, and when he was being constantly bullied at school – and to a certain extent at home – he'd fantasised about how he would redress the balance. When he was expelled, thanks to that horrible gang of boys, he'd devolved further. Then his parents died, and he was left to his own devices, apparently clinging ever more to the animal side of his persona.

But he couldn't bear animals being upset, and he liked to fix things. He couldn't let go of his childhood dream of becoming a vet, and tried to continue helping animals the best way he could – though, it didn't often go well. He took a job at a local fishing shop so he could pay for animal feed, and very little else. His size, and strength, meant that he became respected by the animals he cared for, and it fed into his complex as an apex predator with a territory to defend – a territory that included his family's old mill, and Doke End.

All it took was a nudge. Lindbeck had killed the men after seeing one of them on his beloved Doke End, which had caused a cataclysmic break in Lindbeck's mind. He'd seen one of them in the fishing shop before, and couldn't believe it. He'd try to bury it down, but it was no use. To see one of those boys on Doke End was an affront he couldn't bear. He'd killed the first one. Then he saw another. And then, his rights of territory had been provoked, and he needed them all.

Like any successful predator, he hunted with single-minded skill and potency. He was the alpha now.

Then another alpha had emerged. Another man who was capable of doing what it took, when the time arose.

It was amazing what the mind could concoct when pushed far enough.

Cam had sat with Bix Lindbeck throughout all the interviews, before parting with him, the two alphas having come to an understanding. Lindbeck was on his way to an institution, the most likely outcome following trial, at which there was no doubt in anyone's mind he would be deemed unfit to stand. The cost of Bix Lindbeck was huge, not just to the people he had killed in a warped attempt to redress the balance, but to Lindbeck himself. A man so entirely fractured and broken by what happened in his past that reality, or common senses of right and wrong, no longer applied or carried any weight or relevance. Even then, when he'd caused upset himself, making Conroy cry, he'd tried to fix him.

Conroy had been a pure fluke. When the knife had punctured his heart, by some quirk of physics and geometry, the knife had hit the lowest part of the left ventricle and nicked it. As they would all come to learn, the left ventricle is some 50 per cent thicker than the right – and it was a small piece of ventricle that was stuck in the hilt of that infernal knife Cam had found, the one that had started everything.

It was a fair assumption that when you find a piece of human heart on a knife, the owner of that heart should be dead. Conroy ended up that way, but it took almost six days, after being operated on by his childhood victim, in a crude surgical set-up at the back of a filthy livestock shed. It would take a long time for any of them to come to terms with what had happened here – if at all.

Jess put a hand on Cam's shoulder. 'You doing good?'

'Yes. Thank you for helping me,' he said. 'And thank you for forgiving me.'

She turned to look at him and saw all his hopes, burning so brightly and clearly. She admired him, and a part of her might love him, one day, but all of that felt so distant. There were so many things in the way, and complications to navigate. All she knew was she cared for Cam deeply, and wanted nothing more than to see him happy. If that happiness intertwined with hers, then wonderful. But she couldn't force it. There was too much at stake for both of them.

She smiled softly, and pecked him on the cheek.

'Come on, Wicket,' she said, as she started walking back towards the dinghy. She hopped down into it and Wicket, after a couple of moments of indecision, went with her with a graceless thump. She cast off into the twinkling water, under the watchful eyes of Cam and Nala, and started to row.

'I'll come back and see you in a couple of days,' she shouted.

Cam smiled softly and waved.

Those eyes of his. The things they'd seen. The things they hoped to see.

'I'll have the kettle on,' he said.

Acknowledgements

After the last time out, I'm going to try to keep this shorter and sweeter.

To Becky, Ava, Sylvia and Robin. You're my world, and I couldn't do this without you.

To my mum and dad, your support and love keeps giving me strength. You'll never know, I don't think, how grateful I truly am.

To the TPF, thank you so much. I'm so thankful to you all for being in our corner, and so proud of my nieces and nephews.

To my Henderson family – your support and encouragement really means the world. Thank you.

To my whole family, immediate and extended. I love you all, and can't thank you enough.

To everyone at the mighty David Higham Associates, thank you. Working with you all is like being backed by giants. Particular thanks to Georgie Smith, Jem Dryer, Georgia Glover and Orli Vogt-Vincent. The biggest thank you to Maddalena Cavaciuti, my agent extraordinaire. What you've done for me, and how you've changed my career, is frankly ridiculous.

To everyone at Bloomsbury Raven, and all I work with via association. You are a joy to work with, and another career highlight. Grace Nzita-Kiki, Max Bridgewater, Fabrice Wilmann, Wilhelmina Asaam, Alison Hennessy and Charlotte Phillips. A special thanks to my incredible editor Therese Keating, who is a constant blast to work with, and who inspires and improves me in equal measure every single time.

To all my friends: Wheeey, the Birthday Cake of Faithfulness, the Y-Files Agents, the Hungry Boys, the Croft FDT, my Pod Dojo family, the White Doves, all our wonderful neighbours, and everyone at The Plough in Croft, especially Drew and Charmaine. Additional thanks to Phil Gray, Danny Middleton, Pele Hall, Sarah Sharpe, Stacia Briggs, Siofra Connor, Simon Ward and Karl Mercer.

My fellow authors, bloggers, reviewers, and booksellers – thank you all for everything you do. The lifeblood of our industry!

Norfolk, thank you for showing me, Cam and Nala such an amazing welcome. This is still a dark love letter to your beautiful county; any mistakes in geography are my own, or required for narrative purposes!

Lastly, thank you, reader. I wouldn't get a chance to live this dream if it weren't for you. My gratitude really is endless.

A Note on the Author

ROB PARKER is the author of *Far From the Tree*, the No. 1 bestselling thriller for Audible Original and the first instalment in the *Thirty Miles* trilogy, as well as eight novels for independent publishers. He is the host of Crime Central Manchester, a monthly showcase of emerging crime writing talent and blockbuster bestsellers, and, alongside his wife, runs writing workshops for budding young authors around the country. Rob lives in Warrington with his wife, three children and their dogs, and was inspired to write the Cam Killick Mysteries from years of holidays in the Norfolk Broads – during which he has never, he is pleased to say, found a dead body.